Previously by same author

The Final Shah Matt
Published via Amazon
2014

David Middleton was a news reporter in local newspapers and radio before becoming a motorsport photo journalist. Working in commercial PR and exhibitions and conferences also enabled him to travel extensively. In 1988 he had his "green epiphany" standing on a bridge in Pittsburgh. In 1991 he helped launch the MEBC and became CEO of this business group dedicated to sustainable development, was Secretary General of The Urban Renewal Foundation and CEO of the UK branch of the World Business Council for Sustainable Development. He retired from these responsibilities in 2013.

This book is dedicated to my mom, who elected to adopt me when medical advice was telling her not to. She gave me a chance in life that is an unpayable debt.

David Middleton

THE ACIONNA PROJECTS

AUSTIN MACAULEY
PUBLISHERS LTD.

A CIP catalogue record for this title is available from the British Library.

ISBN 9781785546259 (Paperback)
ISBN 9781785546266 (Hardback)
ISBN 9781785546273 (eBook)

www.austinmacauley.com

First Published (2016)
Austin Macauley Publishers Ltd.
25 Canada Square
Canary Wharf
London
E14 5LQ

Printed and bound in Great Britain

Acknowledgments

I remain indebted to my TEABAGs – "The Editorial Appraisal of Book Action Group" consisting of my long suffering wife Jennie, great encourager Debbie Dorman, creative daughter Caroline, supporting son Anthony, and long-time friend Kevin Walsh. They gave me encouragement and guidance during the writing process. Also a variety of others who helped after the book was written.

Introduction

This is the sequel to my first novel, The Final Shah Matt. The same main characters are re-established in another adventure that mixes fact and fiction (see Fact & Fiction Appendix). The focus this time is on water, the essential resource of life. Some say water security is the hottest geopolitical issue of our time. South Korean "chaos entrepreneur" Sum Taeyoung plans to attack three strategically important dams whilst in the Ferghana Valley of Central Asia, the region teeters on the brink of the first modern water war.

Our main character and reluctant hero (who has a contentious surname and a confusing first name) becomes embroiled in a story that includes the north coast of Scotland; the exotic Flying Bird Tea Shop in Seoul; Portcullis House in London, water crisis hit Las Vegas, the Aral Sea and the Ferghana Valley.

Author's Notes

This book is a weave of fact and fiction – see Fact and Fiction Appendix. Most characters and events are pure fiction and drawn from my imagination although most of the places in the story do exist. However, all the information about the state of water on our planet and issues to do with sustainable development are, to the best of my knowledge, accurate. Strangely, during the course of writing this story, friction has developed in the Ferghana Valley in Central Asia where resources, especially water, are under intense pressure. Hopefully, the first 21ˢᵗ century water war will be avoided.

I have had a love affair with the north coast of Scotland for many years, retreating there to a crofter's cottage my wife and I owned near the village of Bettyhill, about half way between John O'Groats and Cape Wrath. I guess this part of the book is a little autobiographical as are my experiences of working in places like the Palace of Westminster and the Flying Bird Tea Shop in Seoul.

Sadly what is not fiction, is the appalling state of our planet and the way we are abusing water, the essential resource of life. If this novel does anything to stimulate people to respond to the challenges and responsibilities we confront, it will have done what I hoped it might.

Chapter 1

He felt as if he was running through treacle. It was a slow motion nightmare but it was impossible to go faster. There were just too many people. But he was reassured by the knowledge that if it was difficult for him, it was equally difficult for the chasing pack.

He had dreamed about this moment – when his legs would just not function fast enough, hindering progress through a sea of bodies and with those in authority bearing down on him. He expected to feel fear. Instead, he felt exhilaration and excitement. Madeleine had said it would be so. She was right. Nevertheless, the consequences of being caught did not bear consideration. So Fiacre rushed headlong down the crowded corridor galleries and pavilions of the historic building, the 12th century fortress that became a King's home, turned later into a sumptuous palace and now, for more than 200 years, a museum of world repute. Irreverent to the almost cathedral-like atmosphere, he darted between people, leapt into any available space, ducked and twisted one way or another and, more often than he wished, crashed into visitors to the museum, shattering their tranquillity and focussed concentration. He left a wake of chaos – startled people, general bewilderment and much abuse shouted in his direction.

It could hardly have been a worse time of the year. Holiday time. Today alone, some 10,000 people would visit The Louvre. That gave him a peak audience but it made fleeing the scene of the violation of an historic ancient artefact, even more challenging. But he was nearly there. Nearly to phase two of his great escape. And with a final lunge through a line of Japanese visitors, Fiacre dived into a toilet – straight into a cubical – ripping off the cloth cap with long hair attached to expose a short and stubby hair style. His jacket and jumper were discarded at the same time to reveal a thin material, royal blue silk bomber jacket. It took less than 10 seconds. Much practice had ensured that. Now transformed, he strolled casually from the toilet, rubbing his hands as if to rid himself of the excesses of a hand wash. He nearly collided with the first of the posse of security people who had been hot on the heels of the perpetrator of the abuse to the museum's most historic piece of antiquity.

Fiacre was all too aware that the Museum's security system would now be fully alerted. Equally he knew, like all museums, funding constraints meant that The Louvre was under provisioned both in terms of manpower and technology when compared to the value of the assets they were trying to protect in this complex building. His research revealed that of The Louvre's 2000 staff, more than half have security responsibilities. They provide a 24/7 reception and surveillance service and are employed by The French Ministry of Culture and Communication. But in the huge areas of the Palais du Louvre with its long and narrow galleries, its halls and pavilions, all packed with tourists, their task is challenging. In just the last 20 years alone, dozens of major paintings have been pulled off the museum's walls including 20 works by Vincent Van Gogh. So apprehending the fleeing culprit was no easy task.

"Louvre comes from the word Louveterie – a place where dogs were trained to chase wolves," Madeleine had told him. "You will run like a wolf being chased by a pack of dogs," she had said, giggling.

5

What he had done was, he knew, foolish. It was reckless and even dangerous. He knew if he was caught, he would face the wrath of the courts. Imprisonment was a distinct possibility even if his violation of an historic and invaluable piece of antiquity did not physically damage it. But youthful impetuousness overwhelmed sensibility. He was absolutely bursting to hint to the world what they planned. He knew he was not supposed to. The big man from South Korea had given them clear warnings. His cautioning about the consequences of speaking outside their closed circle was a clear threat. So this moment of madness in The Louvre was crazy but he so dearly wanted the world to know that soon he and his small Paris group of friends, would deliver something of enormity. They would no longer be of no consequence to anyone. They would become notorious.

Streetwise, full of self-confidence, bravado and testosterone but retaining quantities of teenage naivety and an almost asphyxiating sense of frustration, 16 years old, Fiacre lived on the wrong side of the great barrier that divides Paris into those that have and those that have not. That great barrier – the eight lane Périphérique that circumnavigates the city, has within its circle the commerce and culture that makes the French capital internationally famed and respected. On Fiacre's side outside the circle – the 'banlieue' – live the "have nots".

Fiacre was drawn to his group of new friends by his determination to explore anything that might gain him relief from his suffocating ghetto life in Paris. He felt trapped in an urban world where despair and disillusionment were widespread, jobs virtually non-existent, money pitifully scarce, and hope pretty well absent. Here, in squalid suburbs mostly occupied by Arabs, Africans and poor French, one third of the people live below the poverty line. Nearly 40 percent of the occupants are under the age of 25 with more than 40 percent of the youngsters, unemployed.

Fiacre investigated several extremist groups in his search for a release from his feeling of entombed desolation. There were many options to choose from. But Paris Guerriers Urbains – or PGU for short – attracted him for a number of reasons.

Originally an informal gang of environmental activists who came together in the late 1980s, it was formed by a small number of multinational, Paris based postgraduates. Many were from families with communist backgrounds who, with the collapse of the Soviet Union, did what many of their comrades did around the world – they turned to environmental campaigning. This group was also inspired by both the Cult of Santez Anne with its ancient Celtic antecedents, pagan links to water worship and connections to Breton, the French area famed for its extraordinary fountains, and the Gallo-Roman water goddess Acionna, with origins in the ancient Orléanais region of France.

The art lovers amongst the ranks of PGU members recalled that Leonardo da Vinci, whose work is so well represented in The Louvre, said "Water is the driving force of all nature." Al Martin, an American member of the group, countered with a quote from Mark Twain – "Whisky is for drinking. Water is for fighting over." PGU members utterly agreed with both. Water is, they believed, the 'lifeline substance' for life on earth. They saw it to be threatened by modern day demands. To them that epitomised what they believed to be a clash between the greed of today's high consuming modern day society and the finite balances of nature and the resources nature provides. It became their prime subject and their emblem.

A determined but passive group from its inception, its links to urban warriors was originally more in name than in action. But in the 80s, it was its very name that attracted the influences of Action Directe, the French terrorist gang that was determined to destabilise the French government and had links to the infamous German Red Army Faction. For a while, PGU became an attached cell of AD living more closely to its title, with its members executing several bombing acts across central Paris. By 1987, with all AD's leaders imprisoned, it gradually reverted back to being a more passive, predominantly environmental group and its more extreme members eventually faded from the scene.

Fiacre found the group appealing. Environmental issues had been an interest to him from an early age. He attributed it to his distanced Celtic family connections. The Celtic links to the Cult of Santez Anne, tenuous though they might be, would, he thought, please his ancestors. The high profile link to urban terrorism of the not so distant past, added a spicy element of excitement and glamour. And then there was Madeleine with whom he had developed a strong fondness. Small in stature and with a round and pale face and always with the shortest of haircuts, Fiacre was attracted to her by her vivacious enthusiasm, her strong opinions and self-conviction and, he had to admit, her 'petit seins.'

The big man from South Korea imposed himself on the group and left a deep impression on Fiacre as with most if not all members of the PGU. With the attending membership originating from China, India, Pakistan, America, England and France, "Hwanung", as they knew him to be, chose to speak to their meeting in his first language, English, but mixed with Oxford and American accents and hints of his Asian origins in the background. But this was interspersed with bits of French in which he was also fluent. Hwanung was, they all knew, a nom de plume. The man behind the name, Sum Taeyoung, was immodest enough to adopt the name of the mythological first king of the Koreans. He first swore the group to secrecy and spent some time talking about the consequences of loose talk. There was no specific threat. No details of the consequences of non-compliance. But nobody in the audience was left unsure of his message. They feared the consequences of breaking the vow of silence to which Hwanung insisted they stood and swore allegiance to. It was all a bit melodramatic but it certainly made the point.

"The trouble is," the big man with his long hair, cascading beard and colourful flowing Asian robes explained as he paced up and down before them, "human nature being what it is, we rarely take action until the problem has materialised."

"*Il ne sert a rien de se voiler la face et de declarer que nous n'avons rien remarqué et que nous ne voulons rien changer* – it does not help to bury one's head, ostrich-like, in the sand and say that we have not noticed anything and that we do not wish to change anything."

"But that is what we tend to do. It seems to be human nature. And as a community on this planet, I do not need to tell you environmentalists, that we are heading towards calamity. Global warming, climate change, population growth, persistent pollution, waste, pressure on resources – all are heading in the wrong direction yet our politicians seem to do little about it, with little or no plans to meet the consequences. This is a global situation with no global mechanism by which to respond."

"You will also know that water is our most valued natural resource. You recognise that. It is your raison d'être. You know it is the essential nectar of all life. That is why I am speaking to you today. France was the home of the water goddess, Acionna. Pagan people the world over worshipped water. Large numbers of ancient populations collapsed through lack of water. Our modern world is putting pressures on water resources in a way we have not seen before. Our growing population increases the stress on water availability. As it becomes rarer, we see more examples of it being commercially exploited – people having to pay more for it, despite it being a natural resource that nature gives to us for nothing. And, as ever, it is the poor who suffer the most."

Sum Taeyoung had done his homework well. He knew he would pull the emotional strings of everyone in this group if he highlighted environmental issues, the exploitation of the poor, and perceived greed in corporate corridors.

"I believe the time is right for the world to be given a lesson – a wakeup call about the real value of water. I have an idea how to do this. But I need resources by which to do it. I need a small army – foot soldiers – warriors like you. Organisations with links to the Goddess Acionna exist around the world in one form or another. I believe they – you – are my ideal army – my ground troops – for the actions I propose."

"Is this a sort of Greenpeace protest?" someone asked from the audience.

"Sort of," responded the South Korean. "But on a high profile, internationally reported, global scale and simultaneously, to make a worldwide impact. To give you an example, until recently, I had the Mosul Dam in Syria in my plan. It is so strategically important to that part of the world. If it were to be broken, the resultant tsunami would be devastating, putting tens of thousands of people at risk. The subsequent lack of water would be horrendous."

"But the war against the State of Islam overtook my plans and it is now too dangerous a place to contemplate. And, you could argue, the war there has already headlined the importance of the dam and the water it holds. But if you look around the world, there are many similarly strategically important places where water is a more precious commodity than it is elsewhere; Places where its security of supply is taken for granted but in reality, it is tenuous and vulnerable. Those sorts of places are my target."

And he went on to tell them about his ideas, where the action would take place, why and how. He also told them he had a date for their global campaign. It would be March 22nd, International Water Day. That gave them nine months. What he did not tell them was that the impact he planned would be devastating. It would wreak havoc. It would create bedlam and major political unrest. What they did not know was that creating global chaos was Sum Taeyoung's prime role in life. But as far as he was concerned, they did not need to know. They would merely be pawns in the game. The analogy with chess pleased him. It had echoes from his last campaign in which the game of chess had been central.

The membership of PGU was excited by what they heard. After the meeting ended, Fiacre and Madeleine talked eagerly about it. Hwanung stimulated their desire to know more. Madeleine, an immature young girl with latent intelligence and an inbred, dogged and insatiable curiosity, set out to expand their knowledge about water conflicts around the world and ancient water wars, and to find out more about this man from South Korea with the monstrous physique and outrageous use of a God-name. She had surreptitiously photographed their new mentor on her phone and sent the image to a friend who worked on the administration side of the gendarmerie. It was through this research activity that Madeleine found that the earliest known official water war dates back some 4,500 years and, by wonderful coincidence, has powerful connections to Paris and especially to The Louvre. It also uncovered for her the real name of the man from South Korea. It was information she intended to share with Fiacre. But that never happened.

The ancient conflict over water she found involved the armies of Lagash and Umma, cities near the junction of the Tigris and Euphrates rivers. The King of Umma had drained an irrigation canal leading from the Tigris and that denied water to Lagash. The war, fought with spears and chariots, left some 60 soldiers dead. The world's first water war ended when a treaty was brokered by Turkey and formalised and noted in an etched cuneiform tablet. Fiacre and Madeleine were excited to find the stone treaty – the Stella of the Vultures – is now displayed in The Louvre. That is what sparked their plan. They talked about Hwanung's vow of silence. But they convinced themselves their action was not specific to what he planned and it would be alright.

Now Fiacre had executed their plan. All he had to do was escape. What he and Madeleine did not know was that the consequences of their action would be devastating beyond anything they could imagine.

Chapter 2

As if the work of witchcraft and demons, the previously reassuring solid landscape of the extensive valley before him, transformed into a sea of waves circling out and away for as far as he could see. It was not only very odd, it was hugely disconcerting. What before had been terra firma was now difficult to stand upright on. It challenged the ability to maintain any sort of solid balance or equilibrium. Moments before the valley seemed like a secure place to be. Now it turned into something very insecure, weird and even threatening where the mind involuntarily conjured thoughts of human engulfing bogs and body devouring quicksands. But having been responsible for the creation of those waves, Gene Bond felt he could only blame himself. So he jumped some more.

This energetic but perturbing activity was an impulsive response to both a glorious day and, to unanswered curiosity. Somewhere within him a voice said – "well, why not?" It also counterbalanced his annoyance, frustration and growing anger sparked by the telephone call two days ago at his cottage on the north coast. It had played on his mind ever since. The Georgian accent was unmistakable. The hesitancy and trepidation in the opening words gave evidence that the caller himself was uncomfortable and anxious about making the call. Rightly so in Bond's mind.

"Gene. It's Georgi."

Bond was taken aback. He had not heard from Georgi Patarava in nearly two years.

"What the hell do you want, Georgi?" His response was sharp and perhaps, he thought later, unnecessarily rude. "I'm in the far north of Scotland. Don't spoil my day."

"Gene," came the reply. "You know I wouldn't unless I really had to. And the truth is, I miss you my friend. I truly do. I have nobody to drink with. Nobody to unload my inner burdens onto. I miss you Gene."

Bond said nothing. Eventually Georgi Patarava continued.

"But we've hit a problem, Gene. I think you can help us. And before you say anything, I know you told us quite clearly you didn't want to get involved with us again. But I need some help my friend."

Anger started to swell within Bond. In the two years since his last involvement with Georgi, he had started to retrieve his life from the disastrous consequences of his last escapade with his Georgian friend. The media had hounded him mercilessly. Government writs and secret service agreements piled onto him. Now, with life starting to feel a little more like normality, the last thing he needed was Georgi.

"Go away Georgi." He replied abruptly and somewhat brutally. "I don't want to know."

"It's all to do with water, Gene."

He did not respond.

"And the Goddess Acionna – and the oldest known water war – and some incidents this week in Paris.

Again he remained silent, making it as awkward for Georgi as he could.

"You could help link some things together for me – help me find a starting point. That's all."

"Georgi," Bond responded at last, unable to conceal his annoyance. "I was as clear to you as I could be. I value your friendship as it used to be. But I don't want to get involved. Your world and mine are different worlds. I want it to stay that way. The last time was enough for me for a lifetime. I got shot at, killed a man and ended up in a maritime battle on Lake Geneva. My God, Georgi, that's enough for anyone in one life. And I've had two years of hell since."

"But Gene," implored the voice at the other end, "I just need help to unravel the start of this. I…"

He cut the call off then and stood for a while looking at the phone. Cutting the call from his friend was at best impolite and at worst, downright bad mannered. But he did not want to be persuaded, against his better judgement, and Georgi could be very persuasive.

So he found himself taking out the frustrations of the telephone call in childlike fashion, jumping up and down, hearing his booted feet splosh in the increasingly wet turf, and watching the valley bottom respond in a series of waves that circled away from where they were and into the distance. He would never have contemplated being out here on his own in the desolate but grandiose expanses of The Caithness Flowlands. It was stunningly beautiful but it was seriously dangerous.

Before him, out of view and well over the horizon, he felt he could almost hear the waves thundering up the golden beaches of the northern shores. To his right, now some two miles away and also out of sight, was the main road where he had parked the Porsche, some few hundred yards from Forsinard railway station in which is the RSPB Centre. Behind him, the rolling valleys and their patchwork of lochs and locháns headed down towards Helmsdale and the North Sea coast. And, majestically dominating the view to the left, Ben Griam Beg, Ben Hope and Ben Loyal provided a mountain range backdrop against a rich blue, almost cloudless sky. There was only a light breeze to disturb the tranquillity but, right across the valley, bobs of pure white bog cotton danced madly in the disturbed air.

Only the foolhardy would venture alone into this place. But he was not alone. To his side, the rugged, weather worn and bearded Graham from the RSPB centre, reassured him all was well. In fact, he did more. He encouraged more jumping!

"This is a unique area of bogland" he explained, puffing a little as he continued to jump. "The largest blanket bog on the planet. It's like jumping up and down on a giant sponge which is why you can create these waves."

Earlier, they had walked a fair distance from the road into the soggy wilderness. It was a stroke of luck that saw him meet Graham as he parked the Porsche by the start of the Dubh Lochan Trail, a sort of stepping stone walk designed to give visitors an unconducted, safe but short and limited opportunity to venture into the Flowlands. He had not planned the walk. He intended just to do the Trail. But the call from Georgi had totally thrown him and disturbed him. A real walk into the valley might, he felt, help blow it from his mind.

He did not know Graham particularly well. They had nodded acknowledgement one to another several times in the RSPB centre. Seeing Bond tying the laces to his walking boots, Graham volunteered the news that he was off on a routine patrol of the valley and invited Bond to join him.

"Graham Mackay," said the RSPB man, extending his hand to Bond.

"Not another Mackay." Bond responded, jokingly. Every other person you met in this part of Northern Scotland seemed to have the same name.

"Oh yes" responded the RSPB man. "But what do you expect? After all, you are in the land of the Mackays."

"Gene Bond." Bond responded, grasping the other's hand in a firm handshake of welcome.

Graham Mackay frowned and scratched his head. "I know I've seen you around the RSPB centre in the past. But I recognise that name. And now I think about it, weren't you making headline news a couple of years ago?"

Bond sighed. He was so desperately trying to shake off both the memory and the stigma of what happened two years ago. But, seemingly, it would not go away.

"There was an incident on Lake Geneva. I threw a large chess piece off a paddle steamer before it blew up. It was a bomb designed to sink the boat."

"I remember now," said Graham Mackay. "The press made a lot about this Bond hero. That was you!"

"I'm afraid so," responded Bond. "I'm stuck with a family name that Fleming unfortunately chose for his hero. I can't think of anyone less like Fleming's fictitious spy than me. And to add to the confusion, I've got a feminine sounding Christian name. That's my Dad's fault. He was a Johnny Cash fan. Do you remember his famous concerts in the California prisons? The inmates roared at his song "A Boy Named Sue.""

Mackay nodded. Bond was relieved. Further explanation was not necessary. It was not always the case.

"I guess I should be relieved Dad didn't call me Sue! Gene's bad enough! Anyway, the media made a huge fuss over this Bond person throwing a bomb off a paddle steamer. It's been horrendous ever since. I hoped it would fade into history and leave me alone."

Mackay took the hint and dropped the subject. As they walked further and further into the boggy peat land, he provided a constant commentary about the wildlife, pointing to a low flying hen harrier, identifying various plants and all this against a constant background noise from the local wildlife including the unmistakable call of a distant curlew echoing across the vastness. After nearly an hour's walking, they stopped between two lochs, one slightly bigger than the other. To one side, the smaller of the two was full of shimmering water and apparently home to a family of ducks. To the other side, the larger loch was empty, nearly bone dry.

"Where do you think the water from this loch's gone to?" asked Graham.

"There" responded Gene Bond, pointing to the smaller loch. "But that's too obvious an answer."

"You're right" Graham told him. "It's gone over there – about a mile away." And as he spoke he pointed to a larger loch some distance to their left. "There's a mass of tubers under the top soil that links these lochs together and carry water from one place to another – often not to the closest or more obvious ones. It's what helps make this area so unique."

They returned to the RSPB centre some four hours after setting off and shared a brew of coffee. The sun had dipped below the mountains and there was now a cold bite to the breeze. Graham left him to enjoy his mug of coffee and as he drank, not for the first time, Bond considered what a strange place this was – and not just because of its name – Forsinard.

Some years back, when Gene Bond first discovered this distanced northerly part of Scotland, he found one of the biggest sheep auctions in Scotland was held at this strangely named place called Forsinard. He only visited the auction once and though it was an extraordinary event to witness, he vowed never to go again. Midges – thick, dark clouds of them – dominated the area. He had never seen such numbers of the little pests. The place was packed with people, north Scottish crofters, hill farmers from Cumbria, truck drivers and onlookers. And sheep! Many tens of hundreds of sheep. It had all raised one big question in Gene Bond's mind.

Why hold such an event at such a godforsaken remote place such as Forsinard, in the middle of nowhere? There is not much here. A small hotel, a half dozen houses for estate workers, the RSPB centre in the railway station and the single track railway line. There is just one road – and despite it being designated a main 'A' road, it is a single track bead of tarmac stretching up to the north coast and, in the opposite direction heading south, way down towards the

A9. It has any number of small, narrow bridges crossing the Halladale River and its numerous tributaries. It is not a road fit for monstrous trucks. The battered and scarred buttresses of the bridges bare testimony to the unsuitability of the road to this sort of transport. Yet for year after year, sheep farmers and their contractors from Cumbria, drove their enormous trucks up this challenging route to meet the crofters of the Scottish north lands, to do business at the Forsinard auctions.

For as long as people can remember, the auctions were a major diary date for this remote place and for the population of the North coast of Scotland. So, why here? That was the question Gene Bond tried to find an answer to. The road was not it. It was really unfit for purpose and anyway, the auctions preceded the arrival of the road. Did it have anything to do with the single track railway line that provided the only other means of access to Forsinard?

The answer was no. That was originally cut through the bog land to provide transportation for the good and the mighty to access hunting lodges scattered across the area. And anyway, the auctions also preceded the arrival of the railway. So was it to do with ancient and forgotten pathways like drover's ways or salt trails? Maybe.

After a long period of seeking the answer, Gene came to the conclusion that the consensus view was right. "The auctions are held here" people consistently told him, "because they've always been held here!"

And, in the absence of any better explanation, that is the one Bond had to settle for. Sadly, the auctions are now confined to history as the last was held some years ago and the sheep pens have long since disappeared.

With these thoughts idling through his mind, Bond finished his coffee and left the railway station and the RSPB Centre. It would take him less than three minutes to walk back to where the car was parked but his view of it was initially blocked by a train crawling along the single track line into the station, crossing the level crossing by which he now stood, heading north in the direction of Thurso. The train passed. He started to walk again, looking up as he did so to see his car, some two hundred metres away, had been joined by another, parked behind his. And there she was. His heart seemed to skip a beat. He felt a tingle of uncontrollable excitement. Leaning against the second car was an unmistakable female shape - voluptuous, utterly feminine and so sexy.

Georgi had responded to him cutting off the telephone call by playing a really dirty trick. He had sent Nagriza more than 700 miles to get him.

Chapter 3

The Boardroom is big, palatial and opulent. It makes no apology for its pretentiousness. It is, after all, the epicentre of decision making of a globally operating business. The quality of the carpet, fixtures and fittings, the advanced sophistication of its supportive technology, the gleaming, mahogany table – so long it nearly fills the length of the room – are all in keeping with what would be expected of such a place. Forty people can sit here if need be. The view from the picture window is spectacular with the River Thames heading East towards Westminster and the Houses of Parliament clearly visible with the City in the background, its skyline now dominated by the Shard, Western Europe's tallest building. This evening, a colourful sunset reflected in glowing red off the more than 1,000 glass panels of the City's new skyscraper.

At ground level, the headquarters of Esca International looks like a small town with its enclosed shopping mall, services, bars and restaurants for people who work here. This imperious building is one of the most prominent on the immediate perimeter of London's central area and a landmark for passengers on aircraft heading into Heathrow. It is the working home to some 2,000 employees of the globally operating food and pharmaceutical specialist business that operates in virtually every part of the world with a total work force of some 200,000 people. This highly successful operation sits behind the giant sector leaders but still achieves around £5 billion gross profit annually.

Now assembled around the table, the key decision makers of Esca Int. concentrated on every word uttered by their leader, Esca's Group President, Bernhard Gedeck. There was now no distracting view across London. Matching the technologically advanced interior, the Board Rooms' windows are made of glass that can optionally be transparent or opaque. With the room's lighting dimmed so projected information could be clearly seen, the windows were now in opaque mode to ensure external light did not interfere with the quality of the images on the white wall.

"Let us understand this," Bernhard Gedeck was telling them. "Water is the oil of tomorrow. We have lived through a period of history when oil took over from gold as being the serious currency and profit arena. Sadly, Esca has not been prominent in either gold or oil. But we are a global leader when it comes to water."

One of Esca's major business lines is bottled water, sold under the EscaEau brand. The French element in the title originates from a French bottled water specialist company acquired by Esca some time ago. The French part of the name was retained because marketing research showed the product name EscaEau, stuck in the minds of the public. It also helps denote the international trading nature of the corporate conglomerate.

"And, if you'll excuse my pun," continued Bernhard Gedeck, "the world is at a watershed moment on the subject of water. Without water, life cannot be sustained. But we are asking our planet to do just that – to sustain more and more lives upon it. We have the biggest population the planet has ever known – more than seven billion – and increasing at a rate we have never seen before. At the same time, more countries are transforming from being deprived economies to being consumer driven communities.

Consumers consume water. They do so in vast amounts. They also consume what some people simply call 'stuff' – like cars, washing machines, clothes, and so on. All these things take water to produce – anything from upwards of 40,000 gallons to manufacture a car to around 1,800 gallons of water to grow enough cotton to produce just one pair of jeans. It's known as embedded water – the water embedded into a product at its point of production. It means countries can be exporting vast amounts of their own water in products they have produced. It creates fascinating anomalies. China is the great example. In recent times, the export of goods from China has escalated out of all proportion. Because water is needed to produce what it exports, China is, in essence – through embedded water – exporting vast amounts of something that it is running critically short of. It's a strange dilemma."

"Food production also devours water – 3,000 litres to produce a kilogram of rice; 440 litres to produce a loaf of bread. So the more tens of millions of people who emerge from poverty and demand what we have enjoyed for decades, so the stress on water resources increases."

"It's becoming recognised as a major international challenge. Some say water security is the hottest geopolitical issue of our time. Indeed, there are even mutterings of water wars as nations seek to protect their assets or find ways of tapping into the resources of others. Let me give you one such example."

Bernhard Gedeck turned to the white wall where a large map was now being shown.

"This is the Tibetan Plateau which extends from the great mountain system of Hindu Kush in central Afghanistan, through Pakistan, India, Nepal, Bhutan and on to the borders of Myanmar. Throughout history, the geopolitical significance of Tibet has been tremendous. It was invaded by Britain in 1904 for purely tactical reasons but now it's part of China. Water has always made Tibet important. It has huge reserves of fresh water contained in vast glaciers and huge underground reservoirs. It's the largest repository of freshwater after the two poles, the Arctic and Antarctic. For that reason it's known by some as 'the third pole'. Some huge rivers flow out of the Tibetan Plateau – the Yellow River, Yangtze Kiang, Mekong, Salween, Sutlej and the Brahmaputra."

"As I mentioned earlier, one of the resources China is growingly anxious about is water, which it desperately needs more of to supply its fast growing, massive new cities. So China is looking with increased interest at Tibet's water reserves. But that's making other nearby countries which have rivers flowing from Tibet increasingly nervous about what the Chinese might do. And if you think about those countries – India, Pakistan, even Iran would be impacted – they, and China, have one thing in common. They've all got – one way or another, nuclear military capabilities. It's no wonder experts around the world consider water to be, as I said before, the most sensitive geopolitical subject of our time."

"For too long, we have all taken water for granted and frequently abused it. Indeed, the world has abused many natural resources to a degree that the continued supply of some of them is now questionable."

"For too long, we've treated such resources as being free to us all. In business, we have treated them as externalised issues, not costs on the balance sheet. The world is waking up to this. A big question is how do you put a value on some of these natural resources? An often quoted example is bees. Bees provide an essential service in the process of plant growing, whether the plants are for

25

food or ornamental use. But now bees are in short supply and their value is being recognised. But how do you value a bee? How do you monetise such a value?"

"We're supporting a United Nations programme called TEEB, The Economics of Ecosystems and Biodiversity. TEEB is a global initiative that's trying to put a monetary value to natural resources. To Esca this is a double-edged sword. If a fiscal value is put on water – and I mean water and not the infrastructure needed to get it to wherever it is to be consumed – the cost to Esca would be unbelievable. We have some estimate of the costs and they are astronomical. They are frightening. But, on the other side of the balance sheet, the more the value of water is appreciated, the more we can justify our costs to our markets."

"So, at this watershed moment in the history of the world's use of water, the time could not be better for Esca to seek to maximise its global position in the provision of water. It will be a matter of serious contention. I can envisage the NGO fraternity being up in arms. We are already under their scrutiny. They will accuse us of profiteering and adding to the burden of consumers. But while the objective of profit enhancement can't be argued or denied, we can, in all honesty, say we can significantly improve the accessibility of water to those who currently have no or only limited access."

"In many parts of the world, water is in short supply. Too often that's because of the inefficiencies in the supply infrastructure. Too often it's because of the lack of ability or inexperience of those responsible for the supply. Across the world, Esca has experience and skills second to none. That is why I want to reveal to you our strategic plan for the future of Esca. It has one objective - to dominate the world market in water."

Chapter 4

Fiacre sensed the tension between them, though the big man's voice had from the outset of their meeting, been soft and his demeanour almost paternal. Outside the night deepened and the rain persisted. This part of the banlieue was deserted. The black saloon in which they sat was parked underneath a railway bridge. Only one street light remained on, some distance away, but giving enough light to illuminate puddles rippling in the rain. The street glistened. Outside, nothing moved except a black cat investigating the remains of a burnt out car.

A day had passed since Fiacre's escape from The Louvre. His high speed change of clothing had been a successful tactic and he had walked out of the museum as if just another visitor. Only later, days later, would footage from surveillance cameras match the seemingly two different individuals, the escaping violator and the young man who exited the toilet just as the security people arrived.

This morning he had received an unsigned handwritten note that sought a meeting. It was not a request. It was a summons. It could only have come from the man he knew as Hwanung.

So they had met near where the PGU held its meetings. From there, Hwanung drove them to the spot where they were now parked. He was not, Fiacre noted, dressed this time in his flowing and extravagant Eastern robes but in jeans and a dark jumper. The big South Korean sat well back in his seat, right arm extended across the back of the passenger seat, head up, looking at nothing. Indeed, when Fiacre dared to catch a quick look, Hwanung's eyes were closed. But he was far from being asleep.

"Tell me what you have been up to," Hwanung asked of the young Parisian and Fiacre told the story of how he had been so excited by the big South Korean's plans, he felt he had to do something. It was not as if he had given any secrets away. Clearly Hwanung had told them about the need for silence. All he did, he explained, was make a link between the distant past and today's problems. He was careful throughout to exclude Madeleine from any of the story.

What had attracted Fiacre to the ancient stone artefact was as much its name, as what it is. The Stele of the Vultures, he told Hwanung, just sounds fantastic. It screams excitement, romance and ancient history. It gained stature in every sense when he found it to be the oldest known historical document in The Louvre. And its pertinence – the story of the oldest known water war – to what Hwanung planned, and what Fiacra and his friends would help him execute, was extraordinary.

"You see," said Fiacre with eager enthusiasm in his voice, "4,500 years ago, they were learning the lessons you want to remind the world about now. It's amazing."

With no response forthcoming, Fiacre continued.

He said he had visited The Louvre on several occasions to look at the Stele of the Vultures. It grew in his mind to become an obsession, this link between the distant past and what they now planned to do. He had thought long and hard about what he felt he must do. He did not want to damage the ancient stone but just wanted to leave a message.

"It is as if the old proverb is right – what goes around comes around. Four thousand five hundred years ago water was precious, as it is now. And as it becomes even more valuable, so people will go to war again about water. You said as much to us."

"So I developed my plan. I had a large sash made in red and yellow. I wanted it to be as colourfully loud as it could be. And to give my message an international dimension– and to echo the historic past – the words I had written onto it were "Quid agatur circa venit circum" – Latin for what goes around comes around."

There was a triumphant tone in Fiacre's voice.

Hwanung at last spoke. "This you did all by yourself?"

"Yes – well mostly. I had the sash made."

"The words? They were yours?"

"Yes."

"I didn't know you knew Latin?"

"I looked it up. On the Web."

There was a long moment of silence before Hwanung spoke again.

"And that is all that was written on the sash – Quid agatur circa venit circum?"

"Yes."

More silence. Fiacre could hear the rain beating against the car roof. The big South Korean had started to breathe deeply, almost snoring. A full minute passed.

"That's not quite accurate, is it?" The question was one that Fiacre had worried about.

"Those were the only words," he responded.

"But the press reports I have read tell me there was more than just the words. Am I not right?"

Fiacre knew he was right. Of course he was. There was no escape.

"There were the initials PGU."

"Meaning what?"

Fiacre knew Hwanung knew the answer. "Paris Guerriers Urbains."

"So you left a signature."

Fiacre's enthusiasm was rapidly fading. This interrogation was turning into something bad.

"You could hardly call it a signature, just the initials. And who knows about Paris Guerriers Urbains? A handful of people."

"I told you all not to say anything."

"But I didn't. There was nothing in this that related to what you told us and what you planned."

"So, why do it? Why disobey me?" Hwanung's voice no longer shielded the anger he obviously felt. Fiacre was now seriously worried. He momentarily thought about leaping from the car and running.

"I didn't disobey you. But I wanted to do something that would make people understand we exist, for us to gain some recognition. The PGU is full of people who society seems to have simply forgotten. We are discarded. Of no value," Fiacre responded.

"But you disobeyed me. Despite the pledge you had made."

"But you have given us the chance to feel important. To do something the world will recognise. We have never felt important before. I didn't break your trust. I didn't tell anyone what you planned. I have not betrayed you," Fiacra pleaded but as he did so he felt Hwanung's right arm move from behind his seat to directly behind his head.

"I did nothing to hurt you." The words were becoming slurred and difficult to understand as the arm tightened around Fiacre's neck. The young Parisian fought to try and find the handle to the door. But he could not reach it. Fear was turning to unadulterated terror.

The arm now bent in a tightening grip. The pressure grew. Breathing started to become difficult. Fiacre's legs started to flay in panic. He tried desperately to strike back. But the South Korean just kept applying more and more pressure. Fiacre gulped for air. His face started to turn blue. Under increased pressure, there was a loud crack as the young Parisian's neck succumbed. He died in Sum Taeyoung's arm.

The South Korean sat for a full ten minutes, recovering from the physical effort, thinking about what Fiacre had told him. He was by no means convinced the young man had acted on his own. Sum was fully aware of the relationship with Madeleine. The question was, was silencing Fiacre enough?

With no answer coming to him but his strength restored, Sum leant over the dead youngster and opened the passenger door. With one heave, Fiacre's body was cast into the dark wetness of the banlieue.

Chapter 5

Kevin Forsythe approached his office with his usual sense of foreboding and pessimism. Although he considered himself a born optimist, in the daily swim against a tide of often seemingly insurmountable problems, it was a challenge to remain positive even when surrounded by the many paradise-like offerings to be found in this country of contradictions and contrasts. Yet, there were perhaps, at last, the seedling indications that fortunes here were changing.

The day started well as he followed his established routine. It was already 26 degrees with all the signs of a very hot day to come. It would probably reach the mid to upper 40s by the middle of the afternoon. The short walk down from his apartment to the harbour and then onto the beach, took him to the café bar with its scattering of coconut trees interspersed with tables and chairs underneath parasols topped with palm leaves. With the silver sand reaching down to a sea of gentle, white capped rollers topping almost cerulean blue water it was, he thought, as he sipped his morning cappuccino, truly a scene borrowed from paradise.

Half an hour later, he puffed back up the hill, the day heating up rapidly and already humid and smelly yet still not half past nine in the morning. Hanging in the air was a mixed aroma of the sea, carbon monoxide, human sweat and cow and ox dung. It was normally like this. The once relatively palatial headquarters first established by the

Portuguese senior administrator for Wandora and in which Kevin's own offices are situated, looks a little jaded now. Indeed, the building perhaps reflects the roller coaster history of this West coast African nation on the Gulf of Guinea. Only a few years ago, it celebrated 50 years of independence after a history of occupation going back to the early 1400s when the Portuguese first colonised it. Later the French stamped their Gallic influences on it. Such colonial interest was driven mainly by strategic political manoeuvrings and geographic location rather than by any wealth Wandora could offer. It started as a poor country, remained poor through its colonial years, and is still poor now despite its new independent status. Post independence internal squabbling verging on a civil war that did not quite happen, further deepened Wandora's sad situation.

Democratic elections, apparently by no means as corrupt as people anticipated, introduced the current refreshing period of political stability, prejudiced for a while by the Ebola epidemic that swept over much of this part of Africa but from which Wandora, for no logical reason, mercifully seemed to miss the worst. Stability produced encouraging signs of inward investment and now, perhaps, came opportunity for the country to generate some real wealth.

Kevin turned off the main street with its bustling, chaotic frenzy of cars, trucks, buses, bicycles and occasional livestock all jostling for what bit of dusty highway they could find. The surrounding buildings also provide evidence of the confusion of past and present with corrugated mud huts, colonial-style buildings and square, uninviting more recently constructed, concrete structures mixing together in a kaleidoscopic jumble appropriately representing Wandora's continuing transition from its occupied past to its independent present.

And, as ever, there was the dust. A mixture of sand from Porto Wandora's expansive and stunning white beaches and from the not too distant desert, swirled around in the day's breeze coming off the sea. At other times when the Harmattanzeit desert wind blew in from the opposite direction, there would be so much sand in the air as to make seeing and breathing difficult and daily living most uncomfortable.

Kevin Forsythe had lived here for nearly four years now. He moved here from another African state when the British government decided to close its Consulate there as part of a global 'realignment of resources.' For the first time in his life, career civil servant Forsythe was looking at a future that had nothing to offer him. He was therefore delighted and relieved when an opportunity came along to switch to the private sector. However, the prospect of a significant change in working culture was a worry.

His new job reflected Wandora being at yet another cross roads moment in the history of this small country with its population estimated to be around 10 million. That it does not know precisely how many people it has or what its official language is – Portuguese, French or even, increasingly, English, demonstrates the country's struggle to catch up with a growingly sophisticated world. Consisting of some 60,000 square kilometres in a long, thin stretch that heads from the coast in the south where fossil evidence can be found of a now long gone forest, to the widespread savannah of the north with its thorny scrubs and huge baobab trees, the country has always been poor. But in recent times, things have started to change.

A few years ago, minerals exploration found good evidence of titanium, bauxite and other ores. Starting as a tentative exercise, the more ore was discovered the greater the interest became with, eventually, China sending a team to evaluate the potential. Their findings were sufficiently positive for China Minerals Inc. to invest in more expansive exploration activity which eventually led to the recent opening of production mines.

Of little consequence to start with, the growing minerals extraction programme impacted on Wandora's already precarious water situation. The country has always had a water supply difficulty. The sources of rivers running through it to the Gulf of Guinea are in adjacent countries which tap the river water for their own purposes before anything reaches Wandora. This dependency has been the basis of political negotiations for years and treaties exist with neighbouring nations as to how much water they extract from the rivers and how much is left to flow into Wandora. Those treaties are all well and good but climate change has, like everywhere else on the planet, hit this part of Africa and weather patterns, especially rainfall, have become abnormal with river flows fluctuating as never seen before. It has placed new stresses on the treaties and accusations of transgressions have generated heated political exchanges between neighbouring nations.

Faced by a worry that could become a crisis, Wandora's Ministry of Infrastructure and Services called on Esca Int. for guidance, the Minister having once bumped into Esca's Global President, Bernhard Gedeck, at a Pan-African convention on water. After much discussion and correspondence, Esca agreed to open an office in Porto Wandora from which to base water experts to advise and guide the government on its water provision policies. Advertisements for someone to run the office were posted in appropriate places across southern Africa and it is via this route that Kevin Forsythe got the job.

In no way could he be called a water expert but his diplomatic skills were unquestionable. Apart from managing and developing the office and providing back up support to visiting experts, the job also called for the fostering and maintaining of good relationships with the Minister and his team, other parts of the Wandora civil service and, the growing number of businesses and people involved in the minerals exploration and extraction processes. It was a job that was right up Kevin Forsythe's street and he set about it with optimism and enthusiasm.

But it soon became apparent that this was not going to be an easy ride. Kevin found he really had two masters to satisfy and their agendas were sometimes harmonious but often significantly opposed. Whilst obviously employed to look after the interests and prospects of Esca, he also had the interests of the Ministry to concern him. The speed of operation of the civil service in a small African nation like Wandora is, at best, snail pace which makes getting responses and decisions a daily nightmare and an enormous frustration. Added to that are the often aggressive stances taken by the minerals specialists and the cultural differences of the Chinese teams which seemingly increased in number on a weekly basis.

With water provision to some parts of the country and especially its remote villages becoming more and more of a challenge, Esca embarked on a programme of water exploration, drilling test programmes around the country to discover what groundwater was so far untapped. The results were promising and Esca turned to its other area of skill, bottled water, to try and resolve the growing provision shortfall. EscaEau became increasingly involved with more and more bore holes developed across the country and bottled water distribution to the population wherever it was most needed. The operation was largely subsidised by the Wandora government and for a while it looked as if the problem was solved. But, as Kevin was to discover, it was not.

He was surprised to find Agbonserema Taiwo, Senior Manager at Wandora's Ministry of Infrastructure and Services, waiting for him. Kevin knew him well and also knew he reported directly to the Minister. It was unprecedented for Agbonserema to visit the Esca offices. Normally he summoned Kevin to come to him. Equally unheard of was for an unscheduled meeting to happen. Wandora's creaking administration was fastidious about etiquette on matters like arrangements for meetings.

"We have a problem, Kevin. And it may rest at the door of Esca."

Taiwo sat in his white robes at Kevin's desk, lightly drumming his fingers on the desk top. It was an annoying distraction but an indication of the visitor's nervousness.

"So I thought I would come and talk to you about it, an off-the-record chat. If we have a problem, this hopefully will be an opportunity to kill it off before it gets bigger, spreads and becomes really damaging."

Chapter 6

The two cars headed north to the coast up the twisting and turning single track A897 main road. In this expansive scenery, the crystal clear River Halladale, sparkling on a sunny day such as this, initially flows alongside the road and to its right until, the only bridge north of Forsinard takes the road across the river where it stays until the river joins the sea and the A897 meets a T junction with the East/West running A836, the most northerly A road on mainland Britain. Leaving Forsinard, the vast expanses of the Flowlands are quickly left behind as the road enters a more farmed area extending from the river valley but with high hills to the right, mostly covered with forests. By the time they reached the junction where they turned right towards Thurso, the day was drawing to a close and the light fading. When they turned left onto the track towards the cottage, the distant sea looked gunmetal grey with the slightest tinge of orange from a mostly cloud covered setting sun. As usual, the journey down the track into the valley was obstructed by sheep that stubbornly refused to shift despite the arrival of the two cars. Whilst some scurried into the bracken either side of the track, others remained obstinately immobile with nothing threatening their inactivity.

Bond had led the way from the RSPB base at the railway station, keeping an eye through his rear mirror on the following Nagriza. Mixed emotions flooded through him. He had vowed to himself – and made it as clear as he could to everyone else – that his involvement two years ago with Georgi and his London based espionage team, including Nagriza, would not be repeated. Through a series of events, none of his making, he had been dragged into their battle with the dangerous South Korean 'chaos entrepreneur', Sum Taeyoung. Bond was emphatic. That had been his only such exploit. Despite his name, this Bond had no desire to emulate his fictitious double-O namesake or be shot at again or to kill as he had done. That moment when he found death on his hands, lived on his conscience like a cancer despite Georgi's professional view that he had had no choice. In that split second, Bond's life and that of Nagriza had been in dire peril. Georgi said it was a choice of kill or be killed. It was a survival instinct.

Bond was oblivious to the fact that even now, two years after the event, Sum Taeyoung seethed that Bond was still alive. The South Korean had gone as far as commissioning a professional killer to put an end to Bond. That had failed. So this was, in Sum's terms, unfinished business. He vowed one day, sometime, somewhere, to conclude it.

And then there was Nagriza. Bond felt an uncontrollable stirring as thoughts of their night together in his home in Birmingham came back to him. They had made uninhibited, raw-naked, exhilarating and exhausting love. He could not shake it from his mind. She had been equally rough and gentle, giving as much as she received. She was sophisticated in her lovemaking yet sometimes just downright rude and naughty. Their passion was beyond anything he had experienced before. It was hardly surprising that, despite his best endeavours, he could not get her out of his mind. Now she was back, a hundred yards behind and following him to his Scottish cottage. How the hell was he going to react to this?

The cottage, more than 100 years old and the former home of a crofter now long departed this world, was dilapidated when Bond first discovered it, derelict but standing proud at the end of a valley with the sea behind it. Built of notably well-matched local stone cut by local craftsmen and constructed by local builders, the cottage might ultimately have slowly slipped into ruin over time. But Bond had bought it, stripped it to the bone and rebuilt it with the help of professionals. They used modern materials but preserved the original characteristics of the cottage. It was the ideal retreat from the crazy pressures of business and modern day living.

There was an awkward silence between them as they entered the building, Bond telling Nagriza which of the two rooms upstairs she would use before he busied himself lighting a coal and peat fire in the lounge. His head was full of recollections of the past, of how Nagriza told him of her family home on the shores of the Aral Sea in Uzbekistan and how her father's fishing livelihood, as with all the other fishermen in the area, died because of the diminishing water levels of what was once the fourth largest inland lake on the planet. She was tearful as she recalled what he already knew from his research – that the mighty inland sea became reduced to a sludge of mostly mud, waste and chemicals as its supply rivers were diverted to serve the irrigation systems of the cotton growing industry. It became an economic, environmental and health disaster.

Bond was amazed at the coincidence of Nagriza's link to the Aral Sea because one of the stimulants that originally caused him to become concerned about the appalling state of the planet, was the shameful story of the human abuse of what once had been a magnificent inland sea. He thought it remains as perhaps one of the worst examples of how economic objectives so dominate people's thinking that they forget to consider the potential social and environmental consequences of their actions. The mistake was catastrophic with terminal impact on the people who earned their living from this Sea. It also seriously affected the health of those who lived anywhere near it. The Aral Sea story was one of the reasons Bond became embroiled with the principals of sustainable development in which economic, social and environmental values have equal consideration.

Nagriza, then in her mid-teens, became involved in helping a Belgian scientific team working on the Aral Sea. As they ended their research, they offered Nagriza a job in Brussels. It was to be menial work but a godsend for the young girl, a chance to break the clutches of poverty. But obtaining the documentation needed to leave Uzbekistan proved almost impossible. After days sleeping rough in Tashkent, she was befriended by a civil servant who took a liking to her. It transpired he worked for SNB – the Uzbekistan National Secret Service and he eventually secured a secretarial job for her there.

"Once in," she had told Bond, "I worked hard, I learn quickly and I find out a lot. I find things out about some of my superiors and I get a better job. Then I start working on projects for them and one was about SDBI, Sum Taeyoung's legitimate business. That took me to meeting Georgi. The rest is – how do you say – history!"

Bond knew Georgi from days some years ago when he dealt with the Soviet Embassy in London where he and his Georgian friend used to drink copious amounts of Georgian brandy. The two of them had drifted apart and Bond ultimately concluded Georgi must have died in the short but vicious war between Russia and Georgia. But to Bond's amazement and joy some years later, he bumped into him at a convention and found he was now heading up the very secret, London based element of the European Secret Service.

With Georgi, Nagriza and others, Bond became involved in a battle with Sum Taeyoung out of which came, especially in the eyes of the UK press, a real hero by the name of Bond. As he had told Graham Mackay down at Forsinard, it was something he wished to wipe from his memory. But now here – in his hideaway cottage in the wilds of northern Scotland – was Nagriza. That episode of history seemed reluctant to go away.

By the time Nagriza came downstairs, a good fire was established and the smell of peat was beginning to permeate throughout the cottage. He poured them both a handsome measure of Douglas Laing's Big Peat single malt from the Isle of Islay, the distinct flavour of the drink mixing with the aroma of the fire. As he cast his eyes on the shapely, alluring figure of Nagriza with her hazel hair and brown eyes, this was, he felt, as close to paradise as he could get.

"I've missed you," Nagriza said as she accepted her drink, bending her head down but looking up at him. When she did this, he melted. He did not know if she did it on purpose knowing its impact on him. But intentional or not, he was magnetised by her.

"It's mutual," returned Bond. "To be very honest, however much I try, I can't get you out of my mind. But I've been to hell and back because of Georgi. I know why you're here. Clearly it's to twist my arm and get me to go to London and become involved again. I'll tell you now, I'm not going to. Your world of counterespionage, spies, surveillance, and all the other activity you get up to from your base in Wapping, is not for me. I can't tell you what hell I've been through since that gun battle on Lake Geneva

– as much because of my bloody name as anything else. I'm not getting into anything like that again."

"But we have something between us, Gene. Remember the night in Birmingham. It was wonderful."

"How can I forget it?" he told her. "And my feelings towards you are as they ever were. It's true to say, I can't shake you from my mind. If I'm honest with myself, I don't want to. But the bad times I've had ever since becoming involved with Georgi, are something I'm not going to repeat. No way. You can tell him that."

"Tell me about your life up here." Nagriza sought to change the subject and the mood between them. Bond settled into his favourite chair and Nagriza made herself comfortable on the floor, leaning against him with her arm across his legs. The fire puffed the occasional waft of peaty smoke into the room as the wind outside caught the chimney. They supped their malt whisky as Bond told her about his retreat here on the north coast of Scotland, about this crofting country, where many feudal-like laws still apply and where the pace of life is in marked contrast to what he – and she – experience in their working careers.

Good friendships had developed here over the 13 years since he bought the cottage. And now he knew about things that had previously been alien to him, like sheep farming, the crofting laws, land ownership, the history of the Clearances, forestry management and other matters he would never have encountered as an Englishman based in the Midlands.

The warmth from the fire, the smell of the peat, the malt whisky, the romantic characteristics of the cottage, their unquestionable love for each other. Their mutual memories of their last passionate encounter, her close proximity - there was an inevitability to the outcome. As he talked, Bond gently caressed her hair and he succumbed to the power of her large brown eyes. This habit of lowering her head then looking up towards him, it was a killer move. She was irresistible. And she was here, in his cottage in Scotland, in front of the blazing open fire. And it was here they made love again, not able to wait for the comforts of the bed upstairs. She virtually dragged him off his chair, pulling her jumper off at the same time to reveal her bare breasts. She straddled him and held him down as he tried to bend up to kiss her lips or her breasts but, teasingly, she denied him – for the moment. But it was for only a moment as their passion overtook control and soon two naked bodies writhed on the floor of the ancient cottage.

The following morning it was raining hard, almost horizontally in a strong northerly wind. But it did not stop them leaving the comforts of the cottage. They followed animal tracks through the bracken over the hill behind the cottage and down to the coast where a lively sea was sending huge waves crashing onto the rocks. It was exhilarating and refreshing, wiping their minds of all the dark things they wanted to forget and enabling them to revel in their own company.

Later, back in the cottage, they reluctantly talked about the future.

"I am not going to get involved with Georgi's work," Bond asserted for the umpteenth time. "I'd love to have a drink with him, as in old times, but I know all he'll do is drag me into your terrible world. I'm not going to do that."

"But how will I see you again?" asked Nagriza, clearly emotionally upset that they had no planned future together – in any form.

Bond was silent. He had no answers. He was passionately in love with Nagriza but she was so intertwined with the world in which Georgi operated as to be inseparable. It was a nightmare dilemma.

The silence persisted for some time until Bond had an idea.

"I will come to London. I was going to anyway. One thing that seems to have come from my adventure with you lot is an invitation to a Buckingham Palace Garden Party – of all things! I was astonished when it arrived. I can only assume it's something to do with what happened on Lake Geneva. There's no explanation with it, just a formal invitation to me – and a guest."

He took her hand. "Look, it's not going to resolve anything but why not be my guest? At least it's another chance to be together. Why not?"

"When is it?" she asked.

"Next week. Maybe too short notice for you?"

"No," she replied. "I don't care what day it is, I'll clear my diary. It sounds fantastic."

So he kissed her again. And they held each other tightly and passionately. And with no ability to control their emotions, they made love again.

Chapter 7

Two weeks on from his last visit to Paris, Sum Taeyoung sat back in his deckchair, relaxed and relished this moment of tranquillity in the small island's silence and the sun. Two years had passed since his skirmish with Georgi Patarava, Gene Bond and various law enforcement agencies. As they searched for him in the aftermath of that encounter, he had changed his physique, including losing considerable amounts of weight in next to no time, cutting his hair short and removing his beard. It was an attempt to shake off various forms of surveillance or at least to make life difficult for those looking for him. He had forsaken his Eastern robes for Western attire. But with the passing of time and immediate dangers dissipating, life gradually returned to how it had been. He reverted to the style and image he preferred and wore long, colourful, flowing robes on a body that was as bulky as it had ever been. His hair was long again, cascading down to meet the bushy beard that reached to his waist.

The early morning was still with scarcely a breath of wind and the newly risen sun shone brightly in a virtually cloudless sky. The fact there was hardly any movement in the air suited his purpose admirably although when it came to the real thing, they would have no control over such matters. But for this test run it was ideal.

He sat on the edge of the wood that dominated the hillside, the rising sap of thousands of trees giving a sweetness to the morning air. The stretch of inland water was a short distance below him, less than a quarter of a mile long and nearly as wide. It looked fresh and sparkling as light from the rising sun glistened across its rippling surface. This was Sum's second visit here. He had done an individual recce some months before with only a boatman from the mainland involved. Even in the short time since then, Sum could see the water level of the small lake had dropped, he guessed some six feet. There was a distinct dark area forming a sort of rim around the lake, just above the water line and looking like a tidal mark. But this was a fresh water lake with no such thing as a tide. Clearly since he was last here, the lake had lost a significant amount of water.

They were now well up the hilly hinterland and he could see down to the harbour and onwards to the open sea with a couple of small islets in view. His ears strained for the first sounds of the prototype device they were here to test. Sum prayed it would work. It was a long way to come and then confront failure – and that would be costly. Sum was only too aware that the funding of this project was so far coming straight out of his pocket. The fact constantly niggled but as yet he had found no external backer.

Since arriving on the island of Uido-ri, they had not seen a soul. It was semi-dark then with dawn just awakening. As they sped across the near flat waters of the Yellow Sea, the island finally rose before them like a black lump emerging from a grey sea. They cut their engine and the momentum of the boat drifted them quietly into the tiny harbour. There was no sign of any residents from the small number of houses scattered around. The locals were yet to start their day. With the boat secured to the harbour wall, the task of unloading the large crate began, a labour in which they were all involved including Sum, despite his aversion to physical hard work. A few fishing boats and holiday craft bobbed on the water but at this very early hour, there was still no sign of life anywhere. In fact they had not seen anyone since setting off in the dark from the mainland in the high speed launch that would take them the 20 miles or so across the Yellow Sea, passing numerous islands of varying size on their journey.

Uido-ri is about two miles square and rises to seven hundred feet high at its highest point. It is thickly covered by evergreen trees and based on volcanic rock, a remnant of historic volcanic activity. It is much like any of the other numerous islands scattered around the southern tip of South Korea. This particular remote location appealed to Sum for a variety of reasons. It has the sort of inland water area he needed for his test. It is secluded. It is to the south of South Korea, well away from the military zones of the border with troublesome North Korea. It is to the west of the mainland in the Yellow Sea and though that put him on the Chinese side of South Korea, China was far enough away not to concern him. Other locations he considered were potentially compromised by the security sensitivities and military activities not only of South and North Korea but also of China and Japan. Relationships between these two had been tentative for years as they contest some of the remote, uninhabited lumps of rock that emerge from the oriental seas of the region.

With Sum was Lee Ryang, a technology specialist from Sum's own company, SDBI, and now also trained to operate the equipment they brought with them. Sustainable Development Brokers International based in Seoul is a legitimate, globally-operating business. Sum launched it after a period of education at Harvard and the LSE in London. Sum never properly concluded his academic courses because they were overtaken by an overwhelming desire to launch a business and make money. Initial ideas came to nothing but Sum became increasingly aware of how many so called poor nations around the world were fast emerging into the consumer age. Often referred to as the BRICS – Brazil; Russia; India; China and South Africa, they all faded into insignificance alongside the example of China.

A nation of some 1.5 billion people, China's transformation is high speed and breath-taking as it moves from a frugal, communist, utilitarian country to a fast moving, consumer based economy – a strange, hybrid combination of communism and capitalism.

While Sum saw the positive side of this, he also predicted it would lead to some frightening environmental consequences. His prophesies proved to be right, with the economic growth of some Chinese mega-cities floundering in their self-created fogs of pollution. The demand for water created another problem – often outstripping provision. Challenges as to how to feed these enormous and expanding urban populations also became increasingly difficult.

Sum knew many of these problems had already been met in the West, or at least were becoming more understood there and responded to. So SDBI was formed to broker solutions and applied experience between the BRICS countries and Western specialist expertise. It is a business that flourishes, especially in China.

But Sum's life in New York and London also created within him a hatred and resentment for what he saw to be parasitical Western imperialism which, in his mind, raped many parts of the world and sucked assets from countries in the race for empire building. He saw the British, French and Portuguese to be the historic villains but now put into the shade by America which, he thought, outstripped the rest because of what he considered to be its arrogance and aggression.

So, known only to a few, SDBI provides a legitimate front to the far shadier activities of Sum Taeyoung – the creation of international chaos. It is an activity he finds highly satisfying because it appeases his poisoned view of Western capitalism and, because it generates other money earning activities – arms and drug dealing in particular.

Sum reflected that this small, placid, silent island in the Yellow Sea seemed far removed from any links to his normal life. To his side, Lee Ryang sat with him overlooking the water. Despite being an employee, the young South Korean technical wizard knew little about what SDBI did, let alone the concealed company within it. All he knew was that SDBI's top man wanted to undertake a feasibility test of a piece of kit. He wanted to do this on his own but needed Lee's technical skills and support. He had been told this was a top secret assignment and not to talk to anyone about it. Another SDBI staff man was acting as boatsman and the only other person involved came from another Seoul based company, which had undertaken some specialist work for Sum under strict conditions of confidentiality.

The equipment Sum wanted to test was contained in the large crate. It took Lee, his SDBI colleague, the man from the specialist company and even a minor contribution from Sum, to manhandle the crate onto the boat from the mainland and then to offload it at the harbour of Uido-Ri. Once onto the small island, a further hour was taken extracting the equipment from the crate, assembling it and then towing and pushing it on its wheels up the road leading from the harbour to a point where there are no buildings. Throughout this activity, they saw no one though what they had assembled would be bound to attract interest. It looked like a huge version of what are increasingly becoming fashionable high-tech toys. If anyone were to ask, that is what they would tell them it was – or a product of a group of university students that they were now putting to test.

Sum and Lee left the other two and walked the remaining length of the road up the hill to where it ends by the inland water. They continued to walk along the dirt track that circumnavigates the lake, with tree covered hills extending steeply to their left and the water below them and to their right, before the track dropped down to the water's edge.

Finding a spot to establish a temporary base, Sum Taeyoung busied himself assembling his deck chair while Lee opened the case he had been carrying and took out his laptop and various others pieces of equipment. He spent a while checking everything was in order before confirming his readiness to Sum. Sum nodded in satisfaction, a signal for Lee to radio down to the harbour that they were ready.

The tension mounted in Sum. Today was vital to the project. He needed to test his theory that this was hopefully going to resolve a major operational problem that had been causing headaches for quite a while. It was to do with the Chinese element of the plot for March 22nd. Sum's dilemma was how to import into China the equipment he needed for the task he wanted to undertake there. The option he first considered was to bring it in across the relatively remote Russian/Chinese border, but the road mileage was horrendous and the longer the equipment was on the move, the greater the odds were that it would be detected.

The solution was to utilise equipment made in China, modifying it to meet Sum's specific needs. With that commissioned, a South Korean company built a twin model in parallel to the Chinese one, and that was what was being tested today. Down by the Uido-ri harbour, the technician prepared the prototype model.

Up in the hills, Sum and Lee waited with growing anticipation and, as far as Sum was concerned, a fair degree of anxiety. Everything about today was based on Sum's theory. He had no idea really if the basic idea would work. He had no idea if the technology he had selected was appropriate. And he had no idea if the model he had had built in South Korea, would work, especially as it was a significant departure from the Chinese original. It was all well and good seeing these things on computer screens. What he wanted was to see it perform in real life.

An hour later the test was complete. Sum stood and stretched, stiff for having sat for so long. He and Lee walked down the hill to the harbour, Sum feeling a sense of satisfaction that his ideas had been verified. It had been a perfect test. He now knew the technical side of his new project was viable. All he needed to do now was find someone with money to fund it.

Chapter 8

Their taxi driver recommended they enter the Palace via the South Gate. "When I passed the Palace on the way to pick you up, the queue there looked less than at the other gates," he told them.

"That sounds ominous," Nagriza commented to Bond. "How many people go to these things?"

"I've no idea," Bond responded. "I must admit I've not done any homework on this. I haven't a clue what we're letting ourselves in for."

So they joined a substantial line of people waiting in the late afternoon June sun to enter the Palace. They assumed, from what the taxi driver had told them, similar lines of people were waiting access through other gates at the front of Buckingham Palace. Though dress code was informal, this queue of people had clearly dressed for the occasion with many of the ladies wearing fascinators and elaborate hats. Scattered amongst the gathered throng, a number of uniformed men and women showed all branches of the armed forces were represented. More exotic colourful gowns and headdresses were evidence that many overseas guests were in the party. Nagriza, Bond thought, looked stunning in a silky, flowing, vividly bright green dress that showed enough leg and cleavage to attract many a male eye but without being so risqué as to offend royal etiquette.

Bond had never been to the Palace before. It was something he had never contemplated doing. Without receiving this invitation, he doubted he ever would have. Indeed, he had mixed feelings about the whole event. An occasion such as this would normally never have entered his mind. It was not his kind of scene, this 'rubbing shoulders' with royalty. But, having been given the opportunity, he recognised the honour, felt declining would be insulting, and had become increasingly curious as expectation and anticipation grew the closer the event came. The moment was made even more special now Nagriza was with him.

Their line of people eventually moved forward into the forecourt of the Palace. Bond could not help feeling privileged to be doing this, especially as hundreds of people now gazed enviously at them from the other side of the railings. When they eventually reached the actual building, the experience of being in the Palace was over seemingly before it had begun. The desire to stop and look at everything was gently discouraged by Palace officials and the line of people moved quickly across a wide, red carpeted hallway with marble pillars and an elegant staircase to the left with nearby, a large marble statue of Mars and Venus which they hardly saw before they were into the grand Bow Room. Again, there was no opportunity to admire its content. In next to no time, they were through the open French windows and into the garden, standing at the top of the wide steps that would take them down to the lawn.

"Well, that was the Palace," Bond muttered to Nagriza. "Hardly an extensive conducted tour!"

"Don't be so sarcastic," she responded. She was already loving every minute of it.

Bond viewed the scene before him. He had no idea what he'd expected to see but the sheer size of the event surprised him. It was now obvious he and Nagriza were part of a guest list numbering some thousands – this sunny afternoon.

Ahead of them, the vast lawn was a sea of humanity. To their right, a military band sat and played. To their left, a huge marquee was evidently where tea would eventually be served. As they stood and surveyed the sights before them, the nearby band stopped playing and the musicians relaxed. No sooner had they done so than music wafted across the lawn from a second band, hidden from view by all the people. Puzzled for a moment as to how the change over from one band to another was organised when their respective conductors could not see each other, Bond spotted that when the band nearest to them stopped playing, a flag was hauled up an adjacent flagpole, a signal to the second band that it was their turn to play. It was all very simple but very effective.

"What do we do now?" asked Nagriza.

"I haven't a bloody clue" he responded. "Your guess is as good as mine."

They had not been given a programme. There was nothing displayed that showed an order of events. And as they moved forward onto the lawn to join the throng of visitors, it became apparent that nobody else knew quite what to do either. Throughout the extensive gardens, people were strolling – individually, in couples, often hand in hand, and in small groups. So they did the same – also hand in hand – wandering around the 30 acres of Buckingham Palace gardens and marvelling at this enormous botanical oasis in the heart of London.

With a backdrop of the iconic, globally recognised Palace, the extensive garden with its beautifully sculptured lake, its meticulously presented flowerbeds and its garden ornaments and statues of varying size, description and from various countries of origin, few, if any, could not be in awe of their surroundings on such an occasion.

An hour later a herd instinct seemed to be operating. It was Nagriza who noticed that people were now queuing at the marquee for food and she and Bond duly joined to get their delicate little sandwiches and smart little cakes with the royal coat of arms embossed in the icing tops. Hundreds of seats had been placed around tables on the lawn in front of the marquee but these were all now occupied so Bond and Nagriza wandered back down the lawn towards the lake and found the stone surrounding at the base of a tree adequate enough to sit on.

"It's all terribly, terribly English," observed Nagriza, surveying the scene and speaking in a voice louder than it needed to be and in an exaggerated and not very successful English accent.

"Stop being naughty," Bond said as heads turned to look at this spectacularly dressed lady who was broadcasting her feelings rather too vocally for their liking. But he agreed. It was a classic English tea party, albeit for some thousands of people, with a backdrop of the royal Palace and the military bands. He reflected again that he had no idea why he had been invited here or what to expect, but he felt a sense of being honoured by the invitation to such an impressive event which now had the added glory of Nagriza being with him to share it.

After tea they occupied another hour strolling around. "Naughty Nagi", as Bond sometimes teasingly called her when she was being particularly outrageous, living up to her name by, in one corner of the gardens where the visitors were scarcer than elsewhere, suddenly turning on him, grabbing his back with her left arm to pull him to her but at the same time ensuring her right hand was between them at chest height. There, in the royal garden of Buckingham Palace, she tweaked his left nipple. It was but a few little flicks of her index figure but it was an outrageously sexy act and one that sparked an immediate reaction in Bond. But before he could respond, with a cheeky squeak of satisfaction, she gave him a brief kiss, a wink and then moved away to a more appropriate respectable distance.

The herd instinct was drawing all the guests onto the lawn. They followed suit and became aware that within the crowd, conspicuous by their pinstriped morning suits, top hats and furled umbrellas, a statutory height which seemed to be at least six and a half feet (although some were taller) and ramrod backs, a handful of men of very apparent former military careers, were gently marshalling some thousands of people into lines on the lawn. Now realising what was going on, Bond watched in amazement. They hardly seemed to do anything but these gentlemen oozed authority. They were like sophisticated sheep dogs herding a very large flock.

As they stood in a developing line of visitors, one of the ex-military gentlemen approached Bond and Nagriza, raising his hat to her as he approached.

"Good afternoon Ma'm," he said, pronouncing the word to rhyme with the word spam rather than sounding as if he was addressing his mother. "I wonder if you would mind acting as a corner post? I need to bend this line and I've run out of Beefeaters who would normally do it for me."

Nagriza, highly impressed to have been picked out to do anything even if it was only to be a corner post, was unable to contain her natural instincts and started to flirt with this tall, handsome, immaculate man.

"How can I refuse such an offer?" she said, fluttering her eyelashes at him.

Bond, wanting to get in on the conversation and through real curiosity, said "Excuse me interrupting. But who are you guys? I've been watching you and how you've marshalled us into rows. It's very clever and very subtle. But who are you and what's happening?"

"Good afternoon sir," the ex-military man responded. "What we've done is form four corridors of visitors. One member of the royal family will progress down each corridor. I think you've been lucky. The Queen and Prince Phillip will be attending this corridor."

"But who are you?" Bond was keen to get an answer to the question that seemingly had been avoided.

"I'm a member of the Honorary Corps of Gentlemen at Arms, sir. We're all ex Guards except one in our current ranks. He's a former Marine."

Bond thought the reference to the Marine sounded as if the solid ranks of the Guards had somehow been polluted. He did not know if it was a serious comment or made in jest. He thought it diplomatic not to ask.

"OK, but who are the Gentlemen at Arms?" asked Bond, growingly inquisitive about this small band of men who had so cleverly manipulated a few thousand people without any of them knowing it.

"History says we're the last line of defence for the Monarch," the man told him with obvious pride, tinged with a hint of humour.

"And how do you become a member?" asked Bond.

"Do you know, sir," the response was accompanied by a widening smile and a twinkle of the eye, "I genuinely have absolutely no idea at all! And if you'll excuse me, I have my corridor to manage."

And with that he moved away.

"You bloody flirt," said Bond, turning to Nagriza.

"Well, why not. He was very good looking and refined."

Bond had his iPhone out and busied himself with it. Looking intently at the screen, he nudged Nagriza.

"Look what I've found. The web site says – 'Her Majesty's Body Guard of the Honourable Corps of Gentlemen at Arms provides a bodyguard to The Queen at many ceremonial occasions. Since 1856, when the award was instituted, twelve Gentlemen at Arms have been holders of the Victoria Cross, the highest award for gallantry and conspicuous bravery in the field. The Honourable Corps of Gentlemen at Arms was instituted by King Henry VIII in 1509 and was originally a mounted escort, armed with spear and lance to protect the sovereign in battle or elsewhere. I wonder where our friend has left his spear and lance?"

Before Nagriza could comment, all conversation stopped as one of the bands played the National Anthem and the Queen and accompanying members of her family walked from within the Palace onto the lawn. With the anthem over, the noise level rose as people started to talk again but in noticeably subdued tones as if in acknowledgement that everyone was now in the company of royalty. Bond and Nagriza waited with expectation rising, he noticing that their corridor, as with the others, was now made of two lines of people some ten or more people deep. They were very privileged to be at the front with such an open view of the proceedings.

After some minutes, the Gentleman at Arms with his top hat and furled umbrella returned to them.

"I hope you're enjoying your afternoon," he said to Nagriza.

"It's perfect," she responded. "Very English. How many people are here?"

"About 7, 000," he told her. "And there are three Garden Parties every summer."

All eyes in the corridor were now directed towards to the Palace as the Queen came into view, wearing a bright green summer coat and stopping to talk to people who had been selected from those standing in the corridor. As Bond watched the nearing royal party with growing interest, their new acquaintance walked back to them. He closed in on Bond, putting one hand on his shoulder. He spoke softly into his ear.

"We shall meet tomorrow, Mr Bond. At the Prospect of Whitby. 1300 hours." There was a pause before he added, "this is not a request or an invitation, Mr Bond. You will be there."

And with that, the hand gently patted Bond's shoulder before the man marched off towards the royal group. Bond stared after him in amazement and bewilderment.

"How the hell did he know my name?" he thought. "Me, amongst 7,000 other people?"

And, as he continued to watch the man who was now busying himself with the royal group, a thought dawned on him.

"Bloody hell! I've been set up!"

Chapter 9

While Sum busied himself on the island in the Yellow Sea, in Paris another task he had commissioned was about to be executed. For Yacine Rami, it was a straightforward task in return for exceptionally good money. The approach to him was made by letter. In itself that was unusual. Nowadays, most correspondence to Yacine was by e-mail and mostly via his iPhone. But this letter arrived, delivered by hand, so there was no postal marking to give any clue where it came from. It simply told him what was wanted – a killing – and gave a very generous fee. Also, most unusually, the envelope contained Euros to the value of 50% of the cost of the job. There was no sender's name. There was no address. There was no question as to whether or not Yacine would want to undertake the task. There was simply a clear set of instructions, a faded picture of a young girl, and a promise of the balance of the fee on confirmation the task had been completed.

Yacine was confident he could complete his assignment and escape afterwards, although the commission was made slightly more complicated by the strange specification that the girl was to be killed by knife – and not just any old knife. Confirmation that the task was completed was to be in the form of a photograph and that was to be posted to a website. Yacine checked the site and found it to be an anonymous collection of news photographs and links to extreme videos. The only other part of the communication was also crystal clear. If Yacine failed to deliver, there would be a cost. His life!

Whoever had commissioned this work had obviously done his homework well and knew Yacine would fulfil the task. Thirty years of age and born of Algerian parents he had never known, Yacine had always lived in Paris, always operated in the criminal world since leaving school before he was due to, and graduated from petty crime to more serious activity including some killings. He was known to law enforcement agencies but always escaped being detained by them. His business territories were the banlieues of Paris where he was able to capitalise on the instability and violence in districts renowned for being social problem areas, where unemployment was widespread, youth was without any prospects, delinquency, drug dealing and gang rule held sway.

Finding Madeleine had not been that difficult. Yacine showed her picture around bars and clubs and eventually was able to put a name to the young girl then trace where she lived and worked. Just four days after receiving the anonymous letter, Yacine started a surveillance of his target. Clearly something had upset her normal routine and it did not take long for Yacine to discover that her boyfriend's body had recently been found amongst the burnt out cars of the St. Denis suburb. For a week, Madeleine virtually stayed at home but by week two, she had started a tentative effort to return to normal life, working in the café bar on the junction of the Rue du Faubourg Poissonniere and the Rue Bleue and doing voluntary work in the nearby Laboratoires d'Aubervilliers where she seemed to go quite frequently. After a further three days, Yacine knew Madeleine's normal route between the art centre and where she lived with her mother. He now also knew of her involvement with the Paris Guerriers Urbains and that that is where she had met her recently deceased boyfriend.

From his observations, Yacine guessed Madeleine was very young, maybe as young as 16, maybe 17. She certainly had the looks, mannerisms, uncertainties and insecurities of a teenager and he would have been surprised to find she was actually 20. She was pretty but not yet very feminine. Her short haircut made her look rather boyish.

Yacine developed a simple plan. He armed himself with his killing tool, his long trusted douk-douk pocket knife, a weapon that became the first choice of assassins during the Front de Libération Nationale (FLN) led uprising against the French in Algeria. The killing tool had been clearly specified in the instructions. He waited in one of the narrow, dark lanes down which Madeleine walked between the Laboratoires d'Aubervilliers and her home. The first night she did not turn up which caused him some concern but he assured himself it was merely related to the interruption to her routine caused by her boyfriend's death. Sure enough on the second day, as he waited in the rain on an especially dark and gloomy night, the diminutive figure of his target came into sight walking directly towards him. Yacine wore a raincoat over his shoulders like a cape, one button holding it closed at the front. Underneath the raincoat, his arms and hands were free, his right hand holding the douk-douk.

The distance between them closed. Yacine's luck was holding. Nobody else was using this narrow side road at this time of night. Within ten paces of Madeleine, he undid the one button of his raincoat. The young girl had not even seen him. She had her head bent against the incoming rain and her eyes were more towards the pavement than anything else. As they passed each other, Yacine grabbed her with his left hand across her mouth to prevent her shouting and at the same time, pulled her small body towards him. As he did so, his right hand buried the knife into her back, on the left hand side and as close to her heart as he could judge.

It was over in seconds. The young female body slumped from his grip onto the wet pavement. Yacine looked around. Still the narrow road remained empty. Quickly, he photographed the body with his iPhone and cleaned the knife blade on her coat before slipping away into the dark night. He was lucky. Less than two minutes later, one of the few cars to pass down this narrow side road this evening did so, the driver catching sight of the fallen girl in his headlight beams. Many drivers would have just kept going. This one had a conscience. He stopped, discovered the crumpled heap on the pavement was a young girl, and phoned the emergency services. They arrived quickly and the paramedics found a faint pulse in the young victim.

Ten minutes later, Madeleine was being stretchered into the Hôpital Saint-Louis where she died shortly afterwards. The staff had done all they could but the wound had been fatal. Just briefly, for a flickering second, the youthful Parisian regained consciousness. It was enough of a moment for her to try and communicate to the medical staff around her. In her whispering voice and on the verge of death, she tried desperately to get words to come from her mouth. The medics bent over her, straining to hear what she was trying to tell them. As they exchanged views afterwards, the consensus was that Madeleine had, for some incomprehensible reason, whispered her last words in English. The hardly audible words, they agreed, seemed to say – "Some die young" – followed by some numbers. Was it 2203? Nobody was sure. It was a while before what Madeleine really tried to tell them became understood.

Chapter 10

Bond travelled by train to Wapping station. His mind was a whirlpool of anger, disillusionment, disappointment and fear for the future – a fear as to what he was now being pulled into and what future lay with Nagriza. In the aftermath of events at Buckingham Palace, in terms of the luscious Nagriza, he simply no longer knew what to think. He was obsessed with her yet she had completely hoodwinked him. She had been part of a secret plot on behalf of Georgi.

Into this mix of thoughts came memories of the last time he was in Wapping. He had not seen Georgi Patarava since or his clandestine world of the Communications Centre of the officially non-existent European Union Intelligence Service, more commonly known as the European Secret Service.

"I didn't know there was such a thing," Bond had said to Georgi.

"There isn't – officially that is," Georgi had told him. "It morphed into being. It sort of created itself by accident as other units were formed in the earlier days of the EU – the European Satellite Centre, the Intelligence Division and the Joint Situation Centre. It didn't take much to extract bits off each of them and form something called the EU Intelligence Service which even most Members of the European Parliament don't know exists."

Georgi went on to tell him that when the EUIS was formed in Brussels, it was agreed that the Communications Centre should be in London, close to MI5, MI6 and the sophisticated links the UK's GCHQ in Cheltenham enjoys with the Americans. And, as Georgi explained when he first introduced Bond to the Centre, where better to hide something that officially doesn't exist than in a place that also does not officially exist – the basement areas of what used to be spice warehouses in Wapping Wall. These giant buildings, dating back to the days of the mighty clipper ships, were redeveloped into luxury dwellings some decades ago. But that was before the new Thames Barrier had been tried and tested. There was fear then that the subterranean basements of the old warehouses might flood. So they were sealed off.

Thirty years later, with modern day technology making possible what used to be impossible and with the abilities of the Barrier now proven, these basement areas were secretly reopened to provide an extraordinary but totally unknown home for Georgi Patarava's sophisticated Communications Centre.

Bond arrived at Wapping Station, itself a reminder to him of the last time he was in Georgi's centre of operation. His old friend had been proud to show the emergency exit from the secret Communications Centre – a freshly built tunnel – or, more precisely, an oversized plastic tube just about big enough to walk down – which connects to what originally was the historic foot tunnel built by Marc Isambard Brunel in the mid 1800s to link Wapping and Rotherhithe on the opposite side of the Thames. For Georgi's purposes, it would have been helpful if this had remained a foot tunnel but its use now as an under-river escape route, or for reinforcements to come the other way, was made significantly more hazardous as the tunnel now forms part of the London Overground suburban rail network.

"It's by no means perfect, my friend," Georgi confessed. "But one day we may be very thankful for it, perfect or not."

Much had happened since yesterday's events at the Royal Garden Party including, sadly, a massive deterioration in the relationship with Nagriza who, Bond had quickly come to realise, was materially involved in the plot that also included the member of the Honorary Corp of Gentlemen at Arms. It was clear to Bond now. The ex-military man could have memorised Bond's face but, amongst 7,000 other people, even for someone trained in such matters, that was no easy task. It was far less of a challenge to spot a startlingly attractive lady in a gloriously rich green dress. Find her and you find your man. He had done just that. And it also eventually dawned on Bond, how come he had an invitation to the Royal Garden Party which also gave entrance to an unnamed, undeclared guest? How could that happen in the mega-security conscious environs of Buckingham Palace? He eventually fathomed it out. They had known Nagriza was going to be with him. So back in the cottage on the Scottish north coast, if he had not got round to inviting her, she obviously would have found a way to ensure he did.

He had been suckered – well and truly.

"You walked me straight into that," he complained bitterly as they left Buckingham Palace. She did not answer.

"How could you? To know that all the way through Scotland – and when we were in the cottage. It's obviously a Georgi plot – and you were a central player. What the fuck does that do to our relationship? How can I ever trust you again?"

"I had no choice," she pleaded. "What else could I do?"

"You could have told me."

"No I couldn't."

"Why not?"

"Because if I had, you would never have come to London with me."

"And", she added before he could say anything more. "I had my own selfish reasons anyway."

"And what are they?" he asked begrudgingly.

"It helps me. If you are working with Georgi, I see more of you."

"Bollocks," he retorted. "That's crap."

And the conversation continued in its heated way, verging on a full blooded row. Their first. It was not resolved when they parted company, he notably not extending the suggestion they dined together. So he ate alone, in a scruffy restaurant in the low cost hotel he was staying in overnight.

He was up early, leaving the hotel and walking into a grey, chilly and damp morning. His mood remained as gloomy as the morning and was not helped by the walk from the railway station up Wapping High Street, turning right into Wapping Wall. The old, grey, huge, historic buildings, once spice warehouses but now spruced up as much as they could be to align to their new found use as luxurious homes for people working in the economic hot house of the nearby City of London, still looked dreary and foreboding.

He strode through a misty rain along Wapping Wall parallel to the river but separated from it by these remnants of 19th century tea and spice trading, buildings one of which now contains the spacious apartment in which Georgi lives, with its secret connecting passageway direct to the basement and his place of work, the Communications Centre of EUIS. He did not slow his pace as he passed Georgi's front door and onwards towards the famous London inn. The Prospect of Whitby's history goes back to the days of Charles Dickens and other notables from that period, including people like fellow writer Samuel Pepys and artists like Turner and Whistler.

The frontage of the inn with its bay windows either side of the main entrance provides little if any external evidence of its near 500 years of history. Bond stepped inside and onto the 400 year old stone floor, the oldest surviving element of the building. He was pleased to move into some shelter as the weather was now really deteriorating and a steady rain had set in. It was welcomingly warm and dry in the inn.

The place was crowded, making seeing anyone difficult unless they happened to be extremely tall. Bond spotted the member of the Honorary Corps of Gentlemen at Arms at the bar, talking to one of the barmaids who was bent towards him over the bar revealing a more than generous view of her cleavage. Bond pushed his way through the throng of people to join him.

"Ah, Bond. Here you are. What are you going to drink?" The accompanying hand shake was strong and vigorous. He bought Bond the beer that had been asked for then led him through the crowded inn to where a table lay empty with a handwritten sign on it saying 'Reserved'. Bond observed that no other table had such a sign.

"I'm pleased to see you," said his host. "I wasn't altogether certain you'd show. Did you enjoy the Garden Party yesterday?"

"Most of it," responded Bond. It was difficult to keep the evidence of his agitation out of his voice. "That is I did until I realised I'd been the victim of a conspiracy. What's all this about, Mr – er? I still don't even know your name. But I guess I know what it's about."

"I think the word conspiracy's a bit tough," responded the ex-Guard. "As I told you at the Palace, I have no idea how I came to be invited to become one of the members of the Honorary Corps of Gentlemen at Arms. But I did. And, as one does when one is asked to do one's bit for Queen and Country, I responded."

It crossed Bond's mind that there had been no response to him saying he did not know this man's name. He became resigned that he probably never would.

"So, Mr Bond, when Queen and Country calls on you, we hoped you too would respond positively. After all, what you did on Lake Geneva when you threw that bomb off the paddle steamer was heroic and commendable and demonstrated you are a man of action and of principles. We also know full well that you have resented the focus on you in subsequent years. That's understandable. We sympathise. But, Mr Bond, your help is again needed and, whether you like it or not, when the Queen and the Country call on you, I think I know you will answer the call positively and stand up and be counted."

Bond's heart sank. It was as he had expected and feared. This was all Georgi's doing and despite his unequivocal indications that he never wanted to become involved again, clearly there was no escape.

He stared at his three quarters drunk pint, unsure what to say. He was still staring at it when a hand clasped his right shoulder.

"Finish that off my friend and I'll buy you another." It was the unmistakable voice of Georgi.

Chapter 11

Sum Taeyoung was speaking. "This has to be what I would call a "what if" meeting. A probe into the possible. I must admit a sense of disappointment that Bernhard Gedeck was unable to be here himself or at least speak to me direct. If he'd done so I might find myself able to be more direct, more forthright. That would have been to our mutual advantage. As it is now, I'm doubtful about the value of this meeting."

The two men sat in one of Sum's favourite places. When in Seoul he frequented it daily even though he knew that probably compromised his security. "But then," he told himself, "as a genuine international businessman, why should I not indulge myself in those things I enjoy and be seen to be doing so?"

Which is why the two men sat opposite each other at a small, round, rickety table on the creaky floorboards of the upper floor of the Flying Bird Tea Shop in the Insadong area of Seoul, the gigantean capital of South Korea. It is hardly the sort of place where one would expect sophisticated business to be conducted or international intrigue to be plotted but Sum loved its quaintness which reminded him of his mother's dining room. He adored it for all its quaint knick-knacks, pottery, ornaments, paper lanterns, a variety of curios and no two tables the same. It is a place of sublime tranquillity, quirkiness, with a pervading aroma of herbal teas, and, of course, the infamous small free flying song birds with their startlingly bright colours that basically have the run of the place.

Sum is also virtually addicted to the shop's famous double harmony tea, celebrated throughout South Korea for its powers to fight colds. Nobody seems sure what it consists of but rumour suggests it has a powerful blend of dried roots, ginger, ginseng, cinnamon bark, and other medicinal ingredients. Whether or not it actually does what it claims to do is scientifically unproven, but it certainly smells as it if should do.

The man sitting opposite him, Gordon Knight, was American, smart in appearance with an immaculate suit, recently titivated haircut, manicured finger nails and obvious sharpness of mind. He had the air of someone with great self-confidence and self-belief.

"I am a senior vice president of Esca, Mr Taeyoung. Mr. Gedeck entrusts me explicitly with quite open-ended responsibilities, with negotiating and decision-making powers – within obvious corporate boundaries as I am sure you understand."

Taeyoung smiled and nodded in agreement. "But I am equally sure you will understand that on matters of trust – of governance if you like – or even of shared responsibility, I cannot proposition you as I would he. If Mr Gedeck was here, we would both know what we said and agreed and have joint responsibility for. That doesn't work if I'm talking through an intermediary, whether he be a senior vice president or otherwise."

If Gordon Knight was embarrassed, uncomfortable or even insulted by what had been said, he hid it well.

"That's your decision, sir," he replied. "But I can only reiterate my authority and hope we can progress this so that it becomes a meaningful encounter and not a waste of time and effort – yours or mine."

"Touché," said Sum. "That's a fair riposte. But what I wanted to proposition Mr Gedeck about is not what would be found within the boundaries of normal business or political convention."

He paused, sipping some tea but continuing to hold Gordon Knight's eye contact.

"You are aware of the problems in Wandora." It was difficult to make out whether this was a question or a statement. Gordon Knight said nothing. He waited for Sum to elaborate and continued to hold his stare.

"It was an Esca created problem."

Another pause. Again, no response.

"And resolved by an SDBI solution."

Another pause.

"Which suggested to me that Esca and SDBI could, in certain circumstances, make an interesting partnership. Maybe?"

This time it was undoubtedly a question. Sum waited for a reply. Like a poker game, he would have sat there all afternoon waiting for a reply. Eventually, he got one.

"Wandora is a special set of circumstances and a challenge which we believe we would have resolved anyway without external interventions. With respect sir, it was the government there that brought SDBI in, not us. We had the issue under strong remedial management and would have put the matter right."

Sum thought about that for a while before answering.

"But you didn't. We did", he said, pointedly. "Just to be clear that we understand each other, as far as I know, Esca was called in by the Wandora government because new and more extensive mining operations were impacting negatively on the country's already perilous water supplies and, in some areas, drying it up completely."

Another pause. More tea sipping. More eye contact.

"Esca's solution was to hunt for more groundwater and drill more boreholes to access what you found. EscaEau then bottled it and distributed it. It seemed like a solution. Peasant people in remote villages were no longer dying of thirst, for instance. That was good news. The Wandora government paid you well for the solution. But it didn't work, did it?"

Gordon Knight sat passively, no emotion or reaction evident at all. So Sum continued.

"While EscaEau pulled groundwater from your new boreholes, so water in the wells in many of Wandora's peasant villages dried up. In reality, you weren't solving the problem at all. You were just shifting it."

"So when the government started to investigate this and became suspicious of what was happening, they decided to call in a new independent player. They called in Sustainable Development Brokers International, my company. It didn't take us long to identify what was going on. The new boreholes were syphoning water off subterranean aquifers that normally provided water for village wells. Esca, far from providing a solution, was seriously compounding the problem."

"Clever business! You create the problem then get paid for clearing it up. Some would say that's immoral. Lots of international NGOs did when they got hold of the story. And though Esca fought our findings tooth and nail to start with, eventually you had to concede we were right. Esca has basically been thrown out of the country and ended up paying significant compensation to Wandora. Right?"

Gordon Knight spoke at last. "Is this all there is, Mr Taeyoung? A history lesson?"

Sum Taeyoung lent forward across the small table.

"No Mr Knight. That is not all. And don't antagonise me or I might not get to declare my offer to you. That would be something to be regretted – by you and Esca."

A pause for more tea.

"SDBI came up with a new solution. We took a lateral look at the problem, went back to its origins and hit it there. We found ways of significantly reducing the amount of water the new mining and extraction activities were using and also, recycled much of it. That hugely reduced the pressure on Wandora's fragile water supplies. So, Esca created a problem, SDBI solved it. You lost a lot of money. We earned a lot of money. Interesting – yes?"

"It's still only a history lesson," Gordon Knight said quietly.

Sum Taeyoung sighed and sat back, rocking his chair onto its rear legs.

"It may be only a history lesson to you. To me – it taught me something. It taught me – or reminded me – how precious water is. How essential to life it is. And, most importantly, how people will pay to ensure they can get it."

Another pause. Sum rocked back towards the table and again lent forward to be as close as he could to Gordon Knight.

"So, my 'what if' question to Bernhard Gedeck would have been, if he were here, how much would it be worth to Esca to know in advance, that three major parts of the world are soon to be hit with serious water shortages? I'm not just talking about reductions in supply. I am talking about catastrophic losses of water threatening the lives of tens of thousands of people – possibly millions – wrecking national and local economies and bringing down governments. To a company like Esca – with its global skills and abilities to supply water in tough circumstances, wouldn't such advanced knowledge be of value, Mr Knight? Of perhaps considerable value."

"What sort of catastrophic events are we talking about – and where?" Clearly Gordon Knight's interest was caught, even if it were with a great degree of reluctance.

Sum Taeyoung rocked back on his chair again, lifted his cup and sipped his tea.

"Mr Knight. If Gordon Bedeck sat before me I might tell him more. Not everything – but more than I've told you. Perhaps you would be good enough to relay my message to Gordon Bedeck. And you can inform him please, what I have is more than a history lesson! If he's interested and wants to know, I'll tell him. But it has to be here. Face to face. I won't do so through an intermediary."

Things moved more quickly than Sum Taeyoung could have hoped for but it still took three weeks and numerous calls to various people in the giant conglomerate that is Esca before he received a call on his personal iPhone from Gordon Bedeck. Three days later, they sat opposite each other in the Flying Bird Tea Room, by coincidence at the same table he had sat at with Gordon Knight.

"As I see it," Sum said in his opening shot at this leader of an internationally respected, globally operating corporation who sat opposite him in his lightweight suit, exuding power and wealth in intimidating quantities. "I have something that might interest you and you have something of potential value to me. That has the ring of a prospective business relationship. Do you agree?"

Gordon Bedeck looked at this extraordinary figure before him and wondered what on earth he was doing in this creaking café with its pesky birds and in an offbeat part of Seoul. The man was unusual, to say the least. Big, massively overweight, tall and seemingly with hair everywhere, he was obviously of Oriental Asian origin and that was confirmed by the colourful robes he was wearing. But when he spoke, the accent smacked of upper class Oxford English with a New York drawl mixed to the faintest hint of Asia somewhere in the man's history. Bedeck had done his homework and knew as much as anyone about Taeyoung's background, and that of his company SDBI. What he did not know was the darker side of SDBI and Taeyoung's impassioned hatred of the developed Western world.

"And what, Mr Taeyoung, have I got that is of value to you?"

"Ah, well," replied Sum in an unusually hesitant and stumbling way. "You have the opportunity to, er, invest in a major project I've put together."

"Does this link to the water matter you talked briefly to Knight about?"

"It does. But before we progress Mr Bedeck, I need you to understand my position and I need to understand yours. On my side, I have two business streams. One is legitimate and internationally regarded. The other is, well, er, how best shall I describe it? Clandestine is probably a good description. This second business is very personal to me. It serves ambitions that go way beyond those of business and which need not be of any concern or f interest to you. It is what I do, that should interest you. Not why."

"So, what I am about to tell you is extremely awkward for me to talk about, to anyone. But you have, Mr Bedeck, I know, aspirations to rule the world in the delivery of drinking water."

Bedeck, taken aback by this last statement which so echoed what he had told his executives at their recent private meeting in London, tried to respond but Taeyoung continued.

"Don't ask me how I know what I know. Just accept I know quite a lot about your forward business plans, especially under the EscaEau brand. If I spelt out to you what I know, you would have serious doubts about your internal security. And you should have such doubts. I recommend you take urgent remedial action. But in the meantime, all I know will remain within my confidence. It should show you, Mr Bedeck, you can trust me. But what I have for you should be of significant interest within the context of your ambition. So where I am now – as we sit together today is – I know what you are about, Mr Bedeck. And you can trust me with that information. My big question is – before I tell you anything more, can I trust you?"

Chapter 12

Gene Bond never did find out the name of the former member of the Guards. He slipped away as Georgi took over the meeting in the Prospect of Whitby.

"That was not my idea, Gene," he tried to reassure his friend. "Believe me. Matters were taken off me. We have a case on our hands that clearly has some environmental context and my bosses told me to get you involved. They remembered you from our battle with Sum Taeyoung on Lake Geneva. I phoned you and tried to get your help. You refused. I understand why. I really do. But my bosses are both determined and concerned. They feel your input's essential. That's why we did what we did. It was not my choice. It was not Nagriza's choice. We did it because we were told to. That's not to say, my very good friend, I'm not delighted you can help."

Bond was at a loss to know what to think. Clearly the approach to him left him with few, if any, options – the member of the Corps of Gentlemen had indicated that. It was, the man had said, a matter of 'standing up to be counted when your country calls.' It could only be a matter of hypothetical debate as to what might happen if he refused. Locked up in The Tower of London? In this day and age probably not, but he guessed some sanctions would be applied somehow. Whilst he was only too happy to respond to a call on his patriotism, he was also extremely conscious that some powerful forces were playing in this game and there was an underlying worry as to what might happen if he simply said no and tried to walk away. All his determination to distance himself from Georgi's world of counterespionage was being frittered away. He was going to have to become involved, like it or not. They talked about it over the remainder of their drinks, not specifically about the new case, but in generalities in which listening ears would have found nothing interesting to hear. And slowly, Bond resigned himself to a fate beyond his control.

Drinks finished they moved off and headed for the subterranean offices of the EU Intelligence Service located deep in the basements of the redeveloped spice warehouses in Wapping Wall. Bond found far more people working there now than when he was last in the EUIS Comms Centre. The place had a feeling of well managed busyness with the majority of people working at computers and concentrating on their screens. Most worked individually, some with headphones on, although there were a few groups of people huddled in meetings. There were more large screens around the walls than when Bond was last here. Some were views of locations the EUIS was observing. Two were of the entrance areas to the Communications Centre as part of the security of the place. There was a large map of the world and one screen was devoted to the BBC 24 hour news channel. Clearly, the whole operation had grown in the intervening two years.

Georgi introduced 'the project team' as he called them. It included Jane with whom Bond had worked last time. Jane was the only English representative in Georgi's multinational team. Olivia was from Belgium, Leonie from Switzerland and Oskar from Germany. The team had clearly been fully briefed about Bond, about his longstanding friendship with Georgi and his involvement two years ago with the EUIS.

At Georgi's request, Oskar took the lead. The young German wore a sweater and jeans, had a glistening, shaved head and was, Bond guessed, about mid-twenties. In fact, looking round the room, Bond thought everyone looked extremely young. Georgi was the oldest person by far in the team.

"Mr Bond," said Oskar, launching into a report. He was holding an iPad on which were his project notes but he was so familiar with them, he never once referred to them. "We have been alerted to what appears to be some sort of threat related to water. You know better than most, water is a high priority issue across the planet – a resource under great and increasing pressure. What we know so far all originates from Paris. It concerns an environmental pressure group called Paris Guerriers Urbains. It's basically a group of young protesters – mostly students – from a variety of countries. It's been around for some time and has been pretty harmless in recent years. Its major focus is water. Historically, it has motivational links to the Cult of Santez Anne and its pagan links to water worship, and to Acionna, the Gallo-Roman water goddess."

"A little while back one of their members, a young man named Fiacre Cassel, was involved in an incident in The Louvre where he attached a protest banner to an ancient stone that records the world's earliest known water war. That dates back some 4,500 years and involved the armies of Lagash and Umma, cities near the junction of the Tigris and Euphrates rivers. Cassel attached a banner to it that had on it the words 'Quid agatur circa venit circum' – Latin for 'what goes around comes around.' It also had the initials PGU."

"A day later, Cassel was dead. His body was found lying in the gutter in a down and out area of Paris. His neck was broken. It took the authorities a while to match the body to the CCTV security camera images caught at The Louvre as the young man who had stuck the banner to the ancient stone, made his escape."

"Two weeks later, Madeleine, Cassel's young girlfriend, was also dead. She was killed by someone using an Algerian fighting knife. It's not an unusual weapon for the banlieue gangs of Paris."

Oskar paused and Georgi took over the briefing.

"It took a while to link Madeleine and Fiacre together and then to associate them both with the PGU. Members of the group have been interviewed by the police and other agencies several times but that revealed nothing. Well, not quite nothing. It revealed so little it raised suspicions as to how much information this young group was holding back. Were they not saying anything because they were frightened? And that's not an unreasonable question. After all, two of their group are dead."

"The authorities involved widened the distribution of case information. It crossed our desk. We had very little interest in it until someone looked closely at the dying words of the young girl Madeleine. Why, people were asking, had she uttered them in English? Why had a young French girl not spoken her dying words in her Mother tongue? The medical team who nursed her reported what they thought she had said. It was 'Some die young'. And then there were some numbers. '2203'. Can you make anything of that Gene?"

Bond thought for a moment. His immediate response seemed so unlikely he hesitated, reluctant to say anything. But in view of his last exploit with Georgi, maybe it was not such a crazy idea.

"Some die young," he said directly to Georgi. "Anywhere else I wouldn't have a clue. But here – perhaps there's an obvious answer. Is it too obvious? Have I just clutched at an obvious straw? Or could it be what she actually uttered was someone's name. Sum Taeyoung? Surely not."

Georgi smiled. "Why not? It's the conclusion we've come to. Maybe because Sum Taeyoung's name is so much in our minds. Is it coincidence? And what about those numbers? 2203. Any ideas?"

Bond already had an answer. "Every year, the international charity Water Aid holds International Water Day. It's on March 22nd. So, 2203. It's the only thing that comes to my mind."

"Brilliant!" responded Georgi in triumph. "Now you know why we wanted you involved. I think you've hit it straight away. There's the common theme. Water. The PGU worships water. The ancient stone epitaph in The Louvre is about a water war. And now we have 2203 also linked to water."

"But what does that all mean?" asked Bond. "And how does it link to Sum Taeyoung? What's he plotting now?"

Georgi looked straight back at Bond. "That, my friend, is for us to find out. And quickly. His target date is March 22. We've got eight months to find out. 32 weeks! On the basis of that, I think I'll call this session to an end. Anyone fancy a drink?"

"How about some food and drink?" suggested Bond. "With some music. Some jazz."

With agreement all round, Nagriza, Oskar, and Georgi left Wapping Wall with Bond, bound for one of his favourite London 'watering holes.'

Chapter 13

"I am a benevolent person, Mr Gedeck. Some people who think they know me will find that statement incredulous. I have a very lateral approach to how I can help mankind survive on this planet. It's based on the human trait of waiting for disasters to happen before doing anything about it. One might think, if we are the highly intelligent species we claim to be, that once we realise disasters are likely to occur, we would proactively do something about it – take preventative measures or at least mitigating action. But, mostly, we don't. We wait until the disaster happens – then we respond. In my work, Mr Gedeck, my benevolence is manifested through the creation of disasters."

"So, you may ask, how can someone who creates chaos be helping mankind? I firmly believe I accelerate the process of people learning how to deal with disasters and I stimulate the generation of new solutions. So I am making a tangible – if not unusual – contribution to society. It reminds me of the analysis of how best to accelerate GDP – Gross Domestic Productivity – the measure we use to plot and report the economic wellbeing of communities. In my view, it's a measure that today is wholly unfit for purpose. It measures the wrong things. For instance, one way to accelerate GDP is to have a massive highway accident. So many people and so many businesses are involved in the aftermath that it can ultimately show a positive impact on GDP. How ridiculous is that?"

Bernhard Gedeck sat opposite Sum Taeyoung in incredulous disbelief that he was in this absurd tea shop in Seoul, listening to this outlandishly hairy monster of a man in his preposterously colourful robes who seemed unable to make up his mind whether his psyche belonged in Asia or the West and, who seemed to be a psychotic confusion between a capitalist and a terrorist. But he was prepared to listen.

"As I said to your representative when we met at this very table," continued Taeyoung, his eyes fixed firmly on the man before him. "This is an exploratory discussion based on some 'what if' scenarios. I am prepared to tell you what I wasn't prepared to tell him. That is what those scenarios are. When I tell you, Mr Gedeck, you will understand the sensitive nature of what you are hearing. And, should you be so indiscreet as to repeat this elsewhere – as I am sure you won't – I will, of course, deny everything. It will be a figment of your imagination."

Sum Taeyoung paused, perhaps anticipating a response. But the man opposite him continued to look straight back at him with no expression at all. It was impossible to guess his thoughts or his reactions. "A good poker player," thought Sum Taeyoung.

"So, Mr Gedeck," Sum continued, "For want of anything else, I have called this my Acionna Plan. Does the name Acionna mean anything to you, Mr Gedeck?"

The businessman looked back at his outrageously extroverted companion, maintaining the eye contact that had been constant throughout the meeting. He thought for a moment before responding.

"No, I don't think it means anything to me."

"Maybe for a man so involved with matters to do with water, it should. Acionna was a French-Roman goddess. More precisely, she was a Gallo-Roman goddess – a goddess of water, Mr Gedeck. And for the sake of my plan, the first three letters are the most important. A stands for America; C for China and I for the Iberian Peninsular. So, each element of the plan is called, respectively, Acionna 1; Acionna 2 and Acionna 3."

"What I am not going to tell you is how the plan will be delivered. But I promise you it will be. You will have to trust me, Mr Gedeck, as much as I'm having to trust you."

"Acionna 1 relates to America and more specifically to the city of Las Vegas. I expect a man like you knows Vegas well, Mr Gedeck. One of the most decadent cities in the world. But it's located in a ridiculous place – in the water deprived Nevada Desert. And now it's paying the price with a potential water shortage disaster that could be catastrophic. How can you sustain life in a city that has not got any water, Mr Gedeck? The answer is, of course, you can't. And many ancient cities and civilisations collapsed because of lack of water. Vegas has over half a million residents but a staggering number of people visit it ever year – around three and a half million. Gambling is of course the magnet but would you believe gambling's making a loss in the State of Nevada? It lost an unbelievable $1.3 billion in 2013. An incredible figure but not as incredible as the $23 billion taken by Nevada casinos in the same year."

"So the glossy image of Vegas is based on a precarious existence. It's hardly got any water and now it's losing money! If – and we're back to my 'what ifs' again – water to Vegas dried up, it would be a game closing catastrophe. You'd think that the intelligent officers in City Hall in Vegas and in Nevada State Administration in Carson City, would be putting into place remedial solutions to not only resolve the current problem but to stop it happening again. But they're not. A young Vegas journalist we had some indirect contact with has accused the authorities of using 'sticking plaster' solutions. I think he was right."

"So, what if something happened that turned the prospect of a Vegas disaster into a calamitous event in which Vegas runs dry of water? It would be a human, economic and environmental disaster of unprecedented proportions. But what if, Mr Gedeck, there was a water specialist company on standby ready to leap in with solutions? That company would be the hero of the hour – and could earn millions – if not billions. Don't you agree, Mr Gedeck?"

The man from the water company remained impassive – expressionless. But Sum Taeyoung sensed the level of interest had gone up many degrees. There was not much outward sign of it but Taeyoung was sure Gedeck was now hanging onto his every word.

"My 'C' in Acionna stands for China. What a story this is! Do you know its estimated 250 million people are being moved in China from rural areas into new cities? It's an unbelievable urbanisation programme on a scale never seen before. And it's causing chaos to the water supply. According to World Bank statistics, eleven of China's 31 provinces are in a state of water scarcity, in some cases with less water per head of population than some of the most arid places on the planet. And the Chinese Government admitted some years ago, that half the water from its seven main rivers is unfit for human consumption and, because of overuse, much of its groundwater is now polluted."

"So they have a massive plan – the world's biggest water movement programme costing tens of billions of dollars – to move water around the country. The first scheme is already open and it brings water from the north to the south. The second, sometimes known as the south/north scheme, has seen more than 300,000 people moved to make way for what is a spectacular engineering project with the opening of a new canal over 750 miles long reaching from the Yangzi river to the capital, Beijing. A reservoir in central China is being expanded to feed it."

"But what if, Mr Gedeck, this programme was interrupted and perhaps so damaged as to take years to repair it. The impact would be beyond description. It would create a cataclysmic disaster. But, what if the world's biggest water provision specialist company was able to quickly come forward with a plan to prevent tens of thousands of people from dying because of lack of water? That would be amazing, wouldn't it Mr Gedeck – a miracle! But imagine the commercial consequences. It would be worth a sum of money that is difficult to imagine."

Sum Taeyoung paused to drink his herbal tea. His visitor was repelled by the thought of drinking anything that smelt like the liquid in Sum's cup and was content to have a more conventional drink. With a smacking of the lips and a wipe of them across the back of his hand, Sum was ready to continue.

"The 'I' in my plan stands for the Iberian Peninsular.

Portugal is down river from Spain. It relies on Spain not drawing too much water from the major rivers that flow from Spain across the border then down to the Mediterranean coast. In 1993, the Spanish Government disclosed its National Hydrological Plan without any consultation with anyone, including the Portuguese. It created a new tension between the two nations which was ultimately resolved when the two became signatories to what's called the Albufeira Convention."

"But Spain continues to struggle with the consequences of climate change and a Sahara Desert that is slowly creeping further and further north towards the Spanish mainland. When the city of Barcelona nearly ran out of water, despite introducing stringent water use restrictions, the Catalonian government pleaded for more water to be drawn from rivers like the Ebro. The idea caused uproar including strong protests from Portugal. In the end, the city shipped millions of litres of water from France and a new desalination plant was built on the edge of the city."

"But here, Mr Gedeck, is another 'what if'. What if the water supplies in Spain were hugely interrupted by some catastrophic event? The impact would be felt not only in Spain but right down into Portugal and its tourist dependent south – the Algarve. It would be another human, environmental and economic disaster. But 'what if' the world's largest water provider was ready to step in with a solution? Wouldn't that be worth millions, Mr Gedeck?"

"So, I have a plan. The Acianna Plan. To create cataclysmic carnage in three places. To teach the world a lesson. To teach the political managers of our communities that water is the most vital resource on the planet and we need to treat it with respect now and plan how better we will use it in the future – as our population continues to grow, as more people become consumers, and as climate change continues to impact. My plan will undermine the economies of three regions of the world. It will threaten the lives of millions. And, it seemed to me Mr Gedeck, if I shared my thoughts with the top man from the world's largest specialist water provision company, maybe that man would see the commercial opportunity I am offering. Maybe that man would be interested enough to invest in my Acianna Plan."

Sum Taeyoung sat back in his chair. He still found it impossible to analyse what impact he had had on the man before him. Their eyes remains fixed on each other. It was a battle of wills – of strength of mind.

"I don't get it. You create chaos. We fix it. So we gain the benefit, not you."

"No, Mr Gedeck, we both win. What I am talking about is chaos on a devastating scale. It will take years to mend. You will be a beneficiary because EscaEau will provide an immediate, emergency response. That in itself might last for a considerable time and apart from the initial commercial gain, EscaEau will be incredibly well positioned for years to come. For me? Well, Mr Gedeck, if you respond favourably to my proposals, I will gain financial support to help in the investment this project needs. Once it has been executed, I will enjoy the fruits of the ensuing chaos. How I will do that is up to me and not something you should be concerned with. It will not be activity that is in any way, as it were, on your territory."

"So, Mr Gedeck, have I got the project partner I need?"

The man's eyes stared back at him. His face was expressionless. Time seemed to be suspended. Taeyoung started to feel embarrassed and uncomfortable. There was nothing else to do but stare back. It was perhaps a full minute before Bernhard Gedeck suddenly and very visibly relaxed. He smiled, sighed and leant forward, hand outstretched.

"You have a partner, Mr Taeyoung." The two shook hands.

Chapter 14

They travelled the twenty minute journey from Wapping in Oska's multi-seated Honda, the most spacious car available to carry Bond, Olivia, Nagriza and Georgi - Jane and Leonie opted out because of prior commitments. Bond noticed it was Nagriza who organised who sat where and it was she who sat next to him, far closer than was necessary so he could feel her body tight up against his.

Though still in the aftermath of their recent angry exchanges, he could not help but feel a tingle of excitement at her close proximity.

Only five or six minutes after they had left Wapping, they were driving through some particularly heavy traffic when it came to a halt. Almost immediately, there was a slight bump at the rear of the car. Before anyone could react, a cyclist pulled alongside Oska and acknowledged in an apologetic way that it was his fault and to indicate he was OK and that no damage had been done to the car. Oska accepted his word for it and decided not to cause further traffic problems by stopping to inspect the back of the car. And anyway, if the car had a dent in it, he would see it when they parked up. There was no point in implicating the cyclist. He would be uninsured and there would be no come back on him. So they kept going.

Only a few more minutes passed before Oska reported he thought they were being followed.

"It's always difficult to tell in the dark," he said. "And I'm probably wrong. But let me just test the situation."

At the next traffic roundabout, he circumnavigated it twice before continuing, slowed at the next set of traffic lights so he could cross on the orange light immediately before it turned red, then, shortly afterwards, at the very last moment, turned left into a side road and quickly found somewhere to stop at the side of the road and turn off the lights. Nothing went past. They sat for several minutes. They were reassured when no other vehicle went by.

"My fault," Oska apologised. "Getting jumpy in my old age."

"You can never be too cautious," Georgi responded. "Not in our line of work."

Drifters Nightclub is in a London backstreet which seems to have been largely ignored by progress and which owes much of its current structures to as far back as the industrial revolution. Still standing are buildings dating back beyond two World Wars. The club is accessed by climbing a twisting flight of battered and scarred stone steps with ancient brick walls either side. When the five arrived, it was raining – the sort of misty rain that penetrates everything. Oska volunteered to park the car to save everyone having to walk in the rain. Olivia decided to go with him. The steps were glistening wet, shining brightly in the light from the single, also ancient lamp that illuminates the stairway. At the top, surprisingly to those who have never been before, there is a canal towpath and, to its right, the black strip of canal with its uninviting waters disappears into the darkness. Fortunately, the three of them only had a few yards to cover before the entrance to the club was reached and they could enjoy shelter and warmth.

The name of the club is a puzzle to the uninitiated but is soon explained once the club is entered. Obviously having a history going back to the days when barge traffic thrived on the canals, the building at some time in its history had played an important part in the infrastructure of the canal system, the logistical network of the industrial revolution. It was canals that provided the means by which raw materials were imported into the cities, and they provided the means by which manufactured goods could be exported out of them. Today, the interior of Drifters does not hide its links to the past. Its walls are uncovered brickwork and steel beams are unconcealed. Now, large pictures of racing cars hang in every prominent area. To motor sport afficionados, they have an obvious common theme. They all date back to the 1950s and 1960s – are single seater and GT racing cars – and all are seen in what is commonly known as 'four wheel drifts'. A four wheel drift happens when a car is angled into a bend with its wheels all pointing as if it is going to drive into the corner too soon, but the sheer speed of the car sliding sideways on the road, ensures the bend is navigated. A racing driving technique that especially prevailed in the immediate post WW2 era of the sport, it now provides the inspiration for the club's name.

From the reception and cloakroom area, the club itself is entered through a brick archway, presumably once a door connecting two buildings. Across the dance floor and slightly to the left is a staging area, large enough to accommodate a reasonably sized band and to the right, another arched doorway leads through to 'Drifters Bistro'. As the three of them entered the main part of the club, a few people were sitting at tables around the perimeter of the dance floor, listening to the resident pianist and his interpretation of some Oscar Peterson numbers.

They rearranged tables and chairs so the five could be together when Oska and Olivia joined them, Georgi appropriately sitting at the end. Inevitably, they talked business.

"What we know" Georgi started, "is that Sum Taeyoung is involved. Or at least we think he is based on what Madeleine said with her dying breath. We also think Sum was probably responsible two years ago for the attempt on Gene's life when an Eastern European sniper tried to kill him in Birmingham. Instead, Nagriza decided to launch WW3 and the two had a battle in which the gunman died thanks to Gene. Nagriza was badly wounded. So we must be aware now that Gene is working with us again, that Sum maybe considers this to be unfinished business. We must be vigilant in case he decides to have a second go."

"We also know Sum is up to something to do with water. Two young people have died so far. Madeleine gave us the connection to Sum. They both belonged to the Paris based group PGU. That also links to water and especially the Cult of Santez Anne with its links to the ancient Celtic world and to pagan water worship. PGU also connects to Acionna, the Gallo-Roman water goddess. And Gene has identified the numbers Madeleine uttered to be the date of International Water Day – March 22nd. Is there anything else we know?"

There was a silence from the group and Bond found his mind slipping away to home in on the music emanating from the room next door. His mood was broken when the food arrived. They had all selected the Bistro's very basic steak and chips. As they started to eat, Olivia took them back to the focus of their deliberations.

"We've just had a report in from NASA which has shocked people in the States," she said.

"They're talking about huge areas of the world drying up because of climate change and a billion people having no access to safe drinking water. There's a report from a US intelligence agency warning of the dangers of shrinking resources and saying the world is 'standing on a precipice.'"

"What sparked that off?" asked Georgi.

"The report has some fresh data from NASA satellites that track the world's water reserves," Olivia told him. "It shows some parts of the US to be on the verge of a catastrophic drought with its groundwater back up reserves so low they could be measured by the satellites. That's never happened before."

"Where the hell do you go when your back up's gone?" asked Oska.

"The same report," continued Olivia, "says that already a billion people, or one in seven people on the planet, lack access to safe drinking water. At the same time, parts of the world are in an almost opposite situation. They're drowning in too much water. Twelve years of these satellite reports show countries at northern latitudes and in the tropics getting wetter. But countries at mid-latitude are running increasingly low on water. Wet areas of the Earth are getting wetter – places in the high latitudes like the Arctic and the lower latitudes like the tropics. In the middle latitudes in between, the already arid and semi-arid parts of the world, they're getting drier."

She paused to eat and look up some notes on her iPhone. "And the same report says watering crops, providing drinking water in expanding cities, cooling power plants, fracking oil and gas wells – all take water from the same diminishing supply. And if you add to that, climate change – which is projected to intensify dry spells in the coming years – the world is going to be forced to think a lot more about water and how we use it than it ever did before."

Gene Bond had listened with interest. "I can add to that", he said. "I've got a copy of the recent US National Intelligence Strategy which says the growing impact of climate change could heighten tensions amongst nations and even spark new wars. It says water shortages, as well as fierce competition for food and energy, will continue to give major headaches to world leaders. It talks about the strain of a growing world population coupled with the effects of pollution and climate change putting pressure on many of the water systems that feed the world's people. They're also vital for agriculture. More than half of the world's wetlands have disappeared. Climate change around the world has altered weather patterns and led to water shortages."

"So what would you expect Sum Taeyoung to be plotting?" asked Georgi.

"God knows," responded Bond. "The trouble is, there are so many vulnerable areas. Who knows which he might be planning to hit."

As the dinner continued, so they speculated what the South Korean 'chaos entrepreneur' might be planning. The ideas came thick and fast and eventually Georgi called it a day.

"Gene. It might be helpful if you can try and capture what we've talked about this evening and put it into some sort of list of targets we think Sum Taeyoung might go for. Maybe a priority list. We can then have a look at that in the morning and see if we can whittle it down to some sort of bite-sized chunk that's practical for us to have a go at."

"Are you still monitoring Taeyoung?" asked Bond. "I remember you had very sophisticated surveillance technology tracking him. Are you still doing that?"

"We're back on the case," Georgi told him. "I must admit he dropped of our radar for a bit. We may have very sophisticated equipment at our beck and call but the sad fact of life is, my friend, we're called on to look at so many things we can't do everything. It becomes a matter of priority – often dictated by what our political lords and masters want us to do. But we're back onto Taeyoung. We've only just turned back to him so nothing to report at the moment."

And with that they took their drinks back into the club and stayed another hour just enjoying the jazz. Again, Bond was conscious that Nagriza chose to sit close to him. It was all so difficult. He knew she lived with Georgi and she had confessed to him before that she and Georgi enjoyed sex together – something she described as being 'a convenience. A safety valve to our work.' It was Nagriza who sat so close to him, all he could smell was her intoxicating scent – a blatant reminder to him of her unbelievable sexuality.

Just after midnight, Georgi told everyone they had another big day ahead of them. It was time to break up the party. They moved to leave but found it was raining hard outside. Oska said it was ridiculous for everyone to get soaked and volunteered to go and get the car and to toot his horn when he arrived back at the bottom of the stone steps. He disappeared into the wet night and they formed a small huddle by the door. He had been gone less than 10 minutes when they heard the dull thud of a substantial explosion nearby.

"Oh fuck" said Georgi grabbing Olivia by the hand and disappearing out into the night, telling Bond and Nagriza to stay where they were and telling Olivia to show him the way to where Oska had parked the car.

With growing impatience and worry, they waited more than half an hour before Olivia returned. She was soaked, her hair dishevelled and her face colourless apart from black marks running down from her eyes. She had clearly been crying.

"Oska's dead," she sobbed at them. "It was a car bomb. There's fuck all left."

They were dumbstruck with horror. It was incredulous. The club management, though not knowing the details, understood the level of disaster and showed Bond, Nagriza and Olivia to a side office where they tried to comfort the anguished young Belgian girl.

Half an hour later Georgi joined them, providing more detail and a revelation. The bomb had been underneath the car, towards the front end of its elongated wheelbase. It had been connected to the ignition so as Oska tried to start the car, so it exploded. The car had been ripped apart, killing Oska instantly and clearly would have killed anyone else who had been inside.

"I had a quick look round," Georgi told them. "The back end of the car was still in one piece but lying on its side. It wasn't difficult to see that underneath the rear sill not far from the exhaust pipe, someone had stuck a tracker. My guess is it was the cyclist we had the bump with. It also proves Oska was right. We were being followed but when he took evasive action and we lost them, it didn't matter. They still knew where we were – and where the car had been parked."

Police officers arrived soon afterwards and took statements. Georgi explained to them that much of their work and activities were covered by the Official Secrets Act but they were able to tell the basic story and the officers eventually left with enough to keep them happy.

Ultimately Georgi called a taxi and the four of them left the club in the depths of sadness. As they walked down the stone stairs to the road, Bond said quietly to Georgi "who do you think they were targeting? All of us? You, or me?"

A very sombre Georgi replied, "At this stage Gene, I've no idea. It could have been any of us or all of us."

Chapter 15

Tim Crenshaw felt he was confronting mountainous difficulties in every part of his life – in holding onto his job, within his family, and now, down the very avenue he had travelled to seek help and fortitude – religion – but which was now turning into a harassing cul-de-sac.

A devout Christian in the mould of his parents and grandparents, Crenshaw had suffered from an early age when his sexuality became confused in High School. He gradually realised he was attracted to boys more than girls. In the religious environment of home, such things were taboo subjects and his sexual preferences remained undetected by his family. His highly conventional, church going parents, and especially his mother, expected their son to progress socially and in business as his contemporaries were doing. Marriage was part of that convention and, pressed by the resolve of his mother that her son would himself become a family man, he succumbed to her pressures and to simultaneous overtures from Susan who his mother introduced to him. Not that many men would have objected to the arrival of Susan into their lives. A vivacious, bubbly girl with long black hair and flashing eyes, she had a personality to match her looks. A devout Christian and a member of the church where she met Crenshaw's parents, Susan was attracted to the young man who seemed to be the epitome of respectability. He was tall, good looking, intelligent, a practicing Christian and a civil servant. It was all Susan could hope for.

Tim Crenshaw, despite his sexual preferences, found he enjoyed Susan's company, conversation, wit and intellect. The relationship developed into a close friendship, enough of a bond between the two of them for Crenshaw's mother to manipulate it into the marriage she sought for her son. So by the time he was twenty-four, Tim Crenshaw – almost without realising it – found himself married and a career civil servant working for the Las Vegas administration.

Fifteen years later, Crenshaw headed up a division of the Office of Emergency Management in Vegas. His two children were growing up rapidly and becoming increasingly independent. His wife, as always, was immersed in church activity. And through it all, Tim's bisexual preferences found him in a series of highly secretive extramarital relationships that, had they become known to anyone, would blow his life to bits.

Pressures in business and developing cracks in his relationship with Susan, progressively made life more and more uncomfortable for Crenshaw. His work had brought him into contact with environmental issues, something he found personally interesting. In a local context, the worsening state of Lake Mead was an issue that crossed his desk at regular intervals. It caused him to examine other examples of depleted lakes in the world. He especially found the Aral Sea in Uzbekistan to be a story with great similarities to their own, growing disaster. But it was at a celebration of Epiphany at his branch of the Orthodox Church of America – and especially the Great Blessing of Water – that inspired his particular interest in water and turned it into something which soon developed into a passion bordering on an obsession.

When talk reached Crenshaw's ears that Angel Martin, the Vegas based internationally renowned gospel singer, was launching her own religious order based on her fixation about water, emulating the new National Church of Bey launched in Atlanta by pop singer Beyoncé Knowles, Tim Crenshaw was more than passingly interested. Angel Martin's inspiration and raison d'être was a biblical quotation – John 3:5 – "And Jesus answered, 'Truly, truly, I say unto you, unless one is born of water and the Spirit, he cannot enter the kingdom of God.' And in seeking a feminine dimension to the name of her new order, Angel Martin turned to Acionna, the Gallo-Roman water goddess. So was born the New Church of Acionna.

It was only natural Crenshaw should become involved. Still quite young, sharp minded and very committed, in the initially small group forming the New Church of Acionna, he became the church's senior non-executive officer, a part-time task to run in conjunction with his professional career. Susan attended a few early meetings but resolutely preferred to maintain her allegiance to the Orthodox Church. It became a separation of interests that further opened the divide between the two of them. They both embraced the social activities of their respective churches, adding further burden to their increasingly tenuous relationship and also on their finances. Now money was becoming a further friction in their marriage.

Throughout all of this, Tim Crenshaw built a close friendship with the editor of one of the city's leading newspapers, the Las Vegas Journal. Sam Baldwin was amongst the guest dignitaries at the New Church of Acionna's launch 'Celebration Festival' and he and Crenshaw maintained contact after that, bumping into each other at city activities and extending invitations to each other to various events. It was a friendship that grew in its closeness but in no way reflected Crenshaw's bisexual tendencies.

The initial approach from Sum Taeyoung came as a bolt out of the blue and its content was intriguing. The letter, addressed from a company in Seoul called Sustainable Development Brokers International, was signed by its founder, one Sum Taeyoung. It was sent to Crenshaw in his capacity as non-executive officer of the New Church of Acionna. It talked about the growing challenge Las Vegas faced in the provision of water to its citizens. It was painful in its accuracy about the contradiction – some would say hypocrisy – of City policy which called for more water savings by the population whilst simultaneously expanding urban development, with its intrinsic increased demands on water supplies. It cited the lowering water levels of Lake Mead and highlighted the inherent security risk the water situation caused Vegas.

In the letter, Sum Taeyoung introduced himself and his company and intrigued Crenshaw by saying he was already involved with a French group with connections to the goddess Acionna. It involved a new, global project he was developing. It was proposed there would be an American dimension to it, focussed on Las Vegas, and Taeyoung thought he, Crenshaw, might be interested both from the perspective of his religious activities but also related to his professional position. The letter ended with a telephone number and some optional times for a call to be made if Crenshaw was interested. After considerable deliberation, he decided he was.

Crenshaw made the call from the church. He considered it to be a legitimate action as Taeyoung had mentioned the Goddess Acionna. The phone rang once before being answered by a male voice simply repeating the number he had phoned.

"Is that Mr Taeyoung?" he asked, a little tentatively.

"Good day to you Mr Crenshaw," came the response. There followed a conversation which, when Tim Crenshaw thought about it afterwards, was informative but very guarded. Taeyoung reaffirmed the project was to do with water, a resource, 'he believed had a certain poignancy for Las Vegas citizens'. Crenshaw agreed the subject of water was vitally important and prevailed in both his main roles in life. Taeyoung said he thought Crenshaw's close friend, the editor of the LV Journal, might also be interested. Crenshaw was shocked to find how well informed the South Korean was. How did he know Sam Baldwin was a friend? How much more did he know? The brief call ended when Taeyoung announced he would visit Las Vegas soon and would welcome a meeting with both Crenshaw and Sam Baldwin.

Ten days later they met in the New Church of Acionna. Like Bernhard Gedeck before them, both Tim Crenshaw and Sam Baldwin had feelings of incredulity about the meeting in which they sat listening to this giant of a man who looked more like a colourfully dressed gorilla, so much hair did he possess. A tall man, enormous in every sense and probably weighing around 350 pounds, he was dressed in a silk gown of hideously decorative colours. If you closed your eyes and listened to him, you would think you were in the company of an Oxford educated American. Yet that was not really accurate because mixed into the accents was a hint of the Far East. This guy, Sam Baldwin thought, was a really strange critter. But he and Crenshaw had done as much homework as they could, mainly courtesy of the SDBI web site, which gave them a comprehensive introduction to SDBI including detailed reports on several case studies of projects the company had successfully completed. It made impressive reading. It was, Baldwin concluded, a highly effective calling card.

"It's interesting sitting here in a church with Acionna as its figurehead" Sum Taeyoung told them.

"One has to admire the vision of Angel Martin in launching such an initiative. Who would have thought a gospel singer would create her own religious order? Isn't that quite something?"

"I am known in various parts of the world for my 'what if' discussions. I sometimes leave it to the judgement of my audience as to whether I'm venturing ideas of a rhetorical nature or ideas embedded in reality. I can assure you gentlemen, what I am talking to you about is definitely for real."

"The City of Las Vegas, audaciously built in a desert, is like a fantasy city. It shouldn't exist where it exists and it should not generate wealth based purely on gambling. It takes for granted and abuses the substance that keeps it alive – water. And even now, on the brink of the catastrophic consequences of running out of water, it continues to make matters worse and does little – if nothing – to respond in any responsible way. What it does is to tinker on the parameters of the problem. It has no idea, no desire, no compulsion and no ambition, to treat this as a major, long-term challenge. But that's not unusual. Vegas is a very long way from being unique in that it does nothing on a major scale until the disaster has happened. Then it springs into action. Do you agree?"

The two men opposite him nodded in agreement but almost as if with great reluctance. They remained silent.

"So," continued Taeyoung. "I am planning an action in Las Vegas that could accelerate the city into a chasm of chaos. I don't plan to tell you how I will do this but I can assure you I will. It will be cataclysmic in its magnitude,

111

devastating in its impact. In a few months' time, Vegas could definitely be without water. That being the case, it will become an unsustainable city. It will be in deep trouble. No water – no city."

"Now, the big questions to you two are – 'what if' a senior member of the City's Office of Emergency Management had some prior understanding of what is going to happen and had connections to a company specialising in water provision that was ready and equipped with answers, to respond to the City's disaster – answers no current supplier could turn on as fast as this one could. Potentially, I believe, that would be of enormous value to the City, to make an understatement. More appropriate would be to say, such a company would be the city's salvation. Such a senior member of the OEM would have the prospect of becoming a hero."

"And 'what if' the leading newspaper of the City also had privileged information about the event and was all ready to respond before anyone else knew anything about it. And as the disaster unfolded and the rescue of the city swung into action, if the editor of that newspaper had exclusive information as to what was to happen and when, that would provide a competitive edge that would be of substantial value. In your lingo, Mr Baldwin, you could scoop the competition. Am I right?"

The two men to whom he was speaking looked back at him in disbelief – but they still nodded in agreement.

"And at such a time of disaster and crisis, a church that was well prepared and that could swing into immediate, effective action to provide comfort and succour to distressed citizens, would gain enormously in terms of its stature, its congregation, and from financial contributions. Am I right?"

"And all I ask is for some meagre help – and, of course, your silence. Your silence is essential. Should that be breached I will, naturally, deny everything. I will ask you to produce evidence. You have none. You have one letter of introduction from me. That's all. That's not evidence."

"So," the flamboyant South Korean concluded. "Can I count on your support?"

Baldwin and Crenshaw looked at each other, searching for the right words to say.

"I would have thought 15 minutes would be enough time for you to come to a decision," suggested Taeyoung. "Why don't I stay here and you two have a little walk around the church grounds."

Which is what they did. They left the church and walked round the grounds for a while, deciding how to respond to this very strange man. The starting point was the clear indication that Sum Taeyoung was going to go ahead with his plan whether or not they were involved. On that basis, their decision had to be – does that happen with them or without them? There were clear benefits to both of them to be of whatever help they could be. There would be risks. But, they convinced themselves, those, one way or another, could be managed. They would need more detail. Their view swayed from one side to the other but, on balance, they concluded it would be best to be in rather than out. So on that basis, they returned to the church with their decision.

"You've got a deal," Baldwin told the man from South Korea.

Chapter 16

The mood when they reassembled at Wapping the day after their visit to Drifters nightclub, was sombre and deflated. By the time Gene Bond arrived, everyone in the Communications Centre had been briefed about the happenings of the previous evening. The death of Oska shook everyone and reminded them of their own vulnerability in the business in which they were occupied. Georgi tried to keep the team in order by ensuring everyone was focussed on their own tasks and responsibilities. Those involved in the Taeyoung project assembled around a black glass-topped table.

"Gene. Last night I asked if you could consider where Taeyoung might attack on March 22nd. We know his target relates to water. I asked if you could create some sort of list of potentials and maybe even prioritise that. Have you had any luck?"

"I must admit," responded Bond, "the only thing I wanted to do last night was hit the whisky bottle. But, you tasked me to do something Georgi and I've done my best. It took my mind off what happened last night – for a while anyway. And it reminded me – as if I needed any reminding – that the last thing I wanted was to get involved with you guys again – because of the sort of incident that happened last night. This is not my world. I feel alien within it. But, I have to accept I'm involved now and in memory of Oska, I'll do whatever I can to help you guys bring Sum Taeyoung's crazy exploits to an end."

"Anyway, what I did last night was Google 'ten areas of worst water crisis'. I just wanted to confirm what I thought I knew. It's interesting what turned up. Let me give you a list of general facts to start with:

- Around three and a half million people die every year from poor water, bad sanitation and hygiene related causes.
- Lack of access to clean water and sanitation kills children at the rate equal to a full jumbo jet crashing every four hours.
- Of the 60 million people added to the world's towns and cities every year, most move to slum areas where there's no sanitation facilities.
- 780 million people lack access to an improved water source. That's about one in nine of us.
- More lives are lost through water and sanitation causes than through war.

Google also came up with a list of 10 cities in America that are at crisis level on water. It had a major item on water shortages in California. There was a news headline – 'Water Crisis Squeezes Sao Paulo State' and a story about record breaking heat in Brazil leaving some of Sao Paulo State's 44 million residents scrambling for clean water sources."

"There was just so much stuff, I decided to come at it from another direction. Knowing Sum Taeyoung as we now do, I wondered what parts of the world he would be interested in. If he was going to do something, where might he do it to get the biggest impact? Top of the list has to be America and all the Google entries confirm there's enough water problems for Taeyoung to get his teeth into. And, of course, if you target America, you get global publicity."

"Then there's China. Wikipedia confirmed for me that China has the largest population and I know through my own work, that the revolution that's going on there at the moment, is creating enormous water supply problems. So I put China on my list after America."

"The next largest population is in India – according to Wikipedia. Again, I know a lot about the struggle India is having with water – and it's only going to get worse. So I placed India on my list."

"What I'd written rang a bell. I'd written ACI. I thought I'd seen such a sequence of letters recently and it didn't take much brain power to recall the name Acionna. It was when I first met Oska in this room when he brought us up to speed about Sum Taeyoung's latest activity. Oska told us about the Paris Guerriers Urbains and its links to both the Cult of Santez Anne and to Acionna, the Gallo-Roman water goddess. Acionna – that's where I'd seen the letters Aci recently."

"So last night I began to wonder if the name Acionna is being used by Taeyoung somehow. If A stands for America, C for China and I for India, what could the rest of it stand for? O? I could only think of the Oman. What the hell would Taeyoung have going on in the Oman for God's sake? Then I was stuck with two Ns and at that stage I had a bad headache and decided to give up. It was something for you guys to think about."

"Well, it's a thought," answered Georgi tentatively. "I'm not so sure you're right and there's always the danger it might be a red herring. But it's worth more thought. Meanwhile, Jane – where are we now with surveillance on Taeyoung?"

"I'm still getting up to speed on that, Georgi," replied Jane. "Oska was handling it and I'm waiting for updated reports as to where he'd got to."

"I know we've put a watch on his office again and automatic surveillance too," said Georgi. "The last I heard was we didn't know where he currently is, which is hardly a surprise because we hadn't been looking for him. I've put a global call out and sent his profile to key agencies. We'll find him soon enough. But back to you Gene. Apart from identifying key areas Taeyoung might be targeting, would you like to have a go at considering what he might be planning to do? If you were he, what would you think of doing?"

"I've been wondering about that too," Bond answered. "I guess I'd be looking at where water is captured and stored or at the infrastructure that gets water from where it is to where it's needed – or a combination of both. I think that means dams or pipelines. Both are vulnerable."

"Can you think which are the most sensitive?" asked Georgi.

"On the pipeline side, I just don't know. There are so many options. And, just to add to what I said, especially in China, you'd have to think of the canals as well. They're being used to transport water. They must become possible targets too."

"But if you were looking for a soft target, which would you go for?" persisted Georgi.

"I don't know Georgi," Bond replied. "It must vary from one situation to another. My inclination is to consider pipelines and canals as softer targets than dams but then I think of the situation in Iraq and Syria. The militant ISIS forces have been attacking dams there. They took over two. At the Fallujah dam, they shut all the gates and started flooding the area – using water as a tool of war. They stopped when they realised they were in danger of flooding their own troops and supply lines. Someone in government out there called it a 'heinous crime' to use water as a weapon in a fight to make people thirsty. He was right. It's a scandalous and evil thing to do."

"But the ISIS forces also took over the Mosul Dam, the biggest in Iraq and a massive hydroelectric plant. Experts reckoned the destruction of the dam would trigger a humanitarian crisis far beyond the scope of anything Iraq has experienced so far in that war. Thankfully, before that could happen, Kurdish troops retook it before any major damage was done but you can see how critical dams are, how vulnerable they are and how catastrophic the consequences would be if they were successfully attacked."

"What about America?" asked Georgi. "You're right. If Taeyoung is looking for global publicity, America has got to be on his target list. So where would you hit in America if you were he?"

"The Hoover Dam," Bond replied without hesitation. "It's massive and it holds back Lake Mead, the biggest reservoir in America. It provides water to all the urban areas and especially to Las Vegas which is a crazy city built in the middle of a desert. Who in their right minds would do that? So Vegas is very dependent on the Hoover Dam. It also has enormous hydroelectric generation and feeds electrical power across Nevada, Arizona and California. Around a million tourists visit it every year. It's a modern day wonder of the world."

"How well is it protected?" asked Jane.

"I don't know," Bond replied. "I haven't researched that. I know there are restrictions about what sort of vehicles can use the road across the dam. They also ban a variety of loads that trucks can carry across it. All vehicles are stopped and searched. It was a huge traffic problem because the road was part of a major US highway. Or at least it was, because another bridge has now been built and that carries the highway across the Colorado River with no security restrictions or hold ups. But in terms of any other security to protect the dam, I don't know. There was talk some time ago about siting anti-aircraft missiles around it. That was in the aftermath of 9.11. There was a lot of sensitivity in Vegas because it became known that some of the 9.11 terrorists had been in the city before the attack on the twin towers. It was never resolved why they were there. Was it because they were thinking of attacking the dam or because they were taking flying lessons in the desert? The question was never properly answered. But were any missiles installed there? I just don't know."

"OK," responded Georgi. "Thanks for that Gene. We'll follow up on various issues you've raised and we'll up the ante on Sum Taeyoung. We'll have a collective think about your idea on Acionna. The clock is ticking on this. We need a real breakthrough to know what he's up to. At the moment we're pissing in the wind."

Chapter 17

He cycled towards the offices of the LV Journal with a growing sense of trepidation. Yet again, Ryan Spears tried to gather all his thoughts together into a cohesive story that, hopefully, the editor would buy into. There were many advantages to being a freelance newsman but top of the list was the freedom to do whatever you wanted to do – whenever. That includes pursuing the stories of interest to you rather than having to respond to the calls of the News Desk and being sent on assignments only they think to be of interest. The disadvantages include the lack of a regular guaranteed income to keep the bank and other chasing creditors happy. And at this particular moment in time, the coffers were distinctly low and the creditors increasingly noisy. So it was more than passingly important that the editor bought into the story. With a bit of luck, there might be an advance payment in it. But Ryan had been a self-employed hack newsman for long enough to know nothing is guaranteed.

He pedalled down the seemingly endless Western Bonanza Road with its low profile buildings, occasional trees, Red Rock Mountains in a hazy distance and to the accompaniment of the constant rumblings of traffic on the virtually adjacent Las Vegas Freeway. Twenty-six years of age, Ryan did not consider himself to be a committed environmentalist but matters to do with wildlife, biodiversity and the state of the planet did interest him, and he found cycling around the city not only a satisfying contribution to carbon reduction but often the most efficient way of getting from A to B. Like many major cities, Vegas purports to support the use of bikes and has committed funds to the provision of cycle lanes. But it remains a hazardous activity in a city still obsessed by the car. The compensation, Ryan so often found, was when major roads choke with traffic and everything grinds to a halt, the bike provides a means by which to glide by the stacked up vehicles.

So, when practical, Ryan uses his bike. That had not been the case yesterday when he had driven the 25 miles or so from his apartment in the San Fernando Valley through Henderson and to Lake Mead. Before his meeting there, he took time off to walk across the Hoover Dam Bypass, something he had done several times since it opened in 2010.

Built about 1,500 feet downstream of the Dam, the new single span bridge looks remarkable and is a true wonder of the modern world. Built primarily to redirect US Route 93 away from the security conscious, congestion prone road across the dam, traffic now flows freely across the new bridge. The walkway adjacent to the highway provides an extraordinary view of the river gorge and the mighty dam. Ryan parked his ancient Ford in the parking lot near the dam on the Navada side of the river and joined the line of tourists climbing the lengthy walk up towards the bridge. To their left, the massive wall of the Hoover Dam dominated the view, itself a wonder of the world when it was constructed getting on for a hundred years ago.

The view from the bridge is spectacular. Ryan walked the whole length of the near 2,000 feet long walkway to the dead end on the Arizona side, stopping now and then to look towards Lake Mead, just visible in the distance past the gorge of the Colorado River, with the huge dam far below. It was breath-taking.

The diversion took most of the morning but Ryan thought it was well worth it. Back in his car, he picked up a burger and ate lunch on the move as he headed to the part of the Lake where he would meet Jerry Parker.

He had spoken to Parker over the phone but was keen to meet this man who had spent all his working life on Lake Mead, either fishing or taking tourists on trips around the Lake. He had not really thought about it but when they met and shook hands, Ryan was surprised at Parker's age. He had sounded like a man in his late 40s perhaps. But standing before him on the edge of the Lake, securing his boat to an anchor ring, was a weather-beaten, leather-skinned man whose age was difficult to assess but must be around the 70 mark.

"How long have you been working on Lake Mead?" asked Ryan.

"As long as I can remember." The voice was strong with no evidence of the man's age. "Since I left school – and I left that before I should have."

"You've seen a lot of changes."

"Sure have. Mostly about people. There's so many of them nowadays. And everyone's hustling. Always busy. Even when they're relaxing. Always got their goddam phones with them. All the time. Looking at screens. Pushing buttons. Never seems to stop. Never time to relate to what's around them. Never any time to appreciate what they've got. Never any time for anyone else. No wonder everyone's so screwed and uptight."

"And what about Lake Mead?" Ryan looked past Parker's boat out towards the lake which, as ever, looked beautiful this sunny afternoon.

"It's changed. And it's changing faster all the time." The old man had completed securing his boat and now sat on some fishing boxes.

"What do you mean?"

"Mainly it's losing its water. People I ask say it's all about climate change. But I think the change is too fast for that. I think the change is manmade."

"How come?" asked Ryan.

"Oh well. That's a big question," Parker responded. "I'm no scientist or politician but it seems simple to me. You've got more and more people taking more and more water out of the Colorado and the Lake. And there's not so much water flowing anyway. So I guess at least part of the problem is manmade."

"How fast is it changing?" asked Ryan.

"I don't know exactly. I guess it's dropped five feet since yesterday."

"You're joking!" Ryan was shocked. This was change at a far greater rate than he had heard of to-date.

"Look" said Parker, pointing towards the water's edge some 50 feet away. "You see that strip of bleached rock? Wherever you look around the lake, it's there. We call that 'the bath tub ring.' I had an English friend stay here a little while back. He said that in some places, there's so much bleached rock now exposed, it looks like the White Cliffs of Dover!"

Ryan was amazed. He thought Parker would add some local colour to the facts he had been researching, but this surpassed anything he had expected.

"And, if you look over there," the old boatman pointed out across the Lake. "You see that hill? Well, I used to tie my boat to that rock you can see sticking out. And I guess that's now 100 feet above the water. And you see that island over there? That wasn't there last year. I tell you, this lake is emptying so fast, there'll be nothing left in a few years' time. It'll be dry before I die. Then what will Vegas do for water?"

Ryan nodded in agreement. Parker had hit the nail right on the head.

"It's a shame and a crime," added the old man. "This used to be a great lake. Now it's being ruined. It's tragic."

The words rolled round Ryan's mind as he arrived at the red-bricked, single storey building of the LV Journal. He was ten minutes early for his allocated time slot in Editor Sam Baldwin's hectic schedule. After he had secured his bike, grabbed a cup of iced water and checked in at reception, he was plumb on time.

Baldwin seemed genuinely pleased to see him. Unusually, rather than send a member of staff, he actually came to reception himself to walk Ryan through the editorial hall to his own office, closing the door behind him with his foot in a well-practiced move. His desk looked like a disaster that was pretending to be controlled. A large computer screen was surrounded by copies of the LV Journal, competitive newspapers, files and a confusion of papers and documents. If, as Ryan thought it was doing, the LV Journal was promoting the concept of a paperless world, its editor was hardly a shining example.

"We've got 10 minutes," the gruff, whisky battered voice of Baldwin told him. "So keep this to the point."

"I want your support to feature a story I think is right up the Journal's street," responded Ryan, still feeling uncomfortable that he had not developed and rehearsed this presentation well enough.

"You mean you're looking for an advance?" Baldwin cut straight to the point that Ryan was trying to introduce more tactfully. "You know from experience I'm a tight bastard Ryan. And times are tough. We're under huge spending restrictions. So this had better be good. But I tell you now, an advance is unlikely."

Ryan's confidence might have been further knocked by this but in his experience, Baldwin always started meetings like this – with an attack. Like all the news editors Ryan had ever met, Baldwin barked a lot but behind the aggressive image, was quite a reasonable man.

"Vegas is on the threshold of a disaster," continued Ryan. "It's going to run out of water soon."

"There's nothing new news about that," cut in Baldwin. "We've run that story to death."

"Agreed," responded Ryan. "But despite all the political statements committing to action – the political rhetoric and bullshit and what action has actually been taken, the situation's getting worse. I was out at Lake Mead this morning. It's dropped five feet since yesterday. Can you believe that!? It's visibly shrinking. So I've been puzzled by why the administration continues on its urban development programme, with all the additional water needs that brings, and at a pace that's faster than the remediation programme it's undertaking to overcome the water crisis."

"Yeah, yeah," grunted Baldwin. "Still nothing new here Ryan." Clearly he was already running out of interest.

"I agree," Ryan replied, his voice tightening as he tried to control not only his frustration but his self-belief and enthusiasm for the story. "And I agree the administration has clearly done something. Water use in Vegas has reduced by close on 15%. They're driving the new pipeline as fast as they can – or so they say. But to me these are all sticking plaster solutions. We've got population growth, massive urban development, growing demands for more and more water, and there's the issue of climate change. Around the world, examples of extreme weather are increasing all the time. So here we can expect more droughts. We're responding to the current drought as if it's a one-off problem. Climate change scientists suggest droughts like this will increasingly be part of our lives. So sticking plaster solutions simply aren't good enough."

Baldwin had been sitting forward, elbows on his desk. Now he sat back into his chair, hands behind his head, and sighed. "Ryan. I admire your enthusiasm and I know these things are of genuine concern to you. Hey – they are to me! But where's the new news story? And you're asking me for an advance. Come on! Get real."

The young journalist responded with growing anxiety. The opportunity was slipping from his grasp. "The news story is what the politicians are up to. This should be a matter the Southern Nevada Water Authority ought to be sorting out – which is what we're told is happening. But did you know the Office of Emergency Management is now involved?"

"Yes I did," answered the editor.

"And that they're talking to a French water company."

"Who's that?" asked Baldwin, at last showing some signs of interest.

"EscaEau," replied Ryan. He needed to hook Baldwin in but was reluctant at this stage to give too much away.

"How do you know?"

"I know. I've got my sources. I think that's strange as SNWA has the job of managing our water supply. So why is the Office of Emergency Management talking to an Anglo French water specialist? And why is a South Korean company also involved?"

"What South Korean company?" the editor asked. At last, a gleam of real interest, thought Ryan.

"I have information about a South Korean company with links to the French water company which is also showing interest in the Vegas water story. Why? Well that's the sort of thing I want to follow up."

Baldwin stood up from his chair and walked towards the window. Ryan felt a change of mood within the room. Ryan sensed he had said something that had sparked interest in the editor. He'd hit a nerve. Now, for a brief minute or so, the editor was thinking about it. As he waited for a response, Ryan thought this was a good sign. Baldwin was hooked. The response was a bombshell.

"No, I don't see it Ryan. I don't see any new news here. We've covered this story to death. I'm sorry if you've wasted a lot of time on this but it's not for us."

And despite Ryan's best endeavours to retrieve the situation, he found himself being ushered back to reception where Baldwin politely shook his hand and left with hardly a word but not before Ryan had passed to him a CD file containing headlines from what he had told the editor.

Back outside and mounting his bike, the more Ryan thought about it, the more strange he found it to be. Baldwin had been polite to start with, then bored and only too keen for the meeting to end. Then the whole atmosphere between them had changed. As soon as he had mentioned EscaEau and then the South Korean connection, Baldwin's whole body language had tightened. It was as if he'd struck a real nerve. But then the editor had ended the meeting. Why? Surely the issue of EscaEau and South Korea was worthy of further discussion?

Furious with himself that this money earning opportunity had floundered, the more he reflected on what had happened, the more strange he thought it had been. If he had lit a fuse somewhere with Baldwin, what had sparked it? Did he already know what Ryan knew? It was very, very odd.

Chapter 18

Sum Taeyoung met with the members of Paris Guerriers Urbains at their normal meeting place in one of the dingier parts of Paris. This was, he knew, going to be a tricky reunion with the PGU. He organised the layout of the meeting well in advance of the start time. Although the building was old and dilapidated, thanks to city grants and other support, the technical facilities were quite sophisticated. He dimmed the house lights and arranged the seating so the audience was in a semicircle in front of the screen onto which he would project images from his laptop. He would roam about in front of the screen and close to the audience. There would be no script. He would, he hoped, overwhelm them with his powerful presence, the idiosyncrasies of his character, style and dress and, his charismatic delivery.

Twenty-two members arrived for the meeting, about the same as the last time they met. But, of course, two of their members were absent. Permanently. In a way, he was surprised any of them turned up at all but a combination of allegiance to their fallen comrades, sheer curiosity and maybe a touch of fear, ensured he had an audience. Once they were assembled, he was uncertain whether what he sensed was hostility towards him or fear, or perhaps a bit of both. Did they associate him with the deaths of Fiacre and Madeleine? That was unclear. But there was certainly a tension in the room.

"I think we should start the meeting with a moment's silence in memory of Fiacre and Madeleine," he said to launch the meeting. It was a bold tactic – striking at the potentially contentious weak spot right at the start of the meeting. If people in the audience were linking him to their deaths, here on a plate was an opportunity for them to say what they were thinking. It was time for them to speak out. Instead, there was silence. Nobody spoke. Some heads bowed. Some of the youngsters just stared back at him. With aggression? He could not tell. Yet! It was a young Japanese student who eventually dared to speak up and raise the subject.

"You come and you talk to us. Then later both Fiacre and Madeleine die. Is that coincidence?" he asked.

"And you threatened us if we broke the vow of silence," added an American member of the group. "And Fiacre broke that vow. Then he died. Did you kill him?"

"Do you have PGU blood on your hands?" another asked.

Taeyoung held up his hands. "My friends. My friends. I'm not aware that Fiacre broke our vow. I know what he did in the Louvre. But that didn't break our vow."

"Did you kill Madeleine and Fiacre?" asked another, bluntly and directly. The group was growing in confidence, becoming more capable of challenging him.

"When I met you before, I talked to you about a scheme I have to awaken the world to the perils of our continued global abuse of water. I came to you because Paris Guerriers Urbains sees and understands how we take for granted this resource which enables there to be life. The future wellbeing of millions of people is at stake. If we do nothing, they will perish. Our species is threatened. So I came to you because we have a common bond. Without water, life as we know it cannot exist. And where there is water, there is life. The two are intrinsically interwoven," Sum told them. He had come to Paris for only one reason – to talk to them about his project. He was not here to be quizzed for the rest of the meeting about the death of two of their comrades. They had had their chance. It was time to move on.

"You know that. I know that. The Goddess Acionna who plays such a central role with PGU is representative of concerns about this most precious of natural resources. And since we met, I now have another organisation helping my project. Have any of you heard about the New Church of Acionna?"

A few hands went up. That pleased Taeyoung. He had got a reaction from his audience. Now he needed to build on that, to regain their interest, to get their attention away from the two deaths. And the more he could move the discussion into the future, the more the past would fade into history.

"I am pleased to report to you that the New Church of Acionna based in Las Vegas is now a partner organisation in my plans." And on the screen he showed the church then another picture of two people standing outside it.

"On the left is Tim Crenshaw. He's the senior administrator of the church. On the right is Sam Baldwin, editor of the Vegas Journal. They both support what I propose to do."

And before anyone else could ask more questions, awkward or otherwise, Sum Taeyoung surprised the group by running a sequence from a film. There was a distinct murmur amongst the group as some of them recognised it. One or two explained what it was to their friends.

"What you have just seen is what inspired the idea," Taeyoung told them when the sequence ended. "You might find that a surprise. The people who were involved in those raids by the British RAF in World War II were called, The Dam Busters. Their target was the dams of the industrial Ruhr Valley in Germany. By releasing the waters held back by the dams, the vitally important industrial area of Germany was flooded and incapacitated."

Onto the screen came a slide with the text:

Acionna 1 – America
Acionna 2 – China
Acionna 3 – Iberian Peninsular.

"These are the three target areas for my plan. They are all dams. Now, I don't intend to blow dams up in these places but I want to demonstrate to the world how vitally important these dams are – how essential the provision and proper management of water is. We will show how vulnerable these installations are, how unbelievably valuable the water they manage is, and the catastrophic consequences of their failure. By this act, we will hit the headlines of the world's media and the subject of water and its importance will become the number one talking point around the globe. It will trigger huge public dismay about the irresponsibility of the people entrusted with ensuring a secure supply of water."

He paused to take a sip of water. It was enough of a pause to enable someone in the audience to ask "how are you going to do that?"

"I don't intend to use Lancaster bombers!" responded Taeyoung jokingly. "But I do intend to use these."

And onto the screen came a picture of a large, propeller driven drone.

"Drones used to be confined to military use," Taeyoung continued. "Now anyone can buy one. Small drones have become playthings. Big ones, like the one on the screen, are increasingly involved in non-military applications – filming, building inspection, land management, surveillance, security – even in agriculture and farming. They're becoming a widely used tool of today. But their public accessibility is increasingly worrying for those involved in security. You can imagine why – and when you think of drones and our targets, the security challenges become very obvious."

"What you're seeing on the screen, is a derivative of China's early version of the military UAV WJ-600 model. I say a derivative because ours are made in South Korea, copying what China produced. We had a problem with Acionna 2 – the Chinese part of the project. To get a drone of our own into China was a nightmare prospect. So we've bought one of theirs for that part of the operation. For the other two locations, we needed something that could be transported in sections and easily assembled near to where we want to fly them. They're about 20 feet long and with a similar length wingspan. There are more sophisticated models around nowadays. They're jet propelled. Ours has a propeller. Its simpler technology but easier for us to handle, modify, transport and construct."

"You plan to fly these into the dams?" asked a PGU member.

"Yes," responded Taeyoung. "And at the same time, we will launch a publicity campaign that will tell people what the consequences would be if these had been the equivalent of dambusters. We will tell people how catastrophic the results would be."

"So you intend to blow the dams up?"

"We intend to show the world the consequences of the dams being breached," Taeyoung told them. "When the drones hit, we will release thousands of leaflets around the world"

. "So where do we come in?" another PGU member asked.

"I need help in Spain, America and China. Its help you guys can provide. I don't need many of you – probably four at each location. China is a different situation. I have my own resources there but I will still need some help in China."

"What will be involved?" came another question.

"We're still working on the detailed plans for all three projects", Taeyoung told them. "They will happen simultaneously. We're working on it being twelve noon in Spain, four in the morning in Vegas and eight o'clock at night in China. It's particularly helpful if we're operating in the dark in China. What I need is ground troops to help make this happen. I need you in Spain and I need you working with people from The New Church of Acionna in the States. I have some of my own people in China but I will need help there too. I need your help assembling the drones. I need to train some of you to fly them though most of that will be automatic and guided by GPS. And I need your help in videoing what happens."

Taeyoung waited for more questions. Though there was much muttering around the group, nobody raised any more queries. He wondered what they would say if they knew the true extent of his plans.

After a suitable delay, Taeyoung said "and what I need to know is – are you in? Are you still with me? And I need your renewal of the vow of silence." It was a challenge from the man they knew as Hwanung but he detected that the thought of travel, of training in drone flying, of being part of a global protest of major significance, all added up to an irresistible opportunity for this group of intelligent but frustrated youngsters.

Chapter 19

Sam Baldwin was genuinely shocked but also extremely worried when the news was brought to him by a reporter who had been doing routine morning calls to the Vegas civic services. It was the police who broke the news that the freelance newshound Ryan Spears, had been found dead in his gas filled apartment in The Valley. The reporter also broke the news that officers were on their way to the Journal's offices and were 'keen to talk to the editor.' When pressed by his staff man about this making a news item for the next edition, Baldwin grunted in response. He would write it himself. To reporters in the editorial hall that added further spice to the spreading news about Ryan's death. Nobody could remember the last time the editor undertook to write up anything but an editorial leader.

Minutes later, Baldwin strode from his office and out of the building, telling his surprised PA he would be gone for no more than half an hour. He left in a hurry, spinning the rear wheels of his car as he set off at speed out of the Journal's parking lot and onto the Western Bonanza Road. In less than ten minutes, he was rushing into a bar where he was well-known, asking the manager if he could use a phone.

"Tim," he said as his call was answered. "I don't want to say much now but did you know that Ryan Spears is dead. Yes – dead! Been found in his apartment. It was gas filled. Looks like a suicide."

There was silence from the phone.

"I think we should meet," continued Baldwin. "Six o'clock. Usual place?"

"OK," came the briefest of responses followed by a click and the sound of a dead connection.

Baldwin marched out of the bar without even a nod at a slightly perplexed manager who was surprised by the lack of any conversation – even a curt "thanks" for the use of the phone would have seemed appropriate. Baldwin climbed into his car and headed back to his office. He was there well within the promised half an hour but it had been important for to him to make the call on a totally independent phone line. Who knew who might be listening and even recording anything within the phone network of the LV Journal or potentially breaking into his mobile?

Within the hour, Baldwin was seated in his office confronting two officers from the police department, one in uniform.

"I gather Mr Ryan trained here as a junior reporter?" asked the non-uniformed visitor.

"Yes," Sam Baldwin replied. "He was a promising young journalist. We were sorry he decided to move on. And we're shocked and horrified to learn of his death"

"Why did he do that?"

"What, leave? Well, I guess he was too much of a free spirit. He found working within the confines and parameters of corporate disciplines too uncomfortable. Too restricting. So he went freelance."

"But he continued to do work for you?"

"Yes, every now and then."

"Was he working on anything for the Journal now?"

Baldwin felt uncomfortable. He wished he knew what these people already knew. "No, Ryan wasn't working for us at the moment."

The non-uniformed officer looked through the file of papers he was holding. "But he came to see you recently?"

"Yes," said Baldwin, feeling increasingly concerned.

"What was that about?" asked the policeman.

"He wanted me to commission a story from him," Baldwin responded.

"And did you?"

"No."

"Why not?"

Baldwin hesitated. Were these guys fishing for something in particular? "It was a story about the Vegas water shortages. We've covered it extensively in the past. I told him – he had no new news."

Again, the policeman scanned through the papers before him. "From what we have found, it seems Mr Spears thought he had come across something unusual. He found that an English company with French connections was talking to the City about solutions to the water crisis.

Wasn't that something new, Mr Baldwin? Not something to interest you? Not a 'new news story' as you put it?"

"No sir," Baldwin replied. "Like I say, we've done this story about the water crisis to death. In my judgement, Ryan had got nothing new for us. He didn't tell me about the Anglo French company you've mentioned. But what he did tell me was not enough for me to commission a story from him. Definitely not something for me to put my hand in my pocket and pay him a retainer – which is what he was after."

Again more delving through the file. "But from what we see, Mr Spears was seeking to link what he knew about the water crisis to issues of security. Did you know that, Mr Baldwin?"

"No," the editor replied. This interview was becoming decidedly difficult.

"But security and water provision to the City have been high profile news in the past. Mr Spears makes notes about 9.11 and the fact that five of the perpetrators of that terrorist attack had been seen in LV before 9.11. There have since been questions as to whether they were planning to attack the Hoover Dam. So Mr Spears seems to be making a link somehow between terrorism and water shortages. Wasn't that of interest to you Mr Baldwin?"

There was a short delay as the editor gave consideration to the last question. In the end the answer was again short.

"No."

"I would have thought anything to do with the security of Vegas would be of interest to The Journal?" The question was delivered with a thoughtful sort of tone.

"Ryan didn't make those connections when he came to see me," replied the editor.

"Don't you think that's surprising when it's very clearly part of the notes Mr Spears was developing?"

"I guess Ryan didn't tell me everything when he came to see me," Baldwin said. "Maybe he was keeping something back – not showing me all his cards on that first visit."

"So did you expect to see him again on the same issue?"

"No," Baldwin answered. "I said we weren't interested. That was that."

"So don't you think it surprising that he didn't raise the security issue with you? I would have thought it was his best bet for you to buy the story."

The editor had to agree. And he was genuinely puzzled. He had been ever since he opened the CD report Ryan had left him. The file contained all sorts of questions that were puzzling the young reporter. Why was the City giving procurement authority to EscaEau? What was the South Korean company SDBI's involvement? Was there a security dimension to the story? Were there any connections to the 9.11 terrorists who had been seen in LV before the attacks in New York and Washington? With the City becoming increasingly short of water, was it also becoming increasingly vulnerable to a terrorist attack? Baldwin had read Ryan's note with considerable interest and much concern. Clearly Ryan was looking at issues of security as much as he was about water shortages. If that were so, why hadn't he raised it when he came to see him?

The interview stumbled to an uncomfortable end. The policemen obviously felt it strange that the Journal had not gone for the security story. But, with promises that they would be back, they left.

Sam Baldwin sat in a dazed mood after their departure. He felt as if he was being sucked into something over which he had no control and behind which were serious dangers. Not for a moment did he think Ryan Spears had taken his own life. He was not that sort of a young man. And, it was worryingly coincidental that he had died at a time when he was delving into this particular story.

After a while, Baldwin turned to his keyboard and thumped out a short story about the death of one of their former newsmen. It was less than 200 words long and more or less a factual obituary rather than a news story about a young journalist's puzzling death. He sent it through to the sub-editors with a terse note attached simply saying – PRINT IT.

He was in one of his favourite bars by ten to six. Tim Crenshaw arrived on the dot of six. He looked ragged, like a man who had been thrashed through a tough day. They sat at a table away from anyone else.

"What the fuck is going on," asked Baldwin.

"I've no idea," came the response. "The death of Spears was as much of a shock to me as it was to you. Are you sure it wasn't suicide?"

"You're joking." Baldwin found it incredulous that Tim was even suggesting the idea. "You know as well as I do that someone has stopped Spears prying any more. What I don't know is – who? Do you know?" He almost spat the challenging question at the man sitting opposite him.

Crenshaw was clearly taken aback by Baldwin's attacking stance. "No way! And don't even think it!"

Baldwin was not letting go. "But it was you Spears saw with the man from EscaEau. That was enough for him to start delving. And, he found the South Korean company SDBI also involved. So he either felt that seeing someone from the Office of Emergency Management – you – with people like this was enough for him to think something strange was going on – adding two and two together to make five – or, he had found out more. Whatever, either his conjecture or growing evidence was enough to disturb someone and lead to his death. Now, of course, the cops are involved. And, eventually, our relationship will become known to them. So I get sucked into this more. It stinks, my friend. And we're up to our necks in it."

Chapter 20

Across the planet, the Christian part of the global population gradually moved towards the Christmas celebrations, three months before International Water Day. From August onwards, Sum Taeyoung had been busy on both the legitimate business of SDBI and on the Acionna Project through the more clandestine side of the company. Somewhat nervous about returning to Paris, Taeyoung was aware that the French police had not been in contact with him at all. Unusually, he had dirtied his own hands with the death of Fiacre, but he seemed to have got away it. The stabbing with a douk-douk pocket knife had, as he always hoped it would, led the police in Paris to believe the murder of Madeleine was the act of a banlieue based Algerian gang. There were many such killings in the squalid suburbs.

His meeting in Paris with the members of the PGU had been more fruitful than he had hoped. It emerged that all the members had, unsurprisingly, been interviewed by the police about the deaths of Fiacre and Madeleine but, as far as he could tell, none had broken the vow of secrecy. Whether that was through fear of the consequences of betraying the vow, Taeyoung could not tell. His position seemed secure but he was thankful he had hidden behind the Hwanung name. The meeting seemed to move the group on from the death of their comrades and to rejuvenate enthusiasm for his Acionna projects, especially now the prospect of travel was promised to at best America or China or, at worse, the Iberian Peninsula. And there was the carrot of training which could be the key to future employment. Those at the meeting who volunteered to become more deeply involved, formed into sub-groups, one for each of Taeyoung's three projects – Acionna 1 in America, Acionna 2 in China and Acionna 3 in the Iberian Peninsula.

He would, he told them, need help with the logistics. To spell out the obvious, he, Taeyoung, could not be in three places at the same time. So, he wanted to delegate some responsibilities to PGU members. They would, he told them, be responsible for much of the action in Spain and America and to a lesser extent in China. He also wanted their constructive ideas as to how to broadcast the message to the world – to capitalise on their social media skills. The message was simple. People the world over must take the subject of water more seriously. This precious resource should be regarded with more respect. On the publicity side, he also wanted PGU members to video record what happened at the three dams on March 22nd.

In Las Vegas, the water situation continued to deteriorate. Despite moving from the summer months into winter, the drought continued. The water levels in Lake Mead dropped week by week and further restrictions on water use were demanded by city authorities. The contrast between the desperately water short Nevada County farming community and the uninhibited extravagance of the spectacular fountains of many of the leading attractions in the glittering city of Vegas – let alone the extraordinary lifelike depiction of the canals of Venice - was now alarming. To the more conscientious, such use of water in the prevailing circumstances was utterly vulgar. But still the City fathers pressed on with urban expansion programmes with their added pressure on the troubled water supply.

Tim Crenshaw's activities in the New Church of Acionna continued to grow and seemed to have a proportionate link to the decline of his relationship with Susan. His contact with the South Korean, Taeyoung, was now minimal but sufficient to keep Crenshaw engaged and committed. His extramarital activities continued, still concealed from his family, friends, colleagues and the church. He and Sam Baldwin now had a more or less formal agreement to meet for a beer once a month and swap notes.

The Vegas Medical Examiner had passed an 'Unlawful Killing' judgement on the death of the young journalist Ryan Spears and left the file open as police investigations continued. As time drifted on, there was little evidence of any great commitment on their part. Crenshaw and Baldwin continued to monitor this and both remained worried as to what the police activity might eventually reveal.

The pace of growth of Angel Martin's New Church of Acionna astounded many and was the envy of rivals. It was driven by the vision and energy of the gospel singer and helped enormously by her very effective and well-practiced PR and publicity machines. Her 'reality congregations' were large, noisy and enthusiastic. "Cyber congregations", as Angel called her on-line participants, stretched further and further round the world. The bank balance struggled to accommodate the flow of donations. Crenshaw found it difficult to keep up with her ideas and initiatives and was not surprised, but somewhat overwhelmed, when she called him to a meeting to tell him of her latest thinking.

"Have you heard what Eleanor Revelle from the League of Woman Voters in Washington has been saying?"

Crenshaw confessed he had not.

"She's been talking about water being an increasingly scarce resource. She says many parts of the United States already face serious water shortages and even drought. She attributes it to population growth and climate change and says even in areas where water seems to be abundant, there's need for careful water management. She seems to be on our wavelength. It's prompted me to think – why don't we look to stage an event about the vital nature of water? We could invite her to speak. Our first convention, maybe?"

Crenshaw was unprepared for this and did not know what to say. He just nodded in apparent agreement and wondered where this might lead. Two days later, he knew. The church leader was on the phone eager to tell him about her latest thinking. He always knew when she was in a creative mood. Her normally deep voice went up an octave or so.

"Tim," her voice was quivering with excitement. "Our first convention. It should celebrate our first birthday. That's in March. March is also the month for International Water Day. It's a United Nations event. We should be part of it. Wouldn't that be fantastic? Check it out will you?"

"But Angel. March is only three and a bit months away," he reminder her.

"Tim. We can do anything if we put our minds to it. Look what we've achieved this year."

"But you can't organise a major conference in three months," he told her.

"If you're positive about it, and with the help of the Lord, I'm sure we can. Be more positive Tim. Let's have less negativity. Check out what venues might be able to do it. Talk to Eleanor. See if the UN'll play ball. It's their International Water Day after all. Use my influence. Use my PR people. Let me see some enthusiasm Tim."

Tim Crenshaw put the phone down with a sigh. "What next?" he thought to himself.

In China, the Beijing water shortage continued to worsen. Reports coming out of the city described the depth of despair of some people with, for example, residents in the neighbourhood near Tsinghua University going as far as digging up pavements and roads in desperate attempts to find water. "Who wouldn't dig wells if there's not enough water? There just isn't any," one resident told reporters. His family had been suffering from water shortages on and off for months until they decided to take matters into their own hands.

The North Western side of the city, an area once known for its natural springs and reed-filled ponds, now resembled the rest of the concrete urban sprawl with wide roads, new buildings everywhere and streets crowded with pedestrians. The Wanquan River, once a prominent feature of the area, was now reduced to a puddle filled ditch. The Wanquan was becoming yet another of the thousands of rivers in China to have dried up and disappeared because of declining rainfall, prolonged drought, exploding population and greater use of water.

Taeyoung's focus had turned to Danjiangkou in China's central province of Hubei where modifications to the dam and a new canal system, altogether costing tens of billions of dollars, involved the compulsory movement of some 300,000 people. The objective was to push 13 billion cubic metres of water more than 750 miles from the Yangzi River to water starved Beijing. In an enormous expansion programme, the height of the massive concrete gravity dam originally built between 1958 and 1973, was being raised substantially to double the size of the reservoir. Taeyoung was also acutely conscious that the dam contains six 150 MW turbines and any incapacitation of the dam would enormously impact on power distribution across the region, let alone cause massive flooding and widespread shortages of drinking water.

Meanwhile, in Pyeongtaek, a city in the Gyeonggi province of South Korea about 70 kilometres south of Seoul and with historic and continuing connections to the military, Taeyoung maintained regular monitoring of the progress of a very specialist company chosen to undertake some highly secretive activity. It was here the 'home built' versions of the Chinese drones were being constructed to specifications provided by Taeyoung. He visited the small factory whenever he could. The trials also involved CL-20, a product some American universities devised especially for drone use. It was a new development of particular interest to him. But Taeyoung and his supplier quickly realised they were ahead of the field in converting what so far had only been tested by academic teams. It was becoming obvious, little or no practical application had happened anywhere. It was proving to be a challenge and one to be treated with great respect.

Taeyoung discussed with his young PGU team suitable targets in Spain. Of all the three Acionna projects, Taeyoung expected this to be the easiest. Frustratingly, it was proving to be complicated. His initial view had been towards the Almendra Dam, an obvious target. It is one of Spain's highest man-made structures at 660 feet. But the dam lies on the River Tormes. Taeyoung was more interested in the Guadiana River. The Tormes, he thought, is 'merely' a Spanish river. In contrast, of the 500 miles length of the Guadiana, although the majority of it is, in its East/West flow in Spain, it eventually bends and heads south into Portugal, all the way down to the Algarve in the south, often forming the border between the two countries. Of all the dams along the Guadiana, the largest, newest, most spectacular and the most controversial is the Alqueva, one of the biggest in Western Europe. It creates an artificial lake of almost 100 square miles. An obvious target.

But for Taeyoung it was too far south, just north of the Algarve. He wanted to demonstrate he could create havoc right across the Iberian Peninsula, in both Spain and Portugal. So he had an alternative target in mind – in the Spanish Toledo Mountains where, since Roman times, a series of four major dams created more than 20 miles of reservoirs along the eastern part of the province. They provide irrigation for several hundred thousand acres of land and electricity to the towns and villages of Badajoz and a growing number of businesses in the area.

Taeyoung believed that by targeting this area, they could show how vulnerable large areas of Spain and Portugal were. In Spain, a PGU team of youngsters sent to increase Taeyoung's knowledge of the area, found there to be little consensus about what should be done about the growing problem of water provision. Heated discussions on the subject were often causing journalists and politicians alike to call the tensions and disagreements "water wars." One farmer/politician told a PGU researcher, "Water arouses passions because it can be used as a weapon – a political weapon, just as oil is a political weapon. In Spain, water has set region against region, north against south and government against opposition."

In London, Georgi's team had now got a real fix on Taeyoung. Through tapping into US and UK surveillance activity and using techniques such as GPS tracking, satellite observation, and CCTV, plus their own bugging activity, they were now seeing much of what he was up to, hearing some of his telephone conversations, seeing some of his emails, and even listening in on his meetings in his office in Seoul. Taeyoung's own anti-surveillance technology meant the team in Wapping could neither guarantee to hear everything or know every minute where Taeyoung was, but they had a pretty good picture of his day to day life.

Gene Bond was kept in contact with any progress as it emerged. By arrangement with Georgi, he worked on the project for the European Union Intelligence Service on an ad hoc basis, attended meetings to give his views, being sent material for his consideration, and offering his observations when appropriate. This enabled him to give time to his normal business and to ensure that did not fizzle out through lack of attention. Of importance to him, the EUIS was paying for time he recorded working for Georgi. This suited Bond well because whilst he could not work for Georgi for nothing, neither did he want to appear to be deeply into the pockets of the European Government.

Based as his normal business is from his home in Birmingham, contact with Nagriza was now far from satisfactory. They had not been alone since the garden party at Buckingham Palace. It left Bond stranded with few opportunities to not only enjoy her company but to develop their relationship. Although he did not want to, and despite her reassurances, he could not help feeling in competition with Georgi who had the advantage of near daily contact with her.

In contrast, Bond's relationship with Georgi was, ironically, fully recovered. Bond was delighted with that. In recent weeks, they had met a couple of times at the Russian Bar Georgi frequented where, as they had done so many times in the past, they drank the staple drink – ice-cold, near freezing Russian vodka chasers, served in long stemmed silver goblets with white frozen sugar rims and slammed down between gulps of dark beer. It was a great way to stimulate debate and to gradually become inebriated so as to relieve daily pressures. He so much enjoyed Georgi's company yet every time they said goodbye, it took no time at all for feelings of resentment to grow in Bond. He was feeling almost schizophrenic.

Just before Christmas, Georgi called a project review. The full team, including Gene Bond, assembled around the glass table in the basement HQ in Wapping. They had had one major breakthrough; it confirmed Bond's thinking. The name Acionna was significant. But it was not the whole name, just the three first letters, ACI. They now knew Taeyoung had three targets on his mind for March 22nd – one in America, one in China and the third on the Iberian Peninsula, not India as Bond had originally suggested. Picking out water only related material from the reams of data they had daily on Taeyoung, they knew he had met the top man of one of the world's leading water provision companies, Esca. Its President, Bernhard Gedeck, had met him in the infamous Flying Bird Tea Shop in Seoul. But why? Why did Gedeck fly all the way to Seoul? That they did not know. They were equally perplexed that the meeting should be held in the tea shop. Why? They had found a connection between Esca and SDBI in the African state of Wandora where Esca had hit problems. Taeyoung's legitimate business, SDBI, seemingly bailed Esca out of serious difficulties. Was that the beginning of some sort of link between the two companies? They did not know.

Despite him having concealed his activity behind the name of a Korean God, Hwanung, they also knew Taeyoung had met the group of young environmental activists in Paris to which Fiacre and Madeleine had been connected. But despite their best endeavours, they could not discover what that had been about or what its outcome was. But the fact he was still talking to this group with its links to the Goddess Acionna, was considered significant.

After their meeting, Bond found Nagriza was flying back to her home near the Aral Sea in Uzbekistan so as to be with her parents for Christmas. She had not seen them for a long time and her father was ill. So the trip was important to her and had to be done. Bond fully understood but it came as a horrible shock to realise he would not see her until after the festive period. He was mortified. Christmas had gone significantly downhill.

Also in London, Bernhard Gedeck pondered long and hard as to how to respond to the deal he had struck with Taeyoung. Standing at the window of his office gazing down at the River Thames as it stretched out before him, he felt contented and excited by the deal. In Esca terms, the money Taeyoung was asking for was no great sum. The potential profits to be gained from the deal with the South Korean could be astronomical and an out-of-the-blue surprise to shareholders.

He anticipated the company shares would rocket. As 50 percent of his income was related to share performance, that was all good news. But how to handle the project was the big question. This was a dangerous game – walking on a knife edge between unbelievable corporate damage if the true story ever got out, and astounding business gain if they pulled it off.

He hoped the problem would be resolved by establishing a Task Force. Drawn from senior managers across the corporate empire, three were tasked with heading up Acionna 1, 2, and 3, Gedeck having decided to adopt Taeyoung's denotation of the different geographical projects. The Task Force leaders were told this was a highly sensitive project but a great opportunity. They were sworn to secrecy on pain of instant dismissal if they failed to abide by it. They were also introduced to a highly attractive commission scheme which would see them each enjoy a generous percentage of the profits to be gained. Working with executives from Taeyoung's organisation, a process of introduction was started to ensure EscoEau was considered to be an ally by key politicians in Las Vegas, Beijing and in both Spain and Portugal. This exercise involved conventional ways of doing business but, where appropriate, supplemented by the 'greasing of palms' if necessary.

It was a substantial amount of work, interrupted by Christmas which seemed to make achieving any progress on anything impossible. Yet by January 1st Gedeck felt they were as well placed as he could have hoped. There were now less than 10 weeks to go to International Water Day.

Chapter 21

Gene Bond emerged from Westminster tube station jostling with commuters and tourists in the packed, confined space of the staircase leading up to Bridge Street. Of the latter, the majority by far seemed to be oriental, Chinese in particular. London was packed with people from around the world all rushing around the stores in a frenzy of pre-Christmas shopping. As he emerged onto the street, it was raining. Black clouds pushed inland from the coast and across the capital to create a heavy and threatening sky. It was a cold, dark and uninspiring morning in which the red of the London buses offered a welcomed splash of colour in an otherwise drab scene. Big Ben, immediately opposite as Bond reached street level, started its hourly chime, it now being just nine o'clock.

He turned his coat collar up and hurried round the corner into Victoria Embankment where a biting wind straight off the river met him full on. He cursed as he saw people lined up outside Portcullis House. Clearly, the security system was again causing a backup of visitors who had no option but to stand in the December chill and shuffle forward towards the welcoming warmth of the administration centre for UK Members of Parliament.

It seemed, he thought as he stood in the queue, no time at all since MPs fought for whatever office space they could find in the ancient, historic but rapidly becoming impractical Palace of Westminster, home of the two Houses of Parliament – the Commons and the Lords. It degenerated into a fiasco as the numbers of MPs went up and the available space went down with some MPs having to resort to using cupboards and the like for their administrative offices. Portcullis House relieved the pressure and provides offices and meeting rooms in a modern building suitably designed to reflect the architecture of the Palace of Westminster which dominates this part of London. Thankfully for MPs, bearing in mind the unrelenting frustration of pressing crowds and constant traffic outside, a tunnel links Portcullis House to the Palace of Westminster.

At last, Bond made the comfort of the inside of the building, having safely navigated the circular doors that often catch out the unwary by snagging bag straps and trapping wheeled cases. The security check – thorough but polite as ever – was navigated without incident leading him into the usual crush of people, this morning all wearing coats wet to one degree or another, waiting to sign in. He made it known he was here to see Garry Austin, the no-nonsense Yorkshire MP, Chairman of the all-party Parliamentary Climate Change Group and currently joint Chairman of the European Environment Committee. He was told, as he expected to be, to wait to one side or the other of the entrance and someone would come for him.

The waiting areas were crammed with visitors and the whole scene resembled only partly controlled chaos – as usual. After five minutes, he heard his name shouted out above the general noise and hubbub. He spotted the caller to be a red-haired, tall and elegant young lady who was peering around, waiting in the hope someone would respond. He shouldered his way through to her, shook her hand in reaction to her welcome, and followed her through the security doors into the relative peace of the mall area that constitutes the ground floor of Portcullis House. The PPS led him to a table and three chairs close to the line of trees that creates the central feature.

"Garry is on his way," she reassured him. "Should be five minutes. Can I get you a coffee?"

Bond accepted the invitation and sat so he could see the exit from the tunnel linking to the Houses of Parliament. He had been here many times before and sat at tables in this area. He found it interesting to see the tunnel. It was a splendid place from which to spot the good and the famous from the world of British politics.

As part of a feature article he was preparing for a specialist magazine, he was here to talk to Austin specifically about the aftermath of the disastrous floods in the UK the previous winter and about management of climate change as a generality. He did not expect it to be that positive a meeting. His faith in the political process and the people who run it had faded badly in recent years. His cup of coffee and the MP arrived at the same time. The red headed PPS left them to it.

"Morning Gene," greeted the MP cheerfully. "You OK meeting here?" It was more like a statement of fact than a query. "It's easier than trying to book a meeting room and my little office is overwhelmed with researchers."

Bond confirmed he was happy to stay where they were and launched into the subject. Knowing Austin as he did, there was no point beating about the bush. Straight talk was best.

"I'm looking for any sort of comforting indications that the UK Government has responded to the floods that wreaked havoc across a large proportion of the country so we may hope to be better prepared when it happens again. I'm not going say 'if it happens again' because it will. You know as well as I that climate change will virtually guarantee that."

"Gene, you know the PM's been out to the Somerset Levels – as have I and other Ministers and senior officials," Austin told him. "We've spent more than £300 million in repairing and improving flood defences and undertaken a huge dredging programme. More than 120,000 tonnes have been dredged out of the Parrett and Tone rivers. It's cost about a million pounds a mile but we've reshaped these rivers and improved their capacities by a third."

"That's all well and good," responded Bond. "But you're tinkering with the problem. You're sticking your figure in the dyke. And anyway, there's a big argument that says dredging isn't the answer. As in every aspect of sustainable development, you're playing on the edges, trying to score Brownie points with the electorate but not really tackling the central overall problem."

Garry Austin was obviously unhappy with this. "That's grossly unfair," he retorted. "We were dealing with the aftermath of unprecedented levels of rainfall. These were exceptional circumstances. We had had the longest period of intense rain on record. The ground was saturated. There was nowhere for more water to go. So we got floods. Dredging provides the fastest and most effective solution."

"But it's only a short term answer," pleaded Bond. "Dredging, like many flood defences, just shifts the problem to another area."

"Dredging is what the residents of the Somerset Levels were calling for. We've responded," insisted Austin.

"But it provides no long term solution", Bond argued. "Climate change is increasing the frequency of crisis events, so don't think this is a one off. And the problems on the Somerset Levels, and around the south and east coastline, were as much to do with sea surge as it was about rainfall. In all honesty, it was about both. And there's no doubt about it, we'll get more."

He expected another response from the politician but none came. So Bond continued his attack.

"With sea levels rising and extreme weather conditions happening more frequently, there has to be a more proactive response. Dredging is reactionary. If there was a strategic approach to this, we'd be ensuring we have more trees and vegetation in the uplands to hold back the flow of water. We'd be expanding existing bogs. We'd be creating floodplains and new channels from flood susceptible rivers to take flood waters to those floodplains. And we'd be paying farmers to manage them. We'd even be paying farmers for use of land into which floodwaters would be directed and held."

"A lot of what you say is in our strategic plan that followed the last disaster. We're doing much of what you're on about," said Austin defensively.

Bond would have nothing of it. "No you're not. You're just talking about it. It's political rhetoric. It's bollocks. It may be in your strategic plan but it certainly isn't in any strategic action taking place right now. If you're that concerned, why the hell are you still granting permission for building developments in floodplains? It's incredible! What insanity is allowing more properties to be built on areas that are bound to flood in the future? And more urbanisation means more concreted acres – more space where water can only rush over the surface and travel elsewhere rather than seep into the ground and into aquifers. If you were doing anything like the Dutch are

159

doing, I could understand it. I'd support it. I'd applaud it. You know as much about this as me."

"The Dutch – and Scandinavians and elsewhere round the planet, they've got the message. Things are not as they were. We're having more incidents of extreme rainfall, high winds, rising seas. So they're responding strategically. Changing the way they do things. In the lowlands of the Netherlands, they're actually creating new water worlds. They're breaking dykes and allowing areas to flood in a controlled way. People are being invited to leave and are being paid compensation for doing so. Those who want to stay are being helped with their properties being raised, mounded areas created. It's a totally different approach. It's a holistic way, not a bit here and a bit there as we are doing."

"But Gene, look at the costs," Austin responded. "They're phenomenal."

"Of course they are," Bond replied. "But it's a far more long term solution. The Dutch have accepted that climate change will create more and more crisis events. So they've adopted a long term approach. When the next crisis hits us, we'll go through all the same drama again. And pay the price – again. So what's sensible? Pay now to manage the future or pay later – again and again – for the costs of not doing the job properly in the first place?"

"But where does the money come from?" asked the politician. "You know we've been cutting back in every direction. There's pressure on every department."

"Don't get me going," Bond answered. "You know what I think. You can find the money when you have to. Look what happened when the banks went phut. You printed millions and millions of pounds. And if the economy was more concerned about the important issues rather than being infatuated with growth, there might be some hope. But you lot, whatever your politics, you're all fixated about short termism and growth. So we have no strategic way of responding to climate change, or to growing populations, or to pressures on resources – like water."

"Talking about water," Garry Austin almost grabbed at the reference to water as a way of changing the subject and getting away from a discussion about flooding which was going nowhere and in which they were both entrenched with different views. "Do you know anything about the New Church of Acionna?"

"No," Bond admitted but with the connection now established between Sum Taeyoung and Acionna, anything that came up with that name immediately caught his interest. "But I do know a bit about the Goddess of water. Where's the church?"

"In Las Vegas," Austin told him. "It was only established this year but its growth is amazing. It's like a new cult. Led by this gospel singer – Angel Martin. Got some serious followers and some real clout – and money."

"Never heard of it. Means nothing to me. Why do you ask?" Bond was curious but did not want to give away the reason why. That the New Church of Acionna was based in America was of huge interest. Even more so that it was in Las Vegas where the Hoover dam is located. America was a Taeyoung target.

"Apparently, they're planning this convention on water. In Vegas. This coming March. To celebrate their first birthday – on International Water Day. They've invited me to speak. What do you think of that?"

Bond was amazed. Taeyoung planned something for March 22nd. America was one of his targets. Acionna was his project's code name. The 'A' in Acionna they knew to be America. If the Church of Acionna was in Vegas, did this mean Vegas was Taeyoung's target? And if that was right, was Bond also right about the Hoover Dam? He could not wait to tell Georgi.

Chapter 22

Chloe Lefevre and Adnan Khan exemplified just why Sum Taeyoung was interested in the young group of people who made up the Paris Guerriers Urbains. As he said from the outset, he needed ground troops. For the '1' project in Acionna 1:2:3, he needed more intelligence to refine his target plans. The Iberian Peninsula target, he had decided, would be the River Guadiana. But where? It is a long river that travels East to West through Spain before turning south and, for a considerable length of its remaining journey to the Mediterranean, forming the border between Spain and Portugal. His idea was that any disruption should potentially cause havoc not only in Spain but all the way down to the tourist dependent Algarve part of Portugal. That particularly appealed to the South Korean 'chaos entrepreneur'.

Despite his own research, Taeyoung still remained unsure as to the precise target in Spain. He knew several dams exist in the Badajoz area close to the border with Portugal, but which one to select was a difficult decision because information was hard to come by. So the young couple, both aged 18 with Adnan of Pakistan family origins and Chloe being French, were selected from the small bunch of PGU volunteers and despatched to undertake an Iberian Peninsula recce. Both were very street wise, sharp, keen, intelligent, youthful and healthy. What they lacked was experience. Their lives so far had been restricted to the suburbs of Paris. Neither had passports or any police records. From Taeyoung's perspective they were inquisitive students on a knowledge gaining journey to Spain and Portugal from their home in Paris. Or at least that is what he hoped others might think should they have cause to interrogate them.

Taeyoung organised their documentation and journey via train from Paris to Madrid then on to Badajoz. They travelled light with back packs and a pup tent to keep their accommodation options wide open. On arrival at Badajoz, they checked into the Hotel San Marcos in the centre of the ancient town and only two streets away from the River Guadiana which they started to reconnoitre the following day. However, that was not without its delay as Chloe, from a very Catholic family, insisted they start the day by visiting the large cathedral which dominates the ancient and historic town and its extensive evidence of Roman occupation.

"There is no way I come all the way to Badajoz and not see the cathedral," she told Adnan adamantly. So they walked from the hotel through the quaint and crooked streets now decorated in anticipation of the coming Christmas festival, to the religious centre with its square architecture and small, slit-like windows which gave it a fortress appearance.

It was midmorning when they eventually reached the Guadiana River. They did so at the town end of the suspended bridge that carries the roadway over the river and two small islets. From their desktop research, they were unsure if this was a dam or not. Now they could see it properly, there clearly was no dam here. So they continued walking parallel to the river along the tree lined, boulevard-like Paseo Fluvial with its modern apartment buildings and occasional business premises. It was a splendid, crisp winter day. A good day for walking.

Their map showed a number of structures crossing the river but there was no indication as to whether they were simply bridges or roads over dams. They had been surprised at their first sight of the Guadiana which was much wider than they had expected. When they reached the second bridge, they found it too was only a bridge. No sign of a dam here either. And so their day continued, walking alongside the Guadiana River, looking unsuccessfully for dams but delighting in being in the picturesque town. Eventually they returned to their shared hotel room to consider what to do next.

They had learnt from the day by talking to people, from information they picked up at the Cathedral, and off Google via Adnan's iPhone, about something called the 'Badajoz Plan'. Further digging told them this dates back to the 1950s, the ambition being to use the power of the region's rivers, and mainly the Guadiana, to bring electrical power to communities in the area for the first time and to provide irrigation schemes enabling a wider variety of agricultural produce to be grown. This would transform the lives of thousands of people and help pull them out of poverty. What the two youngsters from Paris could not find from any of the information they had collected, was the location of the frequently referenced dams of Badajoz.

"We could be here for weeks unless we get some specific information," groaned Adnan in frustration.

And while Chloe agreed, it was obvious to both of them they did not have the luxury of weeks. Taeyoung had allowed for them to be in Badajoz for four days. It had seemed a generous allocation of time. Now they were not so sure.

Adnan acquired a map of the area over which he poured for some considerable time. Eventually it sparked a thought which he tested on Chloe.

"Look, if you track the Guadiana east from Badajoz, there's another river that flows into it. It's the Arroyo de Albarregas which comes down through the town of Merida and eventually joins the Guadiana. Not far further east of Merida is a dam – the Cornalvo Dam. From what I can see on the map, it appears to be located in some sort of national park. Now it seems to me, if you broke that dam, the impact would be felt all the way to Badajoz, through all the Badajoz dams and the floodplains created in the Badajoz Plan, and onwards down into Portugal. It could work?" It was obviously more of a question than a statement made with any conviction.

Chloe looked closely at the map with Adnan.

"That's a sizeable area of water behind the dam. It says it's the 'Embalse de Cornalvo'. Does embalse mean reservoir? I bet it does."

And they confirmed it did. They also found it was about 40 miles from Badajoz to Merida. The more they researched, the more excited they got. They discovered the dam is a declared ancient monument dating back to Roman days. It was thought to have been constructed around 130 AD.

"That must make it one of the oldest surviving dams in the world," said Chloe. "And if that's right, that does wonders for getting maximum publicity for Hwanung."

With growing excitement and conviction that they had found something to excite their South Korean paymaster, they developed their plan for the following day. They would take a bus up to Merida and there, hopefully, hire bicycles for the rest of the journey to the dam, a further six miles on.

The morning presented them with another crisp and bright winter day. They walked away from the historic town centre and the short distance to the coach station located in a bright and modern part of Badajoz that looked like any other of a thousand modernised European cities. The journey to Merida took them just over an hour and, despite their youthful curiosity and the spectacular scenery through which they travelled, both slept most of the way.

They researched this Spanish town but nothing prepared them for what they saw. They knew Merida was declared a World Heritage Site in 1993 but they did not expect to find themselves in the most extensive archaeological site in Spain. The main Roman amphitheatre, capable of seating 6,000 and still with two storeys of magnificent pillars and sculptures, took their breath away. They were told by people they spoke to on the site that more Roman theatres have been discovered in recent times and these facilities are used annually for the International Festival of Classical Theatre.

They were in awe of what they saw. It was, they thought, small wonder Merida was growing as a tourist centre. The evidence of that was everywhere but especially in the shops and stores, filled with souvenirs and trinkets although, like the rest of the town, now decked out for the coming Christmas festivities rather than for summer tourists. It made hiring bicycles more of a challenge than they expected. Cycling tourists are more evident in the summer not the winter. Several places advertised bikes but none were in sight. It was only when Chloe used her feminine charms on one young storekeeper that two cycles were conjured up from the depths of the store. He won a quick kiss on the cheeks from Chloe and a nod of thanks from Adnan.

Neither being regular cyclists, there was much giggling and banter between them as they wobbled off out of the historic town for the comparatively short ride to the protected natural park in which the reservoir and the ancient dam are located. After a few near scrapes and close encounters, they safely reached the park's visitor centre where they picked up a leaflet and map of the extensive parkland. It showed the protected area covers some 50 square miles and informed them the reservoir has a capacity estimated at around 11 million cubic meters of water.

"What does that mean?" asked Chloe.

"I have no idea," Adnan responded. "But it sounds like one hell of a lot of water to me. If you let that lot go, it would be pretty spectacular!"

There was no denying the beauty and tranquillity of the park, a predominantly flat land generously scattered with holm and cork oak trees. They had little time to take in the splendid plants and wildlife as they concentrated on heading to the dam. When they arrived, it was not what they had expected although they had not really talked about what a Roman dam would look like. They found it to be well over 700 feet long and about 60 feet high with a sloping wall on the reservoir side angled at about 30 degrees. Their visitor information leaflet told them it is a gravity dam, earth based but with a stone cladding on the water side.

"I wonder if the sloped face of the dam will cause Hwanung any problems?" Adnan said. "And it seems to have some vegetation growing from it. I wonder what that is?"

Chloe confessed she could not answer either question.

"I think we should find out about the greenery," Adnan said. "I'll go and have a look."

"No," pleaded Chloe. "You might fall in."

"I won't," the young Asian responded. "It's not that steep a slope."

And ignoring Chloe's further pleas, Adnan walked onto the angled wall of the reservoir. The 'greenery', whatever it was, started about a third of the way across the dam. Chloe watched in trepidation as her Asian friend progressed carefully further and further away from where she stood at the end of the dam and at the water's edge.

He reached the vegetation without difficulty and called to her. As his back was towards her, she could not make out what he was saying. She called back, telling him she could not hear. She watched as he started to turn so she could better hear what he was trying to tell her. But half way through the manoeuvre, he slipped. In horror, she watched Adnan slide further and further, closer and closer to the water.

"Help me Chloe," she heard him distinctly now. "It's so slimy. I can't get a grip."

He was trying to grab anything to stop the slide, kicking his feet to try and get a purchase. But the slide continued.

"Help," he called again. "I can't swim!"

"Now he tells me," she thought as Adnan's feet reached the water's edge.

Chapter 23

Tim Crenshaw had hoped Christmas would be OK. He could not hope for more than that. But it was fast degenerating into one disaster after another. On the domestic side, Susan was becoming increasingly agitated about his involvement with the New Church of Acionna. It was now in her mind that this would split the family over Christmas. A lifetime committed Baptist with a deep suspicion about any of the new religious orders seemingly springing up all over the place, there was no way she would step through the door of the New Church of Acionna let alone participate in any ceremony there. Her allegiance to her own church, which she had attended all her life – indeed the one in which they were married, was solid. That is where they always celebrated Christmas. This Christmas would be no exception. Now Tim was telling Susan that because of the high profile role he played in Angel Martin's church, she would expect him to attend services there, hopefully with his family. Susan would have none of that. It lead to one of the worst rows of their marriage and the tension between them was now constantly at boiling point.

Angel Martin's decision to stage a convention to celebrate their first year was not only an horrendous addition to his workload because of what, in his mind, was a ridiculously short period of time in which to organise it, but it was now creating problems at work. Water was something his department dealt with on a day to day basis. It dominated their working lives. The continuing lack of water was slowly tightening a noose around the city's neck and increasing numbers of politicians were now responding to pressure NGOs had been trying to apply for some considerable time. Two distinct camps of opinion had emerged. There was the 'business as usual' group and one advocating 'action now.' In addition, the whole scenario was becoming more and more complicated by the day as plans to build new pipelines from where groundwater could be found to where it was needed – in the city – were thwarted or at least severely stalled as questions arose as to who owned the land on which the pipeline would be developed. When the fathers of Las Vegas – visionary entrepreneurial pioneers and explorers – started the process of building a city in a desert, land was acquired through deals done over poker tables in spit and sawdust bars filled with tobacco smoke. It was far removed from today's lawyer driven sophisticated complexities.

The proposed new pipeline is to pump billions of gallons of water extracted from aquifers in the rural valleys in Lincoln and White Pine counties along the Nevada-Utah line to Las Vegas. But it is a highly contentious scheme with loud opposition from environmental groups, the farming community, local governments and Indian tribes, the latter concerned the project will seriously deplete rural groundwater resources and imperil delicate species, including sage grouse. It could also jeopardise the essential water supplies of the Nevada farmers.

Sitting in the middle of this was the Las Vegas Office of Emergency Management. Unfortunately for him, the division responsible for matters to do with water provision was the one headed by Tim Crenshaw. By now its leader felt he was slowly drowning in the problem.

Public opinion was divided. Some citizens were becoming vocal about their concerns as to how they would survive if climate change continued to cause weather patterns to shift and for more extreme forms of weather – like droughts – to become normality. Others pontificated about the drought only being part of a natural cyclic programme of change.

The scientific community provided no solace. As soon as one piece of scientific evidence was published looking utterly compelling and conclusive, some renegade somewhere would offer an alternative theory. Crenshaw, like many others, was exasperated by how the opinion of one person against ninety nine others could generate so much headline news and dominate coverage.

"Climate Change Hot Air" screamed the headlines from the Las Vegas Sun because some scientist somewhere had challenged one set of data. But like an avalanche, one viewpoint from one person generated one headline which spawned others and cascaded a load of doubt into the minds of a confused public.

Some in Vegas remonstrated about their worries over the future and viability of the city as climate change manifested itself in continuing drought conditions. Others were more anxious about anything that could prejudice economic growth and continuing prosperity. Some simply wanted the status quo to continue. Life was OK, they said. Leave it like it is. Into this mix came the violently different opinions of individuals – politicians – the media – and now the churches.

Angel Martin had no doubts. Jesus had said, she reminded anyone given half a chance: "Truly, truly, I say unto you, unless one is born of water and the Spirit, he cannot enter the kingdom of God." So water was, she preached, as important to human life as was the spirit of God. To that end, it needed to be respected and revered. It also needed to be the central subject of the first anniversary convention of the Church of Acionna. It was absolutely natural to her that her senior officer should take responsibility for its organisation, especially its content. So now another level of pressure was burdened onto Tim Crenshaw. How could he organise a convention that treated water as being more important than oil – or any other resource – when major players in the life and prosperity of the city thought of it only as a means to an end? Their maxim was – if there is not enough of it simply throw more money at the problem.

Under Angel Martin's demanding pressures, Crenshaw was developing the programme for the convention. The founder of the church would lead the day. Key speakers so far agreeing to speak were, Eleanor Revelle from the League of Woman Voters whose proclamations about water had sparked the idea for the convention within Angel Martin, US Secretary of State John Pine who had recently told a UN event that climate change was the most important issue facing mankind, and the Englishman Garry Austin in his capacity as joint Chairman of the European Environment Committee. The UN had been invited to send a speaker, the convention being on International Water Day which the UN organises. They had yet to respond.

Working with Angel Martin's PR consultancy, the event was already generating media interest not only locally but nationally. The convention would be held in the Las Vegas Convention Centre. Officials there originally told Crenshaw they were fully booked in March. He almost cheered! That potentially was a game ender. Everywhere else was also booked solid. He told Angel. She exploded! And three days later, the Convention people phoned him to say an event had been cancelled and a hall was now available. Had that been through her influence – or money? He did not know and did not ask. Annoyingly to Crenshaw, it meant the event was back on and Angel set him a maximum target audience of 500. Through her work, sponsorship for the event was now also arriving on his desk at regular intervals. He was constantly amazed at her ability to attract money.

One of his toughest days was just before the Christmas break. Three things happened. Jack Bundy, Senior Administrator for the City of Las Vegas, called him to an urgent meeting. They met in Bundy's office. He was conscious that Bundy's PA was present, clearly taking notes.

"This is very difficult, Tim." Bundy was clearly uncomfortable about what he was having to say to a head of department. "And I am the last person to interfere with the private lives of people who work for the City. But your involvement with the New Church of Acionna has been brought to my attention, especially its first anniversary convention. I gather you hold an office in the church?"

"Yes," Tim responded. "I'm its non-Executive Officer."

"A completely voluntary position I assume?" asked Bundy.

"Of course," Tim replied.

"This convention. I'm told the subject is about water. Is that right?"

"Yes," responded Tim. He had a horrible feeling this was now going to head in a difficult direction. He was right.

"And this church. It holds out water as something special?" probed the Senior Administrator.

"Yes," replied Tim. "Acionna was a Goddess of water. We believe water to be the very essence of life."

"Is there any conflict between what you are doing for the church – and especially this convention – and your work in your department? I'm fully aware that you are on the front line of dealing with the challenges we face about water."

"I don't think there's any conflict," Tim replied knowing full well there was; he was terrified of the very obvious extreme differences of opinion about water being promoted by the church, by some City officials, by politicians and by prominent business people.

"Is anyone from the City speaking at the convention?" asked Bundy.

"Not as yet," Tim told him.

"Will there be?" asked Bundy.

"I expect so," replied Tim. Up until now he had not contemplated having anyone speak from the City of Las Vegas. It was such a contentious subject with locals.

The Senior Administrator was silent for a moment as he thought through what Tim Crenshaw had told him. Eventually he said, "This is difficult Tim. Water is becoming very tricky. A sensitive subject. Triggers peoples' nerves. Impacts on our economic planning. Has environmentalists crawling all over it – and the media. Some of our political paymasters have very radical views about it. Most have very entrenched positions. Unless we resolve how better to manage water shortages, we're heading towards real difficulties. Your church convention on the subject could not be more badly timed. So I need to be kept informed about its programme as it builds. You keep me up to speed. You understand? And you find somewhere in that programme for someone from the City to speak. You got that? You and I will work out who. But I hope you're hearing properly what I'm saying. You're right in the firing line here and if you get it wrong for the City, your job might be threatened. You got that?"

Tim Crenshaw confirmed he had, indeed, got it. It could not have been more clearly spelt out. As he returned to his office, the phone was ringing. The voice at the other end of the line was familiar and his heart dropped. Not today. Not after the meeting he had just had.

Taeyoung broke the unexpected news he was in town, just for the afternoon, and wanted a meeting. When Crenshaw said he would welcome such a get together but it was far too short notice, the South Korean's tone chilled and the request turned into a demand.

"You will meet me this afternoon, Mr Crenshaw. You would find it regrettable if you do not."

It sounded like a threat. This was a new side of the South Korean as far as Tim Crenshaw was concerned.

"Are you threatening me?" he responded, deciding attack was the best form of defence. But he soon realised it was a bad tactic.

"Persuade might be a more tactful word but your first interpretation may be more accurate. That is why you will meet me this afternoon. Until you meet me, you cannot be sure which word is more correct – persuade or threaten. You cannot determine that until you hear what I have to say. And as you can't afford to gamble that I'm being persuasive rather than threatening, you will come and hear what I have to say."

"I have other diaried commitments," Tim answered.

"Of course you do, Mr Crenshaw. Who would expect a busy man like you not to? But it's all a matter of priorities. And I tell you, Mr Crenshaw, there is no greater priority in your life right now than me."

The South Korean paused, expecting a response. But there was none. Tim Crenshaw did not know what to say.

"So we will meet," confirmed Taeyoung with a heavy emphasis on the word 'will'. And he spelt out a time and a place.

Resigned to there being no way of escape, Tim Crenshaw capitulated. The call ended. Worried now what Taeyoung's threats meant, the Las Vegas civil servant tried to get his mind onto his day's work but no sooner had he started to do so than his phone rang again. It was Susan.

"You haven't forgotten the school Christmas play this afternoon? I'll meet you there."

Tim Crenshaw's heart sunk. He searched desperately for an appropriate response. He could not find one.

"Tim. Are you there?" Susan had her shrill voice on. It was one he was familiar with. It was the one she used when she was angry. She was often angry with him these days. Crenshaw thought she could cut steel with her angry voice so sharp was it.

"Yes, I'm still here," he answered, resigned to this all ending badly. "I'm afraid I'm double-booked this afternoon. I can't make it. Believe me, I wanted to. But you'll have to go by yourself."

It was as if someone had detonated her. Susan exploded. "You shit of a father. It's bad enough when you let me down – which you do constantly. But to let the children down. And at Christmas! It's unforgivable! I don't believe you, Tim Crenshaw, that you could sink this low."

There was a click and the line died. For some time afterwards, Tim Crenshaw sat as still as a statue, staring at the phone.

Chapter 24

Four weeks on from being in Las Vegas, Sum Taeyoung now stood on the shore of the gigantic reservoir in his black trench coat and black fedora, a marked contrast to the colourful and even garish figure he frequently presented to the world. But here, in modern China, where the predominant ambition everywhere seemed to be to change everything – structurally, environmentally, culturally – and as quickly as possible, he felt out of place in lavish, vibrant clothing. And here, unlike other parts of the world, he wanted to be as inconspicuous as possible. As the waters slopped against the shore close to where he stood, he turned his coat collar up against the chill wind and looked across the reservoir to the extraordinary sight of the Danjiangkou Dam, still with considerable evidence of construction activity on it.

He had never been to this part of China before although he was a frequent visitor to the country, especially to Beijing. He could have left the management of Acionna 2 to his local team but the sheer scale of what the Chinese were doing with the South/North water programme, and the modifications to the Danjiangkou Dam in particular, were something he wanted to see for himself.

Now, as he looked at the awesome structure less than a mile away from where he stood, he could not help but feel a twinge of doubt creep into his mind. Would what he planned work? The team back in Pyeongtaek kept reassuring him, they were convinced the technology would perform as he wanted it to. However, he was acutely aware that they did not know what the actual targets were. They were working to his specifications and against those, the experts said they were happy. But they had not seen the Danjiangkou Dam! Neither did they know the Hoover Dam was on his hit list. They were both such huge, formidable and solid structures.

Thinking of the two dams led him to think of the third. He reflected on the strange mix they had ended up with – two iconic representations of modern technology and enormous, complex construction projects, and one from the days of the Roman Empire. How odd! The news received a few days ago that the Spanish police had been called to an incident at the Cornalvo Dam where one PGU member nearly drowned was worrying, but the story the police got from the two young Parisians seemed to be accepted and they were now back in their home city. He was reassured their cover story worked. The authorities accepted they were inquisitive, travelling students.

Taeyoung had agreed with their recommendations about the Roman dam. It appealed to him that such an historic structure should still be so vital to the modern needs of tens of thousands of people on the Iberian Peninsula. From a project perspective, it was, as they suggested it would be, very newsworthy.

Using the PGU youngsters was always going to be a bit of a gamble as the incident in Spain demonstrated. But this project was so ambitious he needed help in its delivery, even if those helping did not know his real intentions. In America, Tim Crenshaw's civil servant position was proving to be incredibly helpful. When they met, the nervousness of the American was obvious. Taeyoung's research on Crenshaw was about to pay dividends.

"There are several ways you can help me, Mr Crenshaw," the South Korean told the civil servant at their speedily organised meeting. "Through your position in the administration of Las Vegas, I want you to ensure the French water specialist company, EscaEau, is an authorised supplier to the city. I also want you to look after two young people from Paris who I will send over shortly before March 22nd. And finally, there's the matter of the convention being organised by the New Church of Acionna."

And he went on to spell out what he would like in the programme.

Tim Crenshaw was horrified by Taeyoung's 'shopping list'. And, nervous though he was, he felt he had to say what he thought.

"I'm not sure how much I can help you," he answered. "The supplier issue to the City is a difficult challenge and I will have to discuss your ideas regarding the convention with the leader of the church."

"Mr Crenshaw," responded Sum Taeyoung. "I think you still fail to understand me. I think you still fail to understand the delicate nature of your position. Maybe you think I will not expose your secret life to your wife, family, friends and employer. But you are so wrong to doubt me Mr Crenshaw, if indeed you do. But as I said before, these are not requests. These are instructions. Do I make myself clear?"

Tim Crenshaw felt sick. "But I'm trying to tell you, sir. I can't guarantee some of the things you're asking me to do."

The South Korean lent closer to the American. "Mr Crenshaw. You will find ways. I am confident you will succeed. If you don't, I am not sure your life will be worth living. You thought your secret life was secret but I can assure you, it isn't. Not to me. There is not much about your life I do not know in detail."

Standing here on the edge of the Danjiangkou Reserviour, Taeyoung could visualise even now the colour draining from the face of Tim Crenshaw. It was, some might say, a defining moment in their relationship. Crenshaw's options were simple. He could agree to do what Taeyoung was asking or he could refuse but then watch as his life exploded and collapsed, his secret sexual activities revealed to everyone. He eventually agreed with the South Korean. And the South Korean agreed with him. Yes, it was blatant blackmail. But there were no options. Tim Crenshaw would do what Sum Taeyoung asked.

Something else niggling away at Taeyoung was the European Secret Service. He was dismayed to learn from his own security team, that the environmentalist Gene Bond was working with the ESS again. That Bond had not died during their previous encounter was a failure that continued to fester. Now the car bomb in London which was meant to kill him to end the matter, had also failed. It would have been a bonus to take out other members of the ESS at the same time. It was disappointing and annoying that Bond still lived. But, he thought, kicking a stone into the water in frustration, another day, maybe. Such things should not divert him from his main objectives. At the moment, Taeyoung was too preoccupied with other demands.

Wherever he looked from his position at the water's edge, some development, some building, some construction was happening. The whole area was in a process of massive transformation. That was evident in the town itself. There were a number of new hotels all filled with construction workers, but only one bar was currently open for business. It meant a lot of thirsty men remained thirsty each day and very frustrated. Driving around Danjiangkou looking for a suitable launch location, he was struck by the vast numbers of new electric cable carrying super pylons and huge sub-stations. They were everywhere. It was like a metallic maze. This south/north water project was of mind blowing proportions. It was a vivid reminder to him that the consequences of what he planned would not only impact on water provision. It would greatly damage the power supply to an unimaginable number of people. How many? It was a question that stuck in his mind. He had never sat down and worked it out. He just knew it would be a colossal number.

Driving around Danjiangkou was fascinating. Not long ago, it was the sleepy centre of a vast agricultural community. Now the town bustled and carried the official title of the 'fount head' of the great water movement scheme. Talking as best he could to people he encountered as he travelled around, many told him they used to work on the farms. Now they were classified as 'immigrants' and their income was dependent on government handouts. He sensed they were not necessarily satisfied with the new arrangements and once proud farm workers were feeling degraded. In Gangkou, he found part of it to be deserted like a ghost town. Modern apartment dwellings stood empty. Traffic free walkways were without people. Gangkou was waiting for the next arrival of forcibly relocated people. From the Hubei and Henan provinces, it was thought some 345,000 villagers had been moved out of the way to make room for the expanded reservoir.

Taeyoung took the opportunity to drive to the nearby Mount Wudangshan, somewhere he had heard of but never before visited. He had a particular interest in Mount Wudangshan, more so than the rest of the mountainous and spectacularly picturesque countryside in which it is located. A tourist leaflet told him the area has 72 peaks, 36 cliffs, 24 gullies, 3 lakes, 9 springs and 10 ponds! But for someone almost addicted to the herbal teas of the Flying Bird Tea Room in his home city of Seoul, what really took him to Mount Wudangshan was its reputation as being a 'natural drug store'. It is said some 600 different Chinese herbs grow on the mountain. Coupled with an opportunity to see the numerous Taoist temples of the area dating back to the reign of Emperor Zhenguan in the Tang Dynasty, it was time out from his work but worth it.

With a view stretching over the nearby valley, Sum Taeyoung sat on the balcony of a tea room and supped the local offering. It was good but, he thought, not a match on the double harmony tea back home. To satisfy the lingering question and as an academic exercise, he did a rough calculation as to how many people would be impacted by his March 22nd Acionna 1:2:3 projects.

Google told him the population of Vegas is around the 600,000 mark although nearly 40,000,000 people visit it every year. That equates to 110,000 a day. The population of towns around the area average about 50,000. He took one quarter of the visitor figure for his equation, thought, maybe, four towns of 50,000 might be involved. That gave him a total well over 10 million. The population of Beijing is just a little under 20,000,000. So if you took a conservative third off but added a similar figure for other Chinese cities that would feel the effect, it moved the total figure back up towards 30 million.

For the Iberian Peninsula, he guessed some headline figures. The Algarve population is about 450,000 but it goes up by over a million during the tourist period. Taeyoung was aware that not everyone there would feel the impact. So he halved that figure but added in 50,000 for other towns in Spain and Portugal that would be affected. His final 'guestimate' for the Iberian Peninsula was another million.

Roughly, very roughly, Sum Taeyoung estimated well over thirty million people would feel the impact of his actions on March 22nd. It was a staggering figure, guesswork though it was. He sat and stared at the number. Against his ambition of creating as much chaos as possible, it was hard to think of anything that could possibly exceed Acionna 1:2:3.

"But," he thought to himself, "If this doesn't cause chaos and shake people's opinions and beliefs, I don't know what will."

Chapter 25

Gene Bond, Georgi, Nagriza, Jane, Olivia, and Leonie together with the newly recruited replacement Peter, met together for a post-Christmas relaunch of the project. Not that work had stopped over the festive period. In particular, the surveillance of Taeyoung had continued. Georgi summarised what they knew.

"We know Taeyoung is going to do something on International Water Day. That's March 22nd. So, to spell out the obvious, it's a safe bet it has something to do with water. We've found the link to Acionna, the Goddess of water. We know Taeyoung has got ties into the international water company, EscaEau. We don't know why. We know he's involved with the Parisian group of young rebels called Paris Guerriers Urbains who also link to Acionna. But we don't know why. We know Taeyoung has taken the initial letters to code his March 22nd plot – Acionna 1, 2 and 3. We know these relate to action he's planning in America, China and the Iberian Peninsula. He's got links into Las Vegas. Vegas has acute water problems at the moment. Gene thinks the Hoover Dam might be his target. The latest news we've got is of a young member of the PGU Paris group being pulled out of a reservoir in Spain just before Christmas. He nearly drowned. We don't know why he was there but he was with a young French girl from the same group. They were climbing on the dam when he slid off. So, we have a second dam. Gene, you've been thinking dams for a while. Maybe you're right."

"Seems so," Bond responded. "But how? What's he hoping to do?"

"We also know Taeyoung has been pretty active all over the place. It's difficult to split out his genuine work from his unlawful stuff but we do know he's been in Vegas lately. He's so elusive. It takes up to 20 people to efficiently track one person under good circumstances. Taeyoung makes it almost impossible. He's all over the place. And there's no way 20 people could track him. We do our best. There's some link to the New Church of Acionna. You've got something on that Gene?"

Gene Bond reported the meeting with Garry Austin.

"Garry's been invited to speak at a convention on water being organised by the founder of the New Church of Acionna. It's on March 22nd – International Water Day. We don't know if that's got any link to Taeyoung."

"How much do we know about the convention?" asked Georgi.

"Only what Garry Austin told me," Bond replied. "The theme is about the critical value of water."

"Do we know who's speaking?" asked Georgi.

"No," Bond told him.

"Might be interesting to find out," said Georgi and Bond agreed to investigate further.

"Taeyoung's been into China several times lately, mostly to Beijing," continued Georgi. "We don't know why. And though we know – or we think we know – he's got a target in China for March 22nd. But we don't know where that is."

"I could guess," said Bond.

"OK," Georgi replied. "Give us something to at least think about."

"Sum Taeyoung doesn't do anything by half measures," said Bond thoughtfully. "So, trying to put myself in his shoes, if I was looking for a dam to target in China what would I look for? Well, I guess I'd look for whatever would cause the most impact. And at the moment there's one that stands out like a glowing beacon. It's the Danjiangkou dam. It's one of the biggest construction projects the world's ever seen with 345,000 people being relocated to expand the reservoir behind the enlarged dam."

"So, if you're right, what's he going to do to these dams?"

"Blow 'em up, I guess", said Bond. "He'd certainly make a big impact if he did that!"

"So, how'd he go about doing that?" challenged Georgi to the whole of the team.

Heads dipped. There was no answer.

"Are we talking 9.11 here?" Georgi pressed for some responses. "Flying aircraft into dams?"

Peter, in his mid-twenties and from Frankfurt, the new boy of the team, tried to help. "I doubt it. Since 9.11 if ATC spots a rogue aircraft on their screens, they'd soon have it checked out – and downed if need be I guess."

189

Olivia joined in with some recent news. "In the past couple of days, we've been tracking emails between some PGU youngsters in Paris. They're being a bit cagey. I guess they've been told to be very discreet about what they put into emails but they seem to be working on some sort of publicity material to do with March 22nd."

"Publicity material?" Georgi queried.

"Well, I think so. It seems to be a sort of "what if" questionnaire. Or maybe a "do you know" sort of document. There's three versions – seemingly for Acionna 1: 2: and 3. One in English. One in Spanish. One in Chinese. It asks how we can take for granted a resource so important to us that if we did not have it we would die. The American version says something about had the dam been breached today, the City of Las Vegas would die and a million people would be without water."

"Did you say the leaflet says 'had the dam been breached?" asked Peter.

"That's right," said Olivia.

"Those words seem to suggest they're not going to blow the dams up after all," Peter suggested. "That answers your challenge, Georgi. You asked how they will do that. Well, maybe they're not going to. Maybe what they plan is to demonstrate they could. That would show how much people depend on these dams. It would make people think. Make people re-evaluate water."

"I agree," said Olivia. "It sounds like the sort of stunt to pull on International Water Day. The sort of thing Greenpeace might do."

"What do you think Gene?" asked Nagriza. She had hardly said a word to him since they all assembled at Wapping. It was the first time he had seen her since before Christmas. She looked wonderful but strangely drawn. Somewhat weary, thought Bond. Perhaps she had just flown back into London. Just travel fatigue maybe? Her absence from his life had made him yearn for her even more and he felt let down and deflated when she barely said hello to him when the team met.

"I'm not convinced," he replied. "If Sum Taeyoung intends to blow these dams up, I've no idea how he'd do that. So, maybe Olivia and Peter are right. Maybe the idea is just to demonstrate a capability and to headline the consequences. I admit, it would make good media stuff. But I'm not convinced. This is Sum Taeyoung we're dealing with and we know he's a bit of a madman with an ambition to create as much chaos as he can."

"I agree," said Georgi. "But at the moment we simply don't know. I don't think we've got enough yet to be able to warn security people in America, China and Spain. If they asked us for substantive evidence, we've not got a lot to show them."

"There's also something going on between Taeyoung and the New Church of Acionna," Olivia told the meeting.

"We know Taeyoung's met Crenshaw," said Georgi. "And we know Crenshaw is the main man at the church."

"No," Olivia responded. "We think Taeyoung's in direct contact with Angel Martin, the gospel singer who launched the church."

"Really! What's that about?" mused Georgi. "I'd assumed anything to do with the church, he'd have spoken to Crenshaw about."

"We don't know yet," Olivia reported.

"I wonder if it's got anything to do with the convention?" Bond suggested.

"You could do some fishing when you talk to them about the programme," Georgi suggested.

"I wonder if Taeyoung's interested because the event's on International Water Day," Bond mused.

"See what you can find out," Georgi said. "And what about EscoEau? Any more on what they're up to?"

"No," reported Olivia. "All gone quiet on that front."

After a meeting summary from Georgi and confirmation of who was to take responsibility for which forward actions, the meeting broke up. Bond made sure he did not lose the opportunity to talk to Nagriza.

"How was Christmas in Uzbekistan?" he asked. "How's the Aral Sea? How's your family?"

The rest of the group had dispersed leaving Bond and Nagriza alone.

"It was a difficult trip," she replied. She was clearly upset. "My father died while I was out there. The day before Christmas," she told him. "I knew he was ill but I didn't know it was that serious. It was as if he'd waited for me to get there before he died."

"I don't know what to say," Bond replied. "How awful. I'm so sorry."

"I could have done with you there Gene. A shoulder to cry on. Your strength. I felt very alone. It was horrible."

Nagriza wiped a tear away. Every instinct told Bond to hold her, to comfort her. But something held him back.

"It's difficult, Gene. I'm getting used to him having gone. But it takes a while to adjust. I need some space – and time. I need to make some adjustments to my thinking. Life goes on for the rest of us."

And that is as far as he got. It left an awkward gap remaining between them.

Chapter 26

"The Brits could have saved themselves a whole lot of young lives if they'd got themselves a few Kamikaze pilots," Basil Jackson asserted. "It was modern day Kamikazes who did for the twin towers on 9.11. More than 50 RAF folk were killed in the Dam Buster operation in '43. Just one Kamikaze pilot in the right sort of aircraft would have done the job. Three dams. Three pilots. At the back end of WW2, the Japanese started flying aircraft into our Pacific fleet. Their pilots believed it was a brave and honourable thing to do for their Emperor. They considered themselves to be samurai warriors. I thought the concept of Kamikaze ended when WW2 was over. But now we've the modern day version – suicide bombers – blowing themselves and other folk up all over the world on a daily basis – or flying aircraft into high rise towers. So you should be getting yourself a few Kamikaze pilots."

Basil Jackson was talking to Sum Taeyoung when the global water project was just a set of embryonic ideas in the South Korean's head. A potential game-stopper was the payload carrying capability of the chosen technology, the Chinese drone. The problem – and the solution – related to how much weight the drone could carry against the amount of explosion needed to achieve a result. Contrary to the smoke screen story Taeyoung was spreading around, he had every intention of blowing the dams up and not just scattering leaflets to say they could. Propaganda was not his way of doing things. Taeyoung wanted to create real chaos – real catastrophic mayhem.

His experts told him the South Korean built, modified Chinese drone could only handle around 1,000 pounds of payload. However, they knew Western military drones could carry three times that amount. So they were looking closely at drones like the Predator B-003 used by the RAF to see how it was able to carry so much more. Was it just a question of engine power or were there some tricks that could be adopted?

Parallel to looking at the performance of the drone, Taeyoung's team was also exploring optional explosive materials. Modern devices were many, many times more powerful than those available during WW2. Taeyoung took it upon himself to talk to Jackson, an ex US army explosives expert he had encountered several times in the past and now knew him to be a global trader in weaponry of one kind or another. Sometimes he supplied to Sum. On other occasions he was a competitor. Each knew the other did business in the murky markets of illicit armament trading and that created a bond of trust between them. It was a strange basis for trust but it did exist.

"And of course," Jackson had continued, "I don't know what your targets are but you'll hit a shit load of trouble. Even getting your aircraft close to the target will be difficult. Since 9.11, it's hard to fly an unregistered flight. There's a lot of twitchy folk around and if you try, it's likely you'd be blasted from the skies, even if you hijack a passenger aircraft. And if you get close to your target, if it's a dam, I don't know if they'd have defences like the Dam Busters encountered. Their problem was getting their bomb past torpedo defences. The Germans had booms across the reservoirs carrying anti torpedo netting to protect the vulnerable part of the dam from airborne torpedo attack. So the Brits invented a way of bouncing a four tonne bomb across the water and over the top of the defences! Crazy, man! When a bomb hit a dam, it dropped and was triggered by a depth switch."

"What sort of explosive did they use? Taeyoung asked.

"Torpex," replied Jackson. "It's a British invention but the American navy was also using it by '43."

"It's no longer around, is it?" queried Taeyoung.

"No," answered the American. "Torpex was too sensitive. It was replaced by HBX and HBX-1."

"And what do you think is the most dynamic explosive today?" asked Taeyoung.

"As far as I know, it's CL-20. I don't know much about it. A lot of military currently use HMX but I'm told this CL-20 is a lot more powerful. It detonates faster and has a higher density. It's four times more potent than the widely used RDX. And its penetration characteristics are the best we've seen to date. There's a lot of folk around the world right now exploring its potential applications."

The reference to the explosive's penetrative abilities together with Jackson's other recommendations was enough for Taeyoung. The next challenge was where to get CL-20 from? He found it originated in California but in a highly unstable form. Chemistry development by the University of Michigan had apparently improved its operational viability and now organisations around the world were evolving it into a usable fighting product. It was Taeyoung's Indian connections who first enabled him to enter the supply chain.

So now he had an explosive material. Long ago, he discarded the idea of flying aircraft into his targets having come to the same conclusions Jackson warned him about. Ever since 9.11, off-course aircraft attracted the attention of the military. In addition, since the disappearance of Malaysian flight MH370, the Boeing 777 that went missing between Kuala Lumpur and Beijing, commercial flights were now monitored and tracked far more intensely than previously.

Which is why he eventually turned to drones. But that left two big questions. How much CL-20 would be needed to do the job? And would his modified Chinese propeller driven drone be capable of carrying the payload? These were the questions the specialist company in Pyeongtaek, south of Seoul, was seeking answers to.

Through his legitimate business activities, Taeyoung moved sufficient volume of goods in and out of China – and had enough corrupt border officials in his pocket – to enable him to transport quantities of the explosive into China on a drip feed basis over a period of time. With one of his supply sources being in America, no such importation problems existed there and he was able to tap into the US/Indian trade route to extract what he needed for his Iberian Peninsula project. But questions around the capability of the drone critically remained unanswered and were now a top priority.

Computer simulations in Pyeongtaek continued to look favourable. A drone had been built based on an early Chinese WJ-600 model but highly modified to accommodate Taeyoung's needs including its substantial payload. On a bitterly cold South Korean winter day, successful trial flights were conducted across a wide strip of frozen water located some 10 kilometres south east of the city. These verified the flying capabilities and range of the drone when carrying the payload demands Taeyoung called for. However, Taeyoung was conscious he had not brought together the drone and the CL-20 but from all the tests and simulations he had seen, Jackson was right about the extraordinarily penetrating powers of the new explosive. He was convinced it would work but remained nervous because a full, real life test run of the drone and the explosive could not happen. Clearly, it would be good to have such a reassurance but the logistics of finding somewhere secure enough to undertake such trials was fraught with difficulties and eventually abandoned.

Taeyoung was happy enough with what had been achieved and, by mid-January, signed off an order for the drones to be built that would be used on March 22nd. Production would fall short of assembly as the drones would be sent off in component parts to be assembled near to where they would be used. Time was running out and things were getting costly. Bernhard Gedeck's EscaEau money was really starting to pay dividends.

Chapter 27

Bond phoned the New Church of Acionna in Las Vegas as agreed with Georgi. Web based research on the church and its founder armed him with enough for him to feel confident in making the call to enquire about the convention being planned for March 22nd. Not that there seemed to be much information available yet about the event even though the convention was now only eight weeks away. He was taken aback when he found out who had answered his call.

"This is the New Church of Acionna. How can I help you?" The very American female voice was strong and authoritative and, somehow, not what Bond was expecting. It was far from being that of an average telephonist.

"May I ask who I'm speaking to?" said Bond.

"Well you surely can." The response simply bubbled with enthusiasm. "I'm Angel Martin. I'm founder of this church of God. And to whom am I speaking?"

"Gene Bond." he replied. "Look, I'm sorry if I sound a bit flustered but I didn't expect a call to the church to be answered by its founder."

"Hey, I'm a hands-on leader," Angel Martin countered. It occurred to Bond that she was almost singing when she spoke. She had great presence and authority, no inhibitions and pervading warmth of character. "So, who are you?"

"I am an Englishman." Bond told her.

"You don't say!" the church leader interrupted sarcastically. "It's not every day I get a call from an English gentleman. I just love your accent! Are you really calling from England?"

It was the first time, thought Bond, he had heard the word England spoken as if it had three syllables.

"Yes," he confirmed. "I'm what might be called a freelance environmentalist. Some call me an environmental entrepreneur. I'm a friend of Garry Austin who's joint Chairman of the European Environment Committee. He told me about the convention you're staging on March 22nd and at which he's speaking. Because of that I was interested to know more."

"It's just fine to talk to you, Mr Bond." The gospel singing church leader was obviously still exuberant that someone from England should call her. "Our event is still being developed. It's the first we've staged. It will celebrate God, water, and the first year of my New Church of Acionna. You know about my church, Mr Bond?"

"I've looked it up on the web," he told her. "And I'm still a bit flustered that you answered my call. Apart from anything else, I've no idea how to refer to you. Do I call you 'My Revered' – or what? I can't think of anything else!"

"Just call me Angel, Mr Bond. Sorry if that sounds like a cliché but that's who I am. It's not necessarily what I am!"

Bond was getting to like her more by the second. A cheeky sense of humour could be added to her other attributes.

"I'm proud of what we've achieved in just one year. And our convention will celebrate that. It will also tell the world how irresponsible we all are about water and how we abuse it – the one natural resource without which we cannot survive. Jesus said in John 3:5 – '*Truly, truly, I say unto you, unless one is born of water and the Spirit, he cannot enter the kingdom of God.*' It is the pivotal concern of our church movement."

Angel Martin never missed an opportunity to recite the biblical quote of her church. "The programme continues to build, Mr Bond. My Senior Administrator, Tim Crenshaw, is responsible for that. We've already got Eleanor Revelle from the League of Woman Voters in Washington. She's expressing concerns about how many parts of the United States are already facing serious water shortages and even drought."

"Garry Austin will talk about how Europe is responding to climate change. Our Secretary of State, John Pine, will tell us why he believes climate change is the most important issue facing mankind. We're waiting to hear from the United Nations who they'll send. March 22nd is after all their day – International Water Day. But tell me, Mr Bond, what's your interest in water?"

"Grief, Angel!" replied Bond, taken aback by a question to which he could offer no easy and quick response. He tried to assemble some words in his mind before saying anything but the mass of high speed thoughts flashing through his head, were difficult to grasp and construct into any sort of cohesive reply.

"That's one hell of a question! I come at it from the direction of sustainable development which is really my specialist subject. My concern is to try and get people to understand that the values of money, the environment, and social well-being are all equal. We should treat them as being equal. But we don't. In our frantic modern world, we're driven by money values first, foremost and very often to the exclusion of all other considerations. So where we are right now is living on a planet which is accommodating the biggest human population there's ever been and that's growing at a startling rate. And we've got widespread changing demographics."

"We've poor nations emerging into the consumer society. So every year we've got tens of thousands more people wanting 'stuff' that's made in processes that consume resources. We've millions of people leaving the countryside to live in cities and we've enormous urban slums growing at an alarming rate."

"Within all of this, the burden on natural resources is like a pressure vessel that's about to blow. Many resources are already at a critical stage – well into the 'about to blow up' zone on the pressure vessel. The danger bells are sounding. Across the planet, water – the most precious of the natural resources because without it we cannot survive – is on the threshold of a calamitous situation."

"Goodness, Mr Bond. You're more of an evangelist than me!" Angel Martin was laughing as she spoke. "My – what a story you tell!"

"It's what I've been preaching for 20 years," Bond told her. "But my success is in marked contrast to yours. Mine is pitiful. Yours is amazing! Just look at how many people are now involved with what you're doing. And you've only been going for less than a year!"

"Ah, but I've got God on my side! Have you got God on your side, Mr Bond?"

It was blatantly obvious that the American gospel singing church leader was now brazenly teasing the English environmentalist. She did not wait for a reply.

"I want to keep talking about you, Mr Bond. Not about my church. What you just said is so interesting. It puts water – and the environmental challenges we face – into a much bigger context. I know Tim Crenshaw is keen to link the issue of bad water management to matters to do with social deprivation. It seems to me you paint the big picture which sets our context."

Bond was delighted with the response. He always found it difficult not to get carried away with his enthusiasm for the subject. "Like I said, Angel, the environment is just one thing to be worried about. Economics and social well-being are the others. But it's imperative they should be equally considered. Too often the three values are managed in isolated silos. They shouldn't be. We should not be concerned about one and forget the other two. Too often in our modern world where money dominates everything, we concern ourselves only with achieving economic objectives. Such a narrow, introverted attitude often causes enormous consequential environmental and social damage. It's just plain ridiculous"

"There you are again, Mr Bond. The evangelist! You should speak at our convention." The so appealing voice of Angel Martin made him feel she was hugging him. But she had dropped a bombshell of an idea! It exploded in Bond's ear. This had been nowhere in his thinking. And how would Georgi respond?

"My goodness," he replied. "That's something I didn't expect."

"Hey Bond." He noticed she had dropped the Mr title. Her voice had seemingly gone up an octave. She was clearly very excited by the idea she had had. "What you say. The way you say it. You've got the big story. I'll pay for you to come over and tell it. Travel, accommodation and food. How can you refuse? You said you were impressed by what we're doing. Come and be part of it!"

"I don't know what to say," Bond was truly surprised by her suggestions.

"Just say yes," the American voice came back to him.

"I need to consider it," he told her. "It's very generous. I'd love to. But I have people here I need to talk to first."

"You talk to them. Then say yes," challenged the church leader. "Let Tim Crenshaw know. I'll let him know. I'll email him and copy you. It will be fantastic if you can be with us. I know Tim is anxious to make this a really special event. He's planning all sorts of things including some video links to other parts of the world. But I would LOVE you to be with us."

Bond locked in on something she had said.

"You're planning video links to other parts of the world? Where? I'm very interested."

"Hey, that's detail Bond. I don't do detail. That's why I've got Tim Crenshaw. But I think it involves China. And I think there's somewhere in Europe. It's all very exciting. When you phone him to tell him you can be with us, you can ask him. I'll tell him to brief you on what he's up to.

Mr Bond, I look forward to hearing you've said yes and to welcoming you to the New Church of Acionna in Las Vegas."

And with that, the phone clicked dead. Bond looked at it for some time almost incredulously. Tim Crenshaw had been talking to Taeyoung. Georgi's people thought Taeyoung had been talking to Angel Martin. Taeyoung was planning something in America, China and Europe on March 22nd. Could it be that what Angel Martin – founder of the Church of Acionna no less – had been talking about – the video sequence in her convention was also Taeyoung's Acionna 1:2:3? The thought was mind blowing!

Bond immediately phoned Georgi.

"Shit! That's amazing," Georgi responded to the news of Angel Martin's invitation and Bond's speculation about linkage between the convention video activity and Taeyoung's Acionna 1:2:3. "You've moaned about getting involved with us again. This is yet another example of how our two worlds cross over and intermingle. There's no escape – double O!"

It was the first time in two years Georgi had joked about Bond's name. He knew Gene Bond was very sensitive about it and in the past, had teased him regularly and mercilessly. With the freezing of the relationship after their first escapade with Taeyoung, Georgi had not had the courage to continue the tease. But their friendship had recovered in recent months.

"If you're right about the link," Georgi continued, "this takes you into the lion's den on March 22nd. We need to find out more about what Crenshaw is planning. If he's establishing a video link to China, you may well be right and the European one will be to the Iberian Peninsula. So there'd be a third link to something in the States, unless that's the convention itself. Maybe that's where Las Vegas comes into Acionna 1:2:3? Maybe it's not the Hoover Dam after all?"

"But why would he need a video link from those places to the convention? And the logistics behind it are stupefying! I'll get the team working on it. Meantime, you talk to Crenshaw and see what you can dig out of him."

Chapter 28

Bernhard Gedeck's plans were progressing well but were about to stumble into something that threatened not only to destroy what he was plotting with Sum Taeyoung, but also discredit the company and be the death of his career.

The South Korean had sent him his mathematical scribblings from his deliberations on Mount Wudangshan. They made remarkable reading. The figures were truly colossal. In particular, the sheer scale of the consequences of what Taeyoung planned in China produced numbers difficult to grasp. At the top end of his predictions, they were in tens of millions. With the best commercial planning in the world, there was no way EscaEau could meet the sorts of demands for water Taeyoung was forecasting. But Gedeck was pragmatic. If he could meet just a small percentage of the opportunity, the sales figures would be extraordinary.

The German had been busy ever since setting up his special task force. The potential Chinese operation was so enormous, he launched a new EscaEau company in China. It took much time and effort and during the set up process, Gedeck suggested to Taeyoung the new venture should be a joint one with SDBI. That got nowhere. It seemed the South Korean was reluctant to formalise any relationships so eventually Gedeck went it alone. The move raised a few eyebrows amongst Esca shareholders but there were no consequences Gedeck considered too worrying. Requiring more serious consideration was not only the logistics of getting drinking water to huge areas of China where vast numbers of people would be without it, but from where to source it. The EscaEau Task Force was exploring and recording all conceivable water supply, and transportation options and ideas were being submitted to Gedeck on a regular basis.

Their research showed that 97% of the world's supply of water is salty, 2% locked in snow and ice, and just 1% available for crop growing, industrial use and for human consumption. However, that 1% represents some 6.5 million trillion gallons! To Gedeck it was simply a matter of getting hold of the amounts he needed and moving them to where they were wanted.

Gedeck's EscaEau Task Force research identified an increasing number of communities around the world already hitting water provision problems. As a consequence, the bulk movement of water was a fast growing business and had become a far more frequent occurrence. Countries such as Argentina, Chile, Mexico, Austria, the Bahamas, Cyprus and Turkey now all exported water, mostly in bottles, with Turkey increasingly supplying Middle Eastern and Mediterranean countries where water scarcity was becoming especially difficult. Israel was one such country with plans evolving for a fleet of super tankers to move 50 million cubic meters of water annually from Turkey to Israel, the water originating from the Manavgat River. Turkey's role as a custodian and supplier of water would have been particularly poignant to Fiacre, as Turkey had been instrumental in brokering the treaty that ended the world's first known water war, the agreement recorded on the tablet of stone the young Parisian attacked in the Louvre.

Having discovered the Turkish water provision business, EscaEau immediately put in a takeover bid which was considered a hostile action by the target company. As part of its defence mechanisms, the Turkish company hit the media with campaign stories showing why the French company's aggressive attention was unwelcome. It was media exposure Gedeck did not need. Although the corporate purchase activity was being undertaken as discreetly as possible, Geldeck found himself having to defend his corporate actions to some anxious and quizzical shareholders and to some NGOs which accused him of profiteering and trying to monopolise the global water industry. Still needing to conceal his real reasons for his actions, all he could do was try and demonstrate the growth of the world's water provision industry and claim his moves were designed to ensure EscaEau remained at the top. And, as he had told his executives when he first revealed his legitimate plans for the company to be the world's number one provider of water, they had the technology and experience to help those who needed help. The Middle East needed help. Therefore it was totally right and proper for EscaEau to try and become involved.

As well as super tankers for the high seas, the EscaEau Task Force considered a variety of different techniques for the bulk transportation of water. Some were already being used and some were under development in various parts of the world. They found one methodology gaining in credence used the standard metal containers commonly stacked on cargo ships. The technique deployed the same practices already used in the movement of 'premium liquids' such as wine and olive oil and experts considered it only a natural progression to transport water in bulk in a similar way.

In trials in New Zealand, the metal containers were lined with a 'bladder' then filled with water. They were known as 'flexitanks'. Large cargo ships have the capacity to carry some 12,500 containers. With each tank capable of storing nearly 6,500 gallons of water, over 80 million gallons of water could potentially be transported in one ship movement. The Task Force was beginning to see this as a solution both in America and on the Iberian Peninsula, with containers being shipped into a point nearest the water shortage areas where the flexitank containers could be transferred to trucks then road hauled the rest of the way. However, that did not solve the China problem and thoughts were turning towards using the same flexitank solution but within military sized cargo aircraft.

In Las Vegas, the water supply situation was continuing to deteriorate. In early February, Tim Crenshaw's team launched the 'CITY OF LAS VEGAS DROUGHT CONTINGENCY AND EMERGENCY RESPONSE PLAN.' The focus remained on conservation although work continued on the ambitious scheme to extract water from aquifers in Nevada and pipe it to the city. But mainly the Plan was *'To establish actions necessary to reduce water consumption during times of emergency water shortage for the City of Las Vegas.'*

Finding a solution was attracting increasing attention. Now the not-for-profit AAAS (the American Association for the Advancement of Science) was testing the City's plan by saying conservation alone was not the answer. They said that even if the City hit its target and curbed the use of water by 20%, there would be a serious shortfall of supply against demand by 2035. Concerned as they were about the reducing water levels in Lake Mead and the future of the Colorado River that fills it, the AAAS believed Las Vegas would not be able to meet future demands if aligned to current growth trends and supply options.

The AAAS said: "We need either more aggressive conservation coupled with slower population growth, or an additional water supply." They pointed out that the population of the Las Vegas Valley had nearly tripled in two decades. Although this growth slowed through the period of recession, Las Vegas, they said, and the surrounding area, was not alone in its thirst. Of the seven states drawing water from the Colorado River, they identified five – including Nevada – as being amongst the fastest growing states in the country. And growth equates to the need for more water.

The instant Angel Martin become aware of the AAAS position on the Vegas water crisis, she made contact and invited them to join the convention on March 22nd. They would, she told them, provide a scientific dimension to the event. It was only after they had agreed that she told Tim Crenshaw what she had done. It produced a rare example of Crenshaw losing his temper with her as he realised she had recruited into the event an organisation that was criticising his City department's approach to the water crisis. The weave of competing pressures in his life took yet another unfortunate step in the wrong direction.

But it was other events in Las Vegas that concerned Gedeck. Though the police department's interest in the death of the young freelance reporter, Ryan Spears, had virtually ground to a halt, a group of his former colleagues maintained a search for the truth about his death. They were far from convinced Ryan had taken his own life. Denied by the police any access to the reporter's note books, computer or phone, progress by his friends was snail paced and their thin file of evidence remained mainly based on anecdotes – until their breakthrough came. The situation changed when one of the team talked the problem through with an IT friend, a computer wizard and a highly active and effective hacker. It was he who enlightened them that though they could not access what the police held, maybe they could via another route – Ryan's cloud based back-up. And through a process of trial and error and an intimate knowledge of his life born from their close friendship with him, ultimately they were able to guess what passwords he used. The group broke into Ryan's computer notes of the story he had been trying to unearth.

They found that following his aborted meeting with the editor of the Las Vegas Journal, Sam Baldwin, Ryan continued to be puzzled as to why the editor became so defensive and ended their meeting as soon as EscaEau and the South Korean were mentioned. It seemed to the young reporter there was a story to be told. Why did Baldwin not want to tell it?

Ryan found the head of the French water specialist company, EscaEau was in town, talking to various officials and most notably to Tim Crenshaw, head of the department of the Las Vegas Office of Emergency Management responsible for water provision. Why? The Southern Nevada Water Authority was responsible for such provision. Why should seemingly extensive conversations be going on with an international company of French origin and why were they so important that the company's group London based CEO should be the one holding those conversations personally and in Vegas?

Deciding on an open attack strategy, Ryan discovered where Bernhard Gedeck was staying during his visit to the city. He phoned him and sent text messages during the day and in the evenings but every time, telephone calls went to voice mail. His messages remained unanswered which was hardly a surprise. After a couple of days of continuing a barrage of calls and text messages but with no response, in his frustration, the young reporter decided to try and intercept the German in his hotel. Ryan established himself in the lobby of the hotel, waiting there for more than half a day and several times having to fend off the interest of the lobby management team. Fortunately, the hotel's manager was a longstanding contact and Ryan used his name to counter the curiosity he was arousing.

It was late afternoon when Gedeck returned from his latest round of meetings in the city. Ryan spotted him as soon as he entered the hotel and as fast as he could, approached him as he walked toward the elevators.

"Mr Gedeck. I'm a journalist working on a news story about the Vegas water shortage. Can you tell me what the interests of EscaEau are in Vegas?"

The question was ignored. Gedeck snubbed Ryan completely, looked straight ahead and continued to walk towards the elevators.

"Vegas water supply is on a long term contract with Southern Nevada Water Authority. Why should you be talking to the city?"

Still no response and they were now close to the elevator.

"I know you've had several meetings with the Office of Emergency Management. If the SNWA has a long term contract, why talk to the OEM?"

Gedeck was now pushing the button to summon the elevator.

"Why aren't you answering me, Mr Gedeck? The water crisis is a major public issue. The people of Las Vegas would be interested to know what EscaEau is doing in town."

The elevator arrived. The doors opened. Gedeck moved forward but blocked the entrance until the doors started to close, only then moving forward, thwarting Ryan's efforts to enter.

Staring at the elevator as the door closed before him, Ryan threw one last question at the German before contact was lost.

"And what's your connection to SDBI? And what's that got to do with Vegas?"

The door clunked to and the elevator buzzed on its way. Ryan cursed and turned away. All that time and effort for nothing. Now what?

As the elevator sped upwards, Bernhard Gedeck took stock of what had just happened. The approach by the reporter had taken him aback but he felt he had handled it properly. What bugged him was the reference to SDBI. What did the reporter know about that? And how?

Once in his room, Gedeck phoned Crenshaw. Crenshaw was obviously shocked to hear of the encounter with Ryan Spears although on reflection, it was perhaps not surprising. Sam Baldwin described Ryan Spears as a keen and effective young reporter. And water shortage was a big story in town. If Spears had found the head of an international water company talking to city officials, it was unquestionably a story any reporter would try and write. Telling Gedeck he would phone him back, Crenshaw phoned Baldwin and told him what had happened.

"Shit," responded the Journal's editor. "I tried to kill the story off with Spears. I obviously failed."

"What do we do?" asked Crenshaw. He sensed this development could prove disastrous.

"I don't know. Spears is good. Gedeck cold shouldering him like that will only make him grittier than ever to find out what's going on. I guess there's two major problems. There's the issue of Gedeck talking to you about EscaEau and the Vegas water crisis. To ask why is a genuine question. Any reporter would. The question you have to ask yourself is how damaging it would be for your official conversations to become public knowledge? Then there's the link to Sum Taeyoung. If Spears is getting anywhere close to knowing what Taeyoung is plotting, that's lethal. For you. For me. For Gedeck. For Taeyoung. I'd hate to think what the South Korean would do."

The conversation with the newspaper man only served to escalate Crenshaw's fears to near panic. Now feeling trapped into an enormous horror story that was out of control, Crenshaw phoned Gedeck back.

"What we don't know is how much Spears knows. It's the reference to SDBI that's the major worry. I tell you, if Spears knows of the linkages between you, me, Taeyoung and Baldwin, that's one hell of a story. That's one hell of a load of shit. It's a fucking disaster."

"What do you plan to do about it?" asked Gedeck.

"I don't know," Crenshaw told him and it was obvious from the voice down the phone line that the civil servant was close to cracking up. "I simply don't know."

Reflecting back, Gedeck wondered if he had taken the right choice of action. Maybe he should have left it to Crenshaw or Baldwin to sort. But he did not know the editor at all and Crenshaw sounded like a man in pieces.

Neither could be trusted. If something had to be done, Gedeck had to organise it himself, which is what he did. It is why Ryan Spears died.

Now he had received a text message from a group calling themselves 'The Friends of Ryan Spears.' They were requesting an interview – anywhere, any time. Knowing that a pack of friends of Spears were fishing around the case, he was fearful Taeyoung's Acionna Projects might be blown asunder. If that exploded, it would inevitably reveal his own role in it, his expectations, his hopes for rich rewards for EscaEau and for himself. He wondered if he should tell the South Korean what had happened, and why.

Chapter 29

Like two ships blindly converging on each other in a pea soup fog, Bond and Taeyoung unknowingly moved towards each other courtesy of Angel Martin's convention, now just four weeks away. And as Georgi Patarava said to Bond, like it or not, there was no escaping the crossover and inter-relationship of Bond's interests as an environmental entrepreneur and those of Patarava's security business.

"As pressures grow on the world's resources, the more valuable they'll become. And the more valuable they become, so the dark forces of evil will increasingly become involved," he had said to Bond during their most recent visit to the Russian Bar, unusually with Nagriza with them to break what had up until then been a male taboo between Bond and Georgi. But responding to how down she still was in the aftermath of her father's death, Georgi invited her along, an act enough to scramble Bond's mind. Still depressed in the aftermath of her loss, Nagriza might not have felt particularly alluring, but she was to Bond. She always would be, whatever her mood and disposition. And now here she was, in the Russian bar of all places, drinking what he and Georgi were drinking albeit in lesser volume and in different glasses, ones more appropriate to the lady she clearly was in the eyes of the long haired, stubble faced barman who, like Nagriza, was also of Eastern European origin – but not Russian.

The combination of near black beer served in thick glass borzoi embossed tankards with ice cold vodka chasers in long stemmed silver goblets, was a recipe that stimulated philosophical discussion. It was at times like this that Bond simply glorified in Georgi's company. It had been so since they first met many years ago when Georgi worked in the Soviet Embassy in London before the collapse of the Soviet Union. Business brought them together but they found great satisfaction in each other's company and their shared common interests including politics, the environment, women and drinking. All those years ago, Georgi introduced Bond to Caucasus brandy which, according to the note on the bottle he opened, boasted great attributes. It read "It attracts by its history, its grandeur, hospitality, beauty of women and nature, braveness of men, love to feasts, respect of guests, polyphony songs and hot dances." It was, they agreed, a drink in harmony with their own interests.

Sadly, the Russian bar did not stock Caucasus brandy but the substitute of beer and vodka served well enough. And while Georgi's Georgian patriotism caused him to hate virtually everything Russian, he was happy to consume vodka. In any case, he supported the camp that insisted vodka originated in Poland, not Russia. And the Russian Bar was no longer owned by Russians.

After a quick round of drinks they retreated to the dining part of the club. The Russian Bar is divided into three small areas – the bar, the dining area and a dance floor. It was relatively quieter in the dining area and something of a refuge from the deep Southern States rock and roll being played loudly through the club's sound system by the Bohemian looking man behind the bar. A few visitors occupied the dance floor, two couples and two young girls dancing together. None were particularly energetic and the two scantily clad girls, described by the barman as locals and regulars, held themselves close together as they swayed to the rhythms.

218

Georgi seemed to be keen to continue the philosophising. "And the really sad part is the more monetary values are put onto resources, the less the poor can afford them. So the gap between those that have and those that have not will widen. The more money comes into it, the more resources are exploited."

"What do you do about that?" Bond probed his Georgian friend, winding him up a little.

"I don't know. You keep on talking about how we don't proactively approach the challenges we face, like water shortages for instance. You say we should hit the problems before they happen and not wait to respond until after there's been a disaster. In a way, I guess the same can be said of the gap between those enjoying prosperity and those living in great deprivation."

"I don't disagree," Bond responded. "But what do you do about it?"

"I don't know," said Georgi despondently pulling his iPhone from his pocket. He busied himself finding the right file of information.

"I've been logging some facts on this. The latest example defies belief. Almost 1,000 migrants were rescued from a cargo ship found adrift in Greek waters. They were mostly Syrians and Kurds. Incredibly, the people traffickers had abandoned the ship, left it on autopilot, and just pointed it at the Italian coast. Can you believe that?! The Italian coastguards brought it under control and docked it at the port of Gallipoli. You have to ask yourself – what sort of hell hole of a place and a hellish life, were people trying to escape from who would risk everything – including their lives – to try and reach Europe?"

"In the Mediterranean areas, the numbers trying to enter Europe from North Africa are astonishing. One report I've got says 2,000 migrants were rescued by the Italian navy within one 24 hour period and another 700 were on board merchant ships reaching ports in Sicily around the same time. 50,000 migrants arrived in Italy last year. 2,200 landed on Malta. The Italian interior minister reckons the number of migrants waiting in Libya to cross the Mediterranean is between 400,000 and 600,000! Can you believe that? It's a movement of people on a biblical scale."

"The Department of Homeland Security in the States estimates there's some 11.4 million unauthorised immigrants living there. Nearly 60% come from Mexico. That's another example of huge numbers trying to escape poverty."

"Australia has adopted what many think to be the toughest responses to deal with illegal immigrants. They've been receiving up to 3,500 arrivals a month. Now they're turning boats back. But it's a political hot potato there."

"These are crazy figures, Gene. Desperate people trying to escape poverty, starvation, lack of water, war and violations. It's pretty awful."

"And don't forget the plight of women and children in all of this," added Nagriza. "The abuse of women and children is another disgrace to the world's community."

"But what do you do?" Bond responded.

"No. What do you do?" Georgi threw it back at him with an emphasis on the 'you'. "It's you that's always saying we need to take proactive action. So, what would you do?"

"I really don't know," Bond admitted with a sigh. "But then clearly nobody knows the answer. In my formula of hitting the problem before it arises, you could argue that those that have should be making some sort of contribution to ensure that those that have not are in less dire straits. The more you can solve the problem at source, the better. The more you can improve people's lives, the less need they have to go anywhere else – less to escape from."

"I love your theory," said Nagriza. "But how do you do it? Thousands of voluntary organisations do their best. Developed countries donate vast amounts of money. But the problems seem to get worse, not better."

"And when money is thrown at these equations it often gets devoured by corruption," added Georgi. "Corruption is another disease. Then you've also got people who delight in creating chaos – like Sum Taeyoung. I really think we should try and finish him."

"You mean kill him?" said Bond pointedly.

"Yes," Georgi replied, defiantly.

"That's summary execution. You can't make yourself judge, jury and executioner."

"Yes I can," countered Georgi. "And so what? The man's a menace to the global society."

"But where's the justice in that? Even Sum Taeyoung qualifies for a fair trial. You're throwing away the very values we're fighting to protect!" Bond was horrified. "Now you see why I feel so alien in your world. We live to different moral standards."

"I don't think it's about moral standards," Nagriza said, defending Georgi. "It's more about being practical, about taking appropriate actions."

"You can't defend summary execution," argued Bond. "It just puts you on the same level as the people you're fighting."

There was silence between them for some time. They retreated from the argument to concentrate on their food. It was Georgi who first spoke again.

"Talking of Taeyoung. Did you speak to the guy at the church in America about his video elements?"

Bond confirmed he had spoken to Tim Crenshaw. The civil servant and volunteer church administrator told him who else had been signed up to speak at the convention. They had spoken at length about what Bond would talk about, the length of time allocated for him, the overall programme, where the event was being staged and the technical support available to speakers. Bond had pressed him about the video links to other parts of the world.

"How come you know about that?" asked Crenshaw. It sounded as though he was niggled that Bond knew.

"I don't know much," Bond told him. "Only what Angel Martin told me."

"And what was that," quizzed Crenshaw.

"She told me you were planning some video links to other parts of the world. She thought it was to China and to Europe. That's all she said."

"That's all there is to know," Crenshaw retorted.

Bond pressed him for more. "And what are the video links about?"

"We're still working on that detail, Mr Bond. Rest assured, you – like Angel – will know all there is to know as soon as it's all arranged."

Although Bond probed some more, Crenshaw clammed up.

"Do you reckon he's got something to hide? Or is he being coy? Or does he simply not know yet, like he says?" Georgi asked Bond.

"Oh I think he knows alright," Bond responded. "But he's not telling anyone, not even Angel Martin."

In fact, Tim Crenshaw knew full well what the video links to the other parts of the world were. Indeed, he now knew far more about the convention on March 22nd than anyone else, including Angel Martin and Sum Taeyoung. The South Korean was now aware who was speaking at the event and had gone nearly apoplectic when he heard Gene Bond was included in the programme.

"Bond!" the name had blasted from Taeyoung in response to the news from Crenshaw that Angel Martin had invited a well-known English sustainable development expert to speak. "How's that happened?"

"Angel Martin invited him. You know him?" Crenshaw asked somewhat timidly.

"Oh yes," Taeyoung answered. "I know him." The South Korean was dumbfounded by the news. The immediate reaction was one of near horror but before he expressed it in those terms to Crenshaw, a flicker of an idea crossed his mind. Without being too specific, he explored its possibilities with Crenshaw.

Crenshaw was far from happy about it. First Angel and now Taeyoung were generally mucking about with his convention programme – with just four weeks to go. Every time a new name was added or the running order changed, the consequential amounts of work were enormous and mostly fell on Crenshaw. But Taeyoung laid down the law. Unless Crenshaw wanted his life blown asunder by the exposure of his secret sex life, he had no option but to do what he was told.

This was entrepreneurial opportunism being demonstrated by Sum Taeyoung. Originally he had planned to video the three attacks on the dams in China, Spain and Vegas. It would be for later publicity. But a new idea now emerged and he was busy training members of the PGU to help. The news that Gene Bond was going to be at Las Vegas, speaking at the convention, was all too much. The instant feeling of horror and outrage was replaced by a satisfying realisation that the plot had thickened – substantially!

Chapter 30

Their target was the sizeable, single storey, flat roofed, whitewashed industrial unit, similar to many others on this massive industrial park with its neat road layout and its carefully manicured and well-managed grass areas. The sprawling building sat in an area surrounded by high security fencing topped with anti-intruder spikes. Security lighting illuminated the expanse of tarmacked space between the fence and the building, most of its light focussed on the building although the extremities of its beam washed against the fencing.

The black Mercedes van with the logo and text on its side from a well-known industrial security company, cruised slowly into the road running alongside the length of the building, its driver being totally aware that someone, somewhere on the estate would in all probability, be watching him on a security monitor. He was looking for a particular spot. It had been there earlier in the night. He had seen video footage from reconnaissance visits. And there it was; a patch of relative darkness between two trucks parked in a line of vehicles at the side of the road. Such parking was not supposed to happen on the industrial park but, not unusually, designers had underestimated the sheer volume of vehicles and had not made enough allowance for overnight truck parking in the compounds. It became the custom for vehicles arriving at night to park on the roads, waiting for the industrial units to open in the morning.

The Mercedes slowed nearly to a stop as it entered the area of darkness, two men in camouflage combat kit and wearing night vision goggles dropping out of its side door and, bent as low as they could, scurrying across the open land between the road and the security fence, both carrying black holdalls. It was, as planned, on the dot of one o'clock in the morning. It was pitch black and a light drizzle persisted but they were thankful for the cloud cover. It protected them from any light the moon might offer. Once against the fence, they lay flat to the grass, one of them taking high-powered wire cutters from his bag, together with wiring and other bits and pieces. He busied himself by-passing the electric current running through the security defence before cutting a hole, large enough for them to crawl through. As he did so, his companion busied himself putting together a high velocity sniper's rifle, its silencer and a small tripod.

In Wapping, Georgi, Nagriza, Olivia, Leonie and Peter watched on two large screens, the images from the two head cameras imbedded into the hard hats of the two men. Being passive spectators always created tension and anxiety. This raid in Pyeongtaek was no exception. It was the result of intense preparation over too short a period of time. From the moment surveillance reported Taeyoung's visit to this high tech facility with its historic connections to military research, development and prototype manufacturing, Georgi used all the options he could think of to find out what Taeyoung was doing there. With March 22nd now only a few weeks away, he was desperate to know what Taeyoung was up to and especially how he intended to attack the dams. It was essential he understood if it was for real or just a very high profile and elaborate publicity stunt. Hitting a brick wall whichever way he turned, Georgi eventually ordered the raid.

Extensive intelligence gathering provided enough information to indicate the best option for accessing the business premises, which part of the interior of the building to concentrate on, and an escape route. Model simulations and mock ups ensured the two men now on site in Pyeongtaek were as well briefed and familiar with the building layout as they could be. But Georgi was all too conscious of it being a rushed job. And rushed jobs habitually go wrong. The chances of the two men escaping were very low.

With the hole cut, the second man lay fully extended on the grass. He manoeuvred himself so the upper part of his torso was through to the other side of the fence. Rifle in position, he searched for his target through the night sights. Repetitive scrutinising of plans of this experimental and manufacturing base in Pyeongtaek ensured he knew precisely where the security cameras covering this part of the large business site were located. It took only seconds before the cross hairs of the night sights centred on the first camera. Holding his breath, he applied a light pressure to the rifle's trigger and watched as the camera shattered. He quickly moved his body and lined the rifle up on the second camera. Seconds later he indicated to his companion this part of the job was complete. They now had the minimum of time to cross to the white building in front of them before security people came to investigate why the cameras had gone down.

The glass window took seconds to shatter under attack from the ultrasonic limpet the men stuck to the glass. It also triggered alarms in the building. From the near total silence of the dead of night, the noise was now ear-splitting. The two men were through and well into the offices before the jeep arrived outside, some five hundred yards away, sweeping the security fence with a high-powered searchlight. Though the hole had been hurriedly patched up, the likelihood was the point of breakthrough would be discovered. It was then just a question of how long it would take before the broken window was also located.

In the building, the two men moved quickly. The broken window gave them access into the warehouse part of the building through which they passed as quickly as they could, heading for the R&D Department and its assembly bays. It took five long minutes to get there. By the time they did, the broken window had been discovered and reported to the security office. Activated when the alarms went off, a well-rehearsed security programme had swung into action and was now directed towards the area where the two men had gained entry to the building.

In Wapping, the progress of the two men was watched with growing anxiety. They saw the R&D Department arrive, come into sight, the two intruders racing in and scanning the massive area with its work stations and engineering bays. The bays were empty. By now, someone was turning all the internal lighting on to ensure security cameras picked up everything. Clearly the two men would be confronted in minutes. They were not trying to escape detection. There was no time for that. But, frustratingly, there was no immediate trace of what they were looking for. While one camera showed the whole area being carefully searched but at high speed, the other showed its operator scrambling as fast he could though files and piles of documents on work benches and desks. It was here they found the clue they were looking for. In one stack of paperwork, was a drawing of a modified Chinese drone. It showed how the machine had been redesigned to be made up of readily assembled components. It looked like a complex Meccano set.

"Bingo!" said Georgi in Wapping, thumping a desk top in satisfaction at the breakthrough. But that was just one element of what they needed to know. What was at the front end of the drone was now the crucial question. Already the team in Wapping were closely examining the plans of the drone that had just been transmitted from Pyeongtaek but there was nothing they could find that gave indications as to whether the nose cone would be full of propaganda leaflets or high explosive.

Eighteen minutes from when the wire fence was cut to herald its start, the raid was over. It was inevitable. With much shouting and waving of a variety of firearms, the company's internal security force arrived in numbers showing that even at this ungodly hour of the night, security was such a high priority and sensitive issue for the company, that a large number of highly trained people could be brought into action very quickly. It was nothing less than Georgi anticipated. His two men gave themselves up immediately. They spread-eagled themselves on the floor in passive submission. There was no shooting. No unnecessary injury to anyone. The raiders were quickly stripped of all their equipment, searched, handcuffed and marched away. In the morning, Georgi would instigate the long process of gaining their release.

At the Wapping Communications Centre of the EUIS, footage from the two cameras was scrutinised by as many people as Georgi could muster. It was tedious work with much of what they were looking at needing translation, two Asian language experts being helicoptered in from GCHQ in Gloucestershire to help. It was late evening when someone asked what CL-20 was. Two unusual looking drums had been spotted in a corner. Once the images had been enlarged and enhanced, the labels showed the drums once contained CL-20. They looked to have been discarded after use, just thrown to where they now lay and the filler caps of two of them were no longer in place. They appeared to be empty but they also appeared to be strange in their structure.

One of the team called out to Georgi. "I've got CL-20 on the web. The headline for one entry about it says: 'The most powerful military explosive tamed for use'. Strange terminology but it seems we've found what we were looking for."

"Bloody hell!" Georgi replied. "Now we know the bastard is for real!"

Chapter 31

"Vy Govorite Po-Angliyski?" Sum Taeyoung spoke slowly into the phone and stumbled through the Russian phrase, praying for a positive answer. Since arriving in this place, nothing had been easy. Now all he needed was a positive answer. Could this person speak English? Even a little.

"Da," came the short response. Taeyoung gave a sigh of relief. "I need to meet Andryey Ginzburg," he said slowly and precisely.

There was a long pause. The telephone line crackled. Had the call been lost? Then an answer – not the one he wanted.

"Andryev Ginzburg is dead," said the voice at the other end of the line.

Taeyoung was shocked. It was not what he had expected.

"Dead. When?" he asked.

There was another pause, then a reply in awkward English. "Two days ago."

Taeyoung hesitated then replaced the phone on its cradle. There was no point continuing the call. He did not really know who he was speaking to and he certainly did not know if anyone was listening in. It would not have surprised him if someone had been. This was a city that seemed to him to be teetering on the brink of progress or recession, advancing into independence and capitalism or slithering back into the uninviting and lawless place it was both in the days of Soviet rule and, in its immediate aftermath. He would be glad to be away from it. But the unexpected events of the last few days made it essential he came to Dushanbe, capital city of the republic of Tajikistan in the Hissar Valley with its surrounding huge, high, snow topped mountains.

The crisis involving Tajikistan and Kyrgyzstan had erupted quickly on March 1st, only three weeks before International Water Day. Already it was impacting not only on Taeyoung, but also on Angel Martin, Nagriza Karimov, Georgi Patarava and Gene Bond all of whom found themselves sucked into this unexpected interruption to their daily lives.

On this day, a group of 30 men from the Tajikistan area of the 300 kilometre long Ferghana Valley, formerly part of the Soviet Union but now a confusion of disputed and badly denoted borders between Uzbekistan, Kyrgyzstan and Tajikistan, crossed the border and illegally entered Kyrgyzstan. Half their number carried tools. The other half, local militia, carried guns. Their determined objective was to retrieve their water supplies. Years of badly developed and maintained irrigation systems for crop growing – mainly cotton and rice – an essential element of Kyrgyzstan's economy, plus dams built by villagers in Kyrgyzstan, had brought the issue of water to a head. There is only so long people can tolerate living without water. That time had long passed. These were very angry people who believed they had a right to seek to restore a daily supply of water they accused their neighbour of depriving them of. The timing was also thought be opportune. The Tajikistani militia were capitalising on a peak in the continuing internal disarray in Kyrgyzstan, a country beset with political difficulties ever since it gained independence.

The group set off on a day when a proper sunrise was compromised by a thick freezing fog. It hung over the snow covered disputed border and gave a white thickness to the morning air. The ground was slippery and the trees draped with a hoar frost. The men plodded and crunched through the deep snow, slithered on ice and crossed frozen streams to reach their first dam undetected. But it was not long before the noise of their dismantling activity attracted attention and a few Kyrgyan locals gathered to protest. With verbal objections ignored and with rifle and shotgun carrying men protecting those dismantling the dam, the locals withdrew only to return soon afterwards, now also armed and in greater numbers. It was an unstoppable scenario leading with some inevitability, to a first shot heralding the start of a shootout that continued and escalated. It was as if a flame ignited a tinder box that for years had threatened to become an inferno. By the end of the day, both sides recorded one death each amongst their small numbers.

This has been a volatile region ever since countries gained their independence in the aftermath of the collapse of the Soviet Union. This latest border skirmish, by far the most serious of many in recent times, stimulated intervention by politicians in both countries. That served only to raise tensions still further. Both sides accused the other of starting the gun fight. Tajikistan logged a formal protest accusing Kyrgyzstan of robbing it of natural resources, especially water. Kyrgyzstan accused Tajikistan of a serious border violation and the unlawful killing of some of its citizens.

By March 3rd, news of the conflict was beyond the confines of the Valley with the UN calling for a cooling of tension and urgent intervention by the major powers with vested interests in the area – China, Russia and the EU. Immediate responses from each of these only served to demonstrate that they too had interests in the Ferghana Valley, and their reactions demonstrated concern only to protect those interests, not to address wider issues or to seek peaceful resolution to the conflict. There was no hint of any humanitarianism in statements from the three superpowers, only a sense of increasing tension and volumes of rhetorical threats. With a shouting match intensifying between China, Russia and the EU, CNN headlined a question about what in reality was still a local skirmish – *'Is This the First Water War of the 21st Century?'*

In Las Vegas, Angel Martin was angry, frustrated and concerned in equal measure. A message from the UN advised her they might now not be able to send a representative to her March 22nd convention. Their focus was turned to the growing conflict in the Ferghana Valley. Her response was to suggest the Church of Acionna's event could be used as neutral territory to try and secure solutions to this water related problem. The conflict, she pointed out to her UN contacts, served as a clear demonstration of the perils of not managing water properly and not respecting it as the most essential natural resource used by man. Initial replies from the UN hinted its officials considered Angel Martin's suggestions to be somewhat naive. That only served to further fuel her anger and frustration. She was used to getting her own way.

At the Communications Centre of the European Union Intelligence Service in Wapping, concern about events in the Ferghana Valley was at different levels, corporate and personal. Corporately, calls were coming in fast and furiously from various parts of the vast EU machinery, anxious to know anything the EUIS could tell them about the growing conflict and tensions. Nagriza, from Uzbekistan, was increasingly worried about her mother and other members of her family. True, the dispute did not yet involve Uzbekistan but as the third nation in the Ferghana Valley, she was concerned it would spread.

The news of the border skirmish and its escalation now embracing the super powers, coincided with Nagriza receiving new information about the continuing plight of the Aral Sea with its 'eastern lobe' now completely dry for the first time in 600 years. New images received in Wapping from NASA's Terra satellite, showed the sea with no water at all in its eastern section, it having divided into two distinct parts some time ago. Originally a freshwater lake, the Aral Sea once had a surface area of 26,000 square miles. In recent history, many towns thrived around its shores. A lucrative muskrat pelt industry and prosperous fishing industry once provided 40,000 jobs. One sixth of the fish brought ashore supplied the Soviet Union. Amongst a vast number of people to become victims of the disaster was Nagriza's fisherman father, recently deceased.

The latest news was like another nail in the coffin of this once significant sea. It also impacted on Gene Bond. The desperate story of the Aral Sea was one reason he made a career out of sustainable development. The drying up of the world's fourth largest inland lake was a classic example of environmental and humanitarian consequences being ignored in a strategy based on short term, narrow, financially led objectives – the Soviet's irrigation of the cotton growing area. When he first encountered the story he thought – "what on earth are we doing to our planet? And what are we doing to ourselves?" It was a turning point in his life.

Georgi Patarava had to respond to this new Central Asian challenge. Though his department was fast becoming overstretched with work and, with the new intelligence on Sum Taeyoung's intentions turning from what was originally thought to have been a publicity stunt but now seen as a potential global threat of some magnitude, Georgi was forced to respond to demands from his Brussels lord and masters. The CCN headline was quickly looking prophetic. The Ferghana Valley was now on a knife edge of war. It gave Georgi enough to worry about professionally let alone personally because the troubled area was not far from his homeland, Georgia. He was thankful the Caspian Sea lay between it and the squabbling trio of former Soviet states. But even so, this quickly evolving dispute was too close to home for his liking. He convened an emergency management meeting from which the decision was made to send Nagriza to the area. The department needed first-hand evidence to respond to calls for information. She was more familiar with the Ferghana Valley than anyone else in the team. She would report back and provide the EUIS with as much intelligence as she could.

Because the spark-point to the new troubles was water, Georgi also decided to send Gene Bond with her. The decision was made with the greatest of professional integrity and concern about diverting him away from the Acionna Project, but it was difficult to ignore personalities and relationships. Sending Nagriza and Bond off together was not without emotional concerns for Georgi. Bond reacted with enthusiasm. It was a chance to visit Uzbekistan. He had never been before. But more importantly, it was an opportunity to see the Aral Sea for the first time. The diminished sea had changed his life – from a great distance. And, of course, there was the undeniably delightful prospect of spending time with Nagriza.

Although at the moment the Acionna Projects were the biggest thing in Sum Taeyoung's life and time was running out, he was also worried about protecting existing business activity. Apart from appeasing his appetite for causing as much damage to Western imperialist interests as possible, his chaos generating activity benefitted his portfolio of illicit businesses in which drugs and guns were an integral part. Tajikistan, a central place in his European drug business, played an important role as a transit country for 'Afghan narcotics' bound for Russia.

When news broke of serious trouble breaking out in the Ferghana Valley, and unable to make contact from a distance with his business connections in the area, Sum Taeyoung reluctantly dropped everything and flew to Dushanbe, Tajikistan's capital located not far from the border with Uzbekistan.

His first action on arrival was to go by taxi to the seedy bar he knew Andryev Ginzburg, his agent in the area, used as his base. But there was no sign of him. Worryingly, nobody seemed to know where he was or when he might return. Taeyoung's questioning of people in the bar – not an easy task given the language problems – got what he judged to be a cold response. He felt uneasy and left having made no progress at all.

Back at the hotel, Taeyoung dug through his iPhone case file on Ginzburg. It gave him two telephone numbers from previous involvement with the drug runner. Unsure about both of them, he reluctantly tried the first. It led him to the information that Andryev Ginzburg was dead.

His second telephone number was of even more dubious reliability and was not even in Tajikistan but in nearby Uzbekistan. He believed the person he was phoning was Ginzburg's main man in that country. It was his best – and probably his only bet in re-establishing the supply chain broken by Ginzburg's death. But it was with great caution that he spoke to the person who answered the phone. The call was short but offered some hope. The Uzbekistan contact was not surprised to hear from him. He would cross the border and meet Taeyoung in the centre of Dushanbe. He would bring with him someone he thought Taeyoung should meet.

It was with nervous trepidation that Tayoung sat in the place where they had agreed to meet, a city centre café. They were late, nearly an hour late. Such lack of punctuality was not uncommon in these parts but nevertheless, it did nothing for the South Korean's nerves.

When they arrived, there were two people. They had obviously done their homework because they immediately recognised Taeyoung and walked straight to him at his table. One was a small man, swathed in dark clothes and with a head piece that made it hard to see his face until he removed the hood. The face was rugged and pockmarked. When he spoke, yellow stained teeth were revealed.

"From South Korea, I believe." It was the opening words they had agreed.

Taeyoung stood. He looked not at the man but at the woman to his side. She was tall and striking, with hazel hair and green eyes.

"This is Nagriza Karimov," said the little man in introduction.

Chapter 32

As top man in a globally operating business, Bernhard Gedeck had done many things in his life. Not all were open to scrutiny. Not all were actions he was proud of. His rule of thumb was always to evaluate the positive and negative impacts on the Esca balance sheet. If profitability could be enhanced, the likelihood was the proposed action would be justifiable. But in the line of corporate duty, never before had he organised for someone to die. In his assessment as to the value of the action to be taken – or not to be taken, the need for the young news reporter Ryan Spears to be silenced, was unquestionable. So Spears had died.

The pestering for a meeting by the group called 'The Friends of Ryan Spears' was relentless and growingly agitating. Gedeck considered it no more than a distraction from the many things he was trying to concentrate on in his myriad of corporate responsibilities but the closer March 22nd got, the more he was obliged to focus on Taeyoung's Acionna Projects. But while operational activity plus Taeyoung's project occupied 99% of his mind, 1% remained stuck on Ryan Spears. It was annoying – as was the constant stream of telephone calls and text messages tracking him wherever he was. There seemed to be no escape. But Gedeck had no plans to return to the USA in the near future and until he did so, he saw no reason to be too worried about pressure to meet from 'The Friends of Ryan Spears'. But it was irritating.

His Task Force continued with their preparatory work in advance of March 22nd. Clearly nothing would happen immediately after the disasters struck on that day. There would be horror and shock and growing concern as to how to respond to the tragedies. EscaEau would be seen to be rapidly evaluating what actions were needed. It would be far too obvious if solutions swung in too quickly. So Gedeck's team planned a phased response but one that would see him still miles ahead of anything any of their competitors might do.

Though across the world, EscaEau assets were being developed and put on standby ready for eventualities post March 22nd, there was little in terms of actual acquisition activity. Everything Gedeck's team was organising was being outsourced, mostly on lease term contracts. In the event, if nothing happened and it transpired Gedeck had backed a loser, the losses to the company would be substantial but by no means a game ender. So as March arrived, ships, aircraft, bottling plant and access to water supplies were mostly on standby in agreements carefully crafted to look as if they were part of EscaEau's widely known global expansion ambitions. Clearly if it all went pear-shaped, there would be penalties to pay, often substantial, and Gedeck's position in the company would be severely undermined – at the very least.

Meanwhile in Las Vegas, with adversity seemingly hitting him from every quarter, Tim Crenshaw needed his faith to enable him to keep going. But his faith was becoming part of his problems. With now only three weeks to the Church's convention on March 22nd, the task of radically changing the timings of the programme to accommodate what Sum Taeyoung now wanted to do was a nightmare. Every speaker needed contacting and advising of the changes or cajoled into agreeing to them. That included, as had been Taeyoung's cynical inspiration, speaking to Gene Bond and inviting him to introduce the video feature – the climax of the event. Because of the high profile of people in the programme, tracking them down and making contact was time consuming and far from easy. It transpired Bond was the worst of the lot because when Crenshaw tried to contact him, he was in Uzbekistan and communication was difficult. Sheer persistence by Crenshaw won the day and they eventually spoke over a badly connected telephone line.

Bond, not unreasonably, still wanted to know what the videos were about. Crenshaw told him what he had told him before – they were live coverage of simultaneous events in America, China and Spain. They would dramatically demonstrate the need for people to better understand the value of water and to treat it, and use it, with greater respect and with regard to its growing scarcity. When Bond wanted to know more, Crenshaw told him "we're keeping a lid on the detail so we create maximum global impact. We don't want the media spreading this everywhere in advance."

And, despite Bond's best endeavours, that is all he gleaned from the call. At the end of his own presentation, he would say a few words of introduction and hit a button. That would introduce the live coverage of events from the three locations around the world. The timing was critical and the striking of the button was to be at precisely 1600 Las Vegas time. Whilst demonstrating reticence to Crenshaw because of lack of clarity as to what would be seen on the screens, Bond simply could not refuse this chance to get closer to what Taeyoung was involved with. On that basis, he agreed to do it.

Working with local show experts, of which there is an abundance in Las Vegas, and, with Sum Taeyoung's experts, Crenshaw planned that when Bond hit the button on the convention lectern, the large screen used throughout the event would divide into three areas, one covering activity not far from where the convention was being staged, one in Central Spain close to the Portuguese border, and the third in Danjiangkou in the north western Hebei Province of China. It would be midnight in Spain and seven o'clock in the morning at the Chinese location.

Bond immediately relayed the information to Georgi in Wapping.

"I've got myself into a ridiculous corner, Georgi. Whatever Taeyoung's planning, I'm hitting the bleeding button that will launch it!"

Georgi was astounded. "My God Gene. I told you our two worlds overlapped. But I never thought it would get to anything like this."

Bond was feeling utterly trapped. But beyond anything else, there were two unanswered questions. How was Taeyoung going to use drones to attack the three dams and further, was it all one hell of a glorious publicity stunt or was he really going to try and damage them – even breach them? He talked about it to Georgi.

"I can't say much over this open line," Georgi told him. "But we are getting close to our main man."

Little did he know just how close they were to him.

Crenshaw was keeping Angel Martin informed of most developments, but not all. She still did not know what the live video links were all about and Crenshaw was grateful for the problems with the UN which acted as a diversion to most other things. Angel was determined to retrieve their involvement and used her many and powerful connections and influences, and her unquestionable PR skills, to eventually win the day. It was finally agreed the UN speaker would focus on the water issues impacting on the Ferghana Valley as a demonstration of the vital socio/political dimensions of water.

This progress, plus the impact of Angel's publicity machine, ensured the first annual convention of the New Church of Acionna was gaining in stature and importance all the time. Now the City of Las Vegas at last acknowledged the international significance of The New Church of Acionna's event. From an initial attitude of indifference, the pendulum swung wildly in the opposite direction and now city officials were almost screaming to be involved and to ensure they grabbed as much of the action and publicity advantages as they could. This in turn turned into a dogfight between the City Mayor, senior officials of the City, and Clark County, the administrative body for the most populated part of the State of Nevada. The ensuing squabble saw Crenshaw again entrapped in the most uncomfortable of positions as his City bosses, knowing of his role within the Church and the event itself, expected him to use as much influence as he could to ensure they were favoured.

Crenshaw, his relationship with Angel becoming increasing tetchy as she constantly pressurised him, felt a deterioration of any spiritual help the Church could offer him in his troubled life. It had been filling the void created by the disastrous relationship with Susan. Now home, work and the church all contributed in equal part to the misery of his daily life.

In China, Spain and America, small groups of PGU students plus a representative from SDBI for each group, gradually made their way to the respective Acionna Project sites. The Chinese drone was being transported to

Danjiangkou in a truck carrying logos of a major construction company, one heavily involved with the expansion of the dam, reservoir and the associated redevelopment activity. Taeyoung hoped it would just merge into the general traffic supporting the vast work being undertaken there.

Contrary to Taeyoung's original plan, the students were now involved at all three locations. Each group would liaise with the separately travelling trucks carrying the drones. They would help unload and assemble all the equipment and one, trained especially in the task, would be responsible for preparing the drone for take-off. That would be triggered from Las Vegas – by Bond hitting the button on the lectern. Take-off was pre-programmed for each drone as were the flight paths which were GPS guided. If anything went wrong with the technical link from the convention, all three drones would be triggered when the American drone was launched, by a manual device. Taeyoung, as anxious as ever to distance himself from any direct action, tasked the suffering Crenshaw with this responsibility in the event of Bond not firing off the drones from the convention lectern.

The students were also responsible for video coverage of the drones hitting their targets. They also had leaflets to distribute after the attacks, supplementing those they believed would explode from the front of the drones on impact.

Meanwhile, since leaving London, Nagriza and Bond spent their first two days together travelling to Uzbekistan and staying overnight in its capital, Tashkent. It was a long, agitating and tiring journey and the closer they got to her home country, so Nagriza's mood became progressively reflective and brooding. Bond quickly realised this was not the opportunity he had hoped it might be to explore their relationship. Though he ached to again experience their lovemaking, which had been to such epic proportions in the past, it was clear this was not the time or the place to encourage it to happen again.

Nagriza's brief from Georgi was to get a personal view of what was going on in the Ferghana Valley and to feed it back to him so he could respond to the demands for information from Brussels. She planned to use personal and family connections to do that, including digging out former colleagues from the time when for a brief while, she worked for the Uzbekistan Secret Service in Tashkent. But she also wanted to talk to family connections back in her home town of Munak. This suited Bond's agenda because it used to be on the shores of the Aral Sea.

Slowed by the state of the roads, an example of the deteriorating infrastructure of the country, and Nagriza stopping to visit and interview various people on the way, it took two days in their hired Toyota 4WD to cover the near 800 miles. Once there, it was immediately apparent to Bond that the town of Munak had seen better days. A strong wind was buffeting clouds of sand everywhere. But the whole town looked played out and sad. A small group of friends and neighbours formed a welcoming party at the home of Nagriza's mother and there was much tear shedding and hugging before attention turned to the stranger she had brought with her. The welcome to Bond was warm and generous – and courteous, as Nagriza stressed to everyone, the Englishman was a business colleague, nothing else.

Later Nagriza drove Bond around the area, firstly heading for the water he so desperately wanted to see. Munak was once Uzbekistan's major sea port. It prospered from the industrial fishing and a canning industry which together employed some 40,000 people. When the sea contracted and those businesses collapsed, thousands of residents fled the city in search of new lives. Today those who still live there, suffer from a multitude of illnesses brought about by the toxic laden dust carried by powerful winds that blow across the desert wilderness picking up contaminated particles from the corrupted sea. Nagriza had to drive more than 60 miles across sand dunes and grey grass stubble to the water's edge, passing numerous fishing boats all keeled over on their sides. It seemed to take an age to reach the water's edge upon which Munak had once so proudly and energetically stood.

They left the relative comfort and shelter of the Toyota to walk alongside the sea that no longer exists. "The local climate used to be kept stable by the Aral Sea," Nagriza told him. "Now it's hotter and drier in the summer and colder in the winter. And we have these winds which pick up residue from salt, pesticides, and fertilizer from the dried up seabed and disperse them all over the place. It's a major factor in contributing to the decline of the local population's health."

Bond knew he would find it all very emotional. This story had been impacting on him for so long. Now for the first time, he was seeing it for himself. It was an appalling situation. Later, they visited the Munak Museum. It provided an insight into what the flourishing town once used to look like with examples of the equipment the fishermen used, pictures of the fishing fleet in action and of the cannery, and local children's paintings of the rusty old ships, the rotting legacy of better times.

Through conversations with a variety of people, Nagriza was beginning to paint a picture of what was going on between the three countries the borders of which meet in the Ferghana Valley. But she needed to get closer to the action. After two days in Munak, they reluctantly decided they needed to split up, Nagriza to concentrate on intelligence gathering and capitalizing on being a local to these parts. Bond would continue his research of the Aral Sea disaster.

It was on a long, dusty, virtually traffic-less road as they headed East from Munak on the 800 mile journey to the border between Uzbekistan and Tajikistan that Bond brought the Toyota to a stop.

"Is this a clever idea?" he asked her.

"What?" she replied.

"Splitting up like this. It's going to worry the hell out of me. You know how I feel about you. Not that I've had much of a chance to demonstrate that over the last few days."

She had turned in her seat to look at him, head slightly down, eyes looking up. He melted. He always did when she looked at him this way. It somehow exaggerated her exoticness, her extraordinary good looks.

"I'm sorry, Gene," she responded, speaking softly. "I know we've been travelling together all these days and I've not been much of a companion – let alone anything else. It's a tough trip, coming home so soon after my father's death and, to see my family in such difficult circumstances. And seeing Munak slowly dying – my home town. It's horrible. So, I'm sorry I've neglected you."

He felt awkward now, feeling selfish and wishing he'd not raised the subject of their relationship. He was only too aware of the emotional turmoil Nagriza had been through ever since they arrived in Uzbekistan. But before he could say anything in response, she leant forward and kissed him, a long and lingering kiss.

"When we get back to London," she told him, "then we will enjoy each other again. Here it is too difficult, too emotional, too much to do."

And on that promise he settled back to drive East again, taking them to the border where he kissed her again, another long kiss but this time holding her tightly to him so he could feel her body against his. She eventually drove off, leaving him to pick up his hire car and turn his attention away for a while from Georgi's world of counterespionage to concentrate more on sustainable development matters. From the border, Bond took the opportunity to track the Syr Darya River. He knew it originates in the Tian Shan Mountains in Kyrgyzstan, over 1,000miles from the Aral Sea. In both Uzbekistan and Kyrgyzstan he had no difficulty in finding evidence of the extensive irrigation activity undertaken during the time of the Soviet Union to expand cotton and rice growing. It was only too obvious; the diversions of the river – and similar activity on other rivers – had depleted its role as a filler river resulting in the shrinkage of the Aral Sea. Undertaken for financial gain, astonishingly the plan eventually resulted in the demise of two major industries, the loss of tens of thousands of jobs and the creation of an environmental disaster as the freshwater sea became more of a chemical residual sewerage sump, with significant and costly health consequences throughout the area. It had been, and continued to be, a cataclysmic tragedy.

He discovered an agreement once existed in which water originating from the Syr Darya River and also the Amu Darya River, was shared by Kyrgyzstan and Tajikistan with Turkmenistan and Uzbekistan during the summer months. In return, Kyrgyzstan and Tajikistan received Kazakh, Turkmen, and Uzbek coal, gas, and electricity in winter. This resource sharing scheme collapsed after the demise of the Soviet Union, gradually leading to the current disputes. Deirdre Tynan, the UN Crisis Group's Central Asia Project Director, was quoted recently as saying: *"Corruption, hidden interests and inflexible positions in all three states hinder a mutually acceptable solution. A common development strategy focusing on reform of agricultural and energy sectors would be in their interest."*

It was clear to Bond that the resurrection of the resource sharing scheme would be entirely sensible and he sent a note to that effect both to Georgi in London and also direct to a personal contact in the UN Environmental Programme. However, he did so with little expectation of anything happening. Tensions in the area were very obviously rising. As he crisscrossed borders in his quest to see for himself why the Aral Sea was in such a mess, the amount of military machinery everywhere and troops on the move, was clear evidence that the Ferghana Valley was on a knife edge of disaster. The tension in the air was palpable. A new water war seemed inevitable.

Chapter 33

Nagriza reached the town of Dushanbe and set about establishing contact with the people Georgi said would be helpful in providing their own views of how dangerous the situation in the Ferghana Valley was becoming. She already had her own impressions. It was not difficult. Like Bond, she found military vehicles and troops everywhere and crossing the borders was now far more time consuming and testing than it used to be until very recently. Unbeknown to her, on reaching the Tajikistan capital, she had established her base at the very same hotel being used by a certain South Korean.

She spent most of her first day in Dushanbe on her mobile phone and the hotel's land line. Communications in the area were clearly suffering from the escalating attention of the world on what was becoming an increasingly political and military hot spot. Of all her calls, one in particular stood out as especially interesting. The man she spoke to said he would prefer to talk to her directly rather than over the phone. They agreed to meet in Rudaki Park, conveniently located close by the town's main administrative building where she was scheduled to meet various local civil servants. There was a strong wind blowing but it was a bright day as she exited the building after discussions with government officials and headed into the well-kept gardens and myriad paved pathways, flower beds and fountains of Dushanbe's central park. Even at this time of the year, it was fairly busy with tourists, locals and students. Her rendezvous was at the dominating decorative arch with its colourful, symbolic hieroglyphics spanning across the statue of Persian poet Rudaki.

He was waiting for her there. There was no way she would not have recognized him from the description he had given her. The small man in a long, thick winter coat and wearing a Russian fur trapper's hat, could not be mistaken. He was rough shaven and equally rough voiced, greeting her in poor English confused by the influences of several other countries.

With a total lack of introduction or formalities, the little man's first words to her were, "there is someone I want you to meet." This man was a distant connection of Georgi's and was on Nagriza's list of people to see. She knew he was from the murky world of terrorism and spying but that was all. She had thought he would give his views on the posturing between the three nations of the Ferghana Valley but instead, after the few gruff words, they walked from the park to the Café Mege, a place popular with the locals and specializing in Turkish food. The little man led the way through the café's door, Nagriza following but with a growing sense of anxiety. She had no idea what she was walking into. Ever since arriving in Tajikistan, a nervous unease refused to go away. Uzbekistan provided the comfort and security of her homeland. Here she was in alien territory, exacerbated by the country's general disquiet and military activity. And the less she felt in control of her circumstances, the more her nervousness grew. Now she was blindly following someone of dubious reputation into somewhere she did not know to meet someone she did not know. It was making her feel significantly uncomfortable.

Of all the people in the café, she was shocked to see there was one person she immediately recognized. They had never met but she had seen hundreds of images of him.

It was unbelievable, the huge man with his long hair and bushy beard could now be rising to greet them.

"This is Nagriza Karimov," said the little man in introduction.

"Sum Taeyoung," responded the South Korean, extending his hand in welcome. Though he showed no signs of emotion, the incongruity of the situation was only too apparent to Taeyoung. He was shaking hands with the girl he knew had frequently shared the bed of a man he had twice failed to kill.

Nagriza hid her astonishment. She was clasping the hand of the man Georgi and the team at Wapping knew as one of the most dangerous men on the planet. She wondered if the surveillance programme at Wapping was tracking this extraordinary meeting. If they were, how on earth would Georgi now be reacting? And what would Gene Bond think if he knew?

"I'm told I might be of help to you," the South Korean said in his Oxford English with American and Asian undertones.

"I'm here on a fact-finding mission for the European Community," she told him. "We're trying to get a good understanding of the tensions in this area."

"There are plenty of those," he agreed.

"What brings you to Tajikistan?" she asked. Her little companion who had made the initial introduction had moved away and was now in conversation with someone else in the café.

"Oh, many things," Taeyoung answered. Nagriza wondered how much of the truth he would tell her.

"Are you a business man, a politician – or connected to the military perhaps?" She asked.

"I run a business called Sustainable Development Brokers International. I'm here to see if I can help the current local difficulties."

"In what way?" Nagriza wanted to test him as much as she dared.

"I don't know until I fully understand what's going on."

"But what sort of skills do you offer through your business?"

"Ah," said Taeyoung, combing his beard with his fingers. "How long is a piece of string, as they say? We act as middlemen between those who have a problem and those who might have a solution. It's very wide ranging."

"So where does sustainable development come into what you do?" she asked.

"You have very testing questions," Taeyoung responded with a smile. "The answer is that we use the experience of people who have applied solutions and offer them to people who have problems – like, for instance, in this area with the problems to do with resources."

"So what solutions have you got? It's a very tricky situation here."

The big South Korean paused, then smiled again although she felt there was no substance behind the smile. This man is very false, she thought.

"If you're buying solutions I might tell you," he said. "I have to be commercial. But tell me more about you. What brings such an attractive lady to a place that's now so dangerous? Which part of the European Community do you work for?"

"It's part of the communications department," she told him, and then, trying to divert him away from a line of questioning she did not want to pursue, she added, "but I was told I should meet you. Our mutual friend seems to have given up on us. Why did he want me to meet you?"

Again. More combing of the beard. "You have contacts that might be useful to me. I have intelligence about what's happening in the Ferghana Valley and that might be of value to you. It seemed to me we could be helpful to each other."

Nagriza was becoming very cautious as to where this might lead. It reeked of untruths and deceptions.

"What sort of intelligence?" she asked.

"Oh, I can offer you troop numbers, weapons deployment – and more."

"And what sort of contacts do you want?"

"Uzbekistan civil servants. Anyone you can tell me about from any of the three countries involved."

She thought for a moment. What he was offering would be like gold to Georgi if it were authentic. But how could she trust this man? After all, Georgi was advocating he should be killed!

"And how do we go about this?" she asked.

He smiled again, that false smile. She felt that on his oriental face, it almost looked like a sneer.

"As an act of goodwill and integrity, I can show you what I have to offer."

"Now?" She asked.

He laughed. "No! Come on! You wouldn't expect me to carry such intelligence with me. I can show you on my laptop. It's back at my hotel."

Nagriza was weighing up the situation as he spoke. She could not trust this man an inch. She knew he was dangerous. On the other hand, what he had to offer was potentially priceless. And, anyway, what danger did he present to her here in Tajikistan?

"OK," she agreed. "How do we do this?"

Taeyoung was delighted. This gorgeous but undoubtedly dangerous member of the European Community Secret Service, was beginning to eat out of his hand. He kept thinking of her relationship with Gene Bond. To be so close to her was an unexpected bonus. Now the question was – how best to capitalise on the opportunity? Control of Nagriza meant some degree of control over both Bond and Georgi Patarava's organisation. She could be of enormous value to him. The opportunist in him was again winning the day. She could provide him with a completely new deck of cards. But what was the next move? Should he kidnap Nagriza? That was the question. Taeyoung already had the answer.

Chapter 34

Gene Bond was only too conscious that Angel Martin's convention in Las Vegas was now only seven days away. It seemed to be something so remote – so far away both in terms of time and distance. Having left the Aral Sea and Uzbekistan, Bond decided to trek along the Syr Darya River as best he could as the history of this river told much of the story of water provision to people living in this part of Central Asia. He was now in the town of Khujand located in the northern 'finger' of Tajikistan that penetrates into what is otherwise Uzbekistan. Today, it is a mixture of Central Asian architecture and culture but with much evidence of Russian/Soviet influences.

Surrounded by dusty, reddish mountains towering in every direction, Bond was enthralled by Khujand's history with much of its foundation related to the ancient Silk Road. The historic architecture and fortifications with Arabic and Persian influences reminded him of stories of Genghis Khan and what he knew from his love of anything to do with the Ottoman Empire. Since his youth, he had been inspired by this ancient realm stretching from the Atlantic in Europe across to the Caspian Sea in Central Asia and to the borders of China. It was a huge geographical area with a kaleidoscope of cultures and religions yet it had been bound into one empire spanning centuries from the early 1300s to modern times. Here in Khujand was an abundance of evidence of the city's long history dating back to Alexander the Great and its significance as a centre of culture and craftsmanship.

But it was the city's struggle with water that brought him here. It was a struggle that had gone on for as long as people could remember – and continued today. Less than two decades ago, there was no access to clean water for the 160,000 or so citizens of Khujand. Drinkable water was available only by boiling whatever water they could find. Bond wondered what life was like living in a city the size of Khujand with no ready access to clean water. It must have been hugely difficult.

The city's history museum provided helpful information but it was by talking to local officials that he found it was intervention by the Swiss State Secretariat for Economic Affairs and the European Bank of Reconstruction and Development that enabled the city to modernise its water infrastructure. That included installing thousands of water meters and improving both an existing waste water treatment plant and systems for collecting wastewater. Bond was relieved to find this work meant further threats to the Syr Darya River – and on to the Aral Sea – were reduced, as were discharges into it.

Mindful of the need to soon be the other side of the planet, Bond was growingly anxious to depart this part of the world. He travelled from Khujand to Tashkent from where he planned to fly out to Moscow then on to Las Vegas. Progress was hampered at the border where Uzbekistan officials looked especially nervous and twitchy, an indication of the mood across the whole of the region. Once into Tashkent it seemed the world's media and political circus had descended there to look from this neutral territory at the squabbling going on between its near neighbours. It would, he realised, take a good two days to get from here to Las Vegas. And while Uzbekistan still remained aloof from the troubles, the dangers of it being sucked in were only too real. If that happened, getting out of Tashkent might become significantly more of a problem.

As best he could in the circumstances, he had kept a regular flow of reports heading to London for Georgi. But contact with Nagriza was lost. It was to be expected but that did not reduce his concern for her. She had her own busy schedule to fulfil and would be trying to move around the area, not easily achieved in a territory now more or less under military control. In many ways, such worrying was, he tried to convince himself, irrational. She knew this part of the world far better than he. She was a trained and experienced counter espionage operator – a spy. She had all the abilities and attributes to be able to look after herself. He knew Georgi was receiving messages from her. That was good and reassuring. But Bond still worried.

His time was now being divided between doing analysis of the growing military tensions in the area for Georgi, analysing the significance of the issue of water and other resources in general as the base cause of the troubles, gathering information for his own purposes but especially related to the Aral Sea, and increasingly trying to commit time to writing his presentation for the Las Vegas convention. It seemed incongruous to make a direct comparison between what happened here in this extraordinary part of Central Asia and what was happening in Las Vegas. Bond found Tashkent and its surrounds positively weird, a mix of cultures and religions as if history put all its elements into a mixing bowl and poured out today's result. To the east is the dominance of China, to the north Russia and to the West, the ever expanding European Community which seemed to be gobbling up countries once part of the Soviet Union. Across centuries, ownership of Uzbekistan had changed hands many times but eventually became firmly established with well-rooted significance to Central Asia at the time of the Silk Road.

This trade and cultural route had been so evident in Khujand, connecting West and East for traders, merchants, pilgrims, monks, armies and nomads. It held a long time fascination for Bond.

Yet, despite the extreme differences between the Aral Sea and Lake Mead, the issue of lakes being deprived of their water now seemed to him to be a common denominator. Today the Aral Sea is reduced to a toxic sump. Now Lake Mead is losing water at a frightening rate. Would it, he wrote into the beginnings of his convention script, go the same way? What then the fate of Las Vegas – the gambling capital built in the desert? It was a scary thought. It would be an interesting question to ask to an audience in the Las Vegas Convention Centre!

While Bond juggled time between various demands and planned his departure from Central Asia to the Nevada Desert, Nagriza was only a little over 250 miles away in Dushanbe. The offer of data from Taeyoung was a fascinating if not dangerous prospect. But weighing up the potential gains against the risks, the gains won and she agreed with the South Korean to explore an exchange of information in his hotel. After all, she thought to herself, how dangerous could it be in such a public place as a hotel?

That she was with this strange, larger than life, exceptionally hairy man – designated by the team in Wapping to be one of the most dangerous terrorists on the planet – both excited and frightened her. She knew him so well from all the research and scrutiny the Wapping team had done on Taeyoung, it felt like being with a long lost friend. But she also knew she was now walking with the devil.

"I will meet you there," he told her. "It solves another problem. I've a car and driver here. But I have a meeting with someone else and he too wants to end this afternoon at my hotel. He's picking me up in his car. It's all an annoying confusion. But now I can send you with my driver to my hotel and you can wait for me there in the bar. I will be ten minutes behind you. Is that OK?"

Nagriza was far from happy about this. She felt as if she was walking into a potential trap. She was unarmed. To have been carrying a weapon as she crossed the borders from one country to another then another would have been asking for trouble. But what Taeyoung was offering was just what people in Brussels were pressuring Georgi for. It was a rich prize to be had. And she had unarmed combat training to call on. As rivals and opponents from the past had found to their cost, she looked stunning, unbelievably sexy but could be lethal. Weighing up the benefits against the risk, Nagriza felt she could cope with Taeyoung's driver if that's what it came to. With those thoughts in mind, she agreed to Taeyoung's plan and he escorted her from the tea room to a waiting limousine. He opened the rear door for her and she got in. He was smiling that false smile when she last saw him.

It took less than five minutes to start realising the car was heading somewhere other than Taeyoung's hotel. Her knowledge and familiarity of Dushanbe was limited but she was pretty certain that between Cafe Merve and Taeyoung's hotel on the airport side of Rudaki Park, there was no need to turn right off the main Hofiz Sherozi Avenue as they had now done. It should have been, she thought, a left turn. Now she could see signs to the Dushanbe Zoo. She conjured in her mind a picture of the city's map. The Zoo was in the opposite direction to the park. Maybe, she thought, this was some sort of local knowledge at work with the driver using side roads as a short cut. But she grew more anxious.

They crossed over the Gissar Canal and were now in a confusion of new roads and modern houses. Without warning, the car skidded to a halt and a man quickly got in alongside the driver. Nagriza, now convinced all was far from right and now outnumbered, reached for the door handle only to find it did not budge. Her door was locked.

"What's going on?" she shouted at the driver.

He turned, looked at her and smiled. It was as false and insincere as Taeyoung's had been.

It was the newly arrived passenger who spoke, pulling a gun from his jacket pocket as he did so. He had hardly drawn it into view when Nagriza, as best she could in the cramped space, lunged forward, right hand poised in an attack position.

The driver's left hand caught Nagriza's right arm before she could strike a blow. It was a tight grip. It stopped her attack before it happened. She brought her left fist over to try and strike the passenger but he was quicker and struck her with a sharp blow to her forehead with the gun barrel. It was a heavy strike, enough to send her reeling back into her seat, blood now seeping down her face.

"Now you be good," said the newcomer in just understandable English.

The situation stabilised, the front seat passenger now holding the gun steadily at her. Her head thumping and holding her hand against the wound opened by the gun, Nagriza sat back in her seat.

"You be good," he repeated.

"What a fool," she thought to herself. Tempted by his offer she had walked straight into Taeyoung's trap. She had analysed the risk and benefits. She had backed her own skills and abilities. She had got it wrong. Horribly wrong. Now she had no idea who these two men were, what they planned for her or where they were going. Breathing deeply to regain control of her emotions and to let the pain subside, her training kicked in as she started to assess her options, few though they might be.

Halfway across the planet, in Wapping, Georgi too was assessing options, both his and Taeyoung's. From the raid on the research and development establishment in Pyeongtaek, they now knew Taeyoung's attack on the dams was for real. He was using modified Chinese military drones with explosive nose cones made from what is currently the world's most explosive material, one known to have exceptional penetrative characteristics. Bond had guessed at the targets in China and America and the one clue they had about the Iberian Peninsula was when the young French student from the PGU group in Paris had fallen from an historic Roman dam into a reservoir in Spain. It was hardly enough to be counted as clear and unequivocal warning bells. And anyway, as Georgi's department did not officially exist, messages to appropriate people in China, Spain and America would have to be sent through proper channels from proper departments in Brussels. It would all take time and time was something they did not have.

And as Georgi and his team took stock of what they knew and what they did not know, their anguish and frustration grew in the knowledge they had no idea of the range of Taeyoung's drones or where he would be flying them from. It made the task of finding them a true needle in a haystack task. And unless they could find them, they could not stop them. Until, that is, the obvious became obvious.

It was Leonie who spotted it. "We don't need to know where the drones are," she told Georgi. "It would be helpful if we did and eventually I guess we'll need to find them to destroy them. But we don't need to know to be able to stop them attacking the dams."

"How come?" asked Georgi. The rest of the team were now all looking towards her, intrigued by this sudden revelation.

"We don't need to know because it's Gene Bond who's been tasked with pushing the button to start the video sequences. That action will launch the drones. If Gene doesn't push the button there'll be no attack."

Georgi thought about it for a moment. "You could be right. But you might not be. There might not be an automatic link between pushing the button and the drones launching. I think we need to know more about what technology Crenshaw's putting into the Vegas convention. But that won't go in until the day before the event. That's cutting everything mighty short. If you're right, Leonie, that's brilliant. But – it's a big but! I think we need to continue to look for the needle in our haystack. But we'll also check out what Crenshaw's technology looks like."

In Las Vegas, Tim Crenshaw was in a sorry state. Everything stacked against him – his wife, his employers, his church. It seemed only Sam Baldwin and Jack Daniels kept him alive. The editor was now more of a shoulder to cry on than a confidant. But unknown to the thankless civil servant, even his journalistic friend was getting bored by the civil servant's constant negative attitude and disposition. Tennessee whisky, once enjoyed in moments of reflection and relaxation, was now more like a lifeline to be downed in volume. As a consequence, to one degree or another, Crenshaw was in an alcoholic state for most of the day, most days. Even his sexual activities – conducted as he saw it to be in a secret, black corner of his life – were now few and far between, pressures from every direction devouring any time he might otherwise have had to pursue such pleasures.

With six days now left until March 22nd, the International Water Day Convention of the New Church of Acionna was somewhere near ready to roll. As ever, obtaining information from speakers and registrations from delegates was irritatingly difficult to conclude. It should have been a manageable irritation to Crenshaw but in his frame of mind, he was seeing every hurdle as a conspiracy by outsiders to ensure he failed. And beyond all his concerns lay the threat from Taeyoung. If he did not deliver what the South Korean wanted, his life would be blown asunder.

Chapter 35

In Dushanbe, the car carrying Nagriza and her two assailants travelled another ten minutes or so, always with the canal to the right and residential roads to the left. A couple of times they passed under main highways and then through a wooded area before returning to more housing. She could see ahead that they were reaching one of the horticultural zones of the town but before they got there the car slowed and turned into a short driveway. An electronic gate swung open and the car passed through to be confronted by a garage, the door of which was also automatically opening. From the short glimpse she caught of the house, it was much bigger and older than those they had been passing in the estates opposite the canal. And this one was located in a small wood backing onto one of the fields of the horticultural zone.

Once in the garage the doors closed and lights flickered on. Both men got out and while one held her tightly the other opened doors, first into the house then to what once might have been a dining room. Now all it contained was a rudimentary bed and a chair. There were closed blinds at the windows. A single light bulb with no shade hung from the ceiling. The place had an unused feel about it. It smelt dank but it was clean.

The man holding her thrust her towards the chair.

"You make no trouble and you won't be hurt," said the man who had struck her with the gun.

The driver was hunting through his pockets, eventually finding a folded up piece of paper and a mobile phone. He thrust the paper at Nagriza who opened it and read the typed note on it.

"I have been kidnapped. I am held by armed gunmen. If Gene Bond does not push the button to play the video sequence at the Vegas convention I will be killed."

There was a telephone number. Nagriza thought she recognised it.

"Who is this to?" she asked.

"Phone and read," demanded the man with the gun. "Just do it."

"Not until I know who it is to," said Nagriza stubbornly.

The man with the gun walked towards her, stood in front of her and grabbed each side of her jacket. The taller of her two captors, he was roughly the same height as Nagriza. He was also strong. He heaved her up from the chair with a sharp jerk, the jacket tearing and splitting as he did so, then thrust her back. She hit the chair which rocked back sending her crashing to the floor. As she lay there, the second man kicked out at her, striking her in the middle of her back. Together the men picked her up and returned her to the chair. She sat, bent double, searing pains cutting through her back while she tried to cover herself up with her ripped jacket.

"Now phone," said the gunman. "No more trouble." He thrust the mobile phone and piece of paper at her.

Regaining strength and control and realising further resistance was futile, Nagriza dialled the number.

It was half past two o'clock in the afternoon in the capital of Tajikstan. In London, Georgi had started the day early. By nine thirty he was on his second cup of coffee and pretty well everyone had arrived for work in Wapping. His phone rang. This was his business mobile phone. Few knew its number. He used it more to dial out than take incoming calls. He picked it up, hit the receiver and two other buttons.

"Who is there?" her quavering voice asked.

As soon as the voice spoke he knew who it was, even though it was more timid and fragile than he was used to.

"Georgi", he said. She had only spoken a few words but it was enough for him to tell she was in deep trouble.

Now her words just kept coming. It was as if he had not said anything. She just kept talking. With what seemed to be the last word uttered, he tried again to speak to her but the line clicked and went dead.

Georgi turned to Leoni who was sitting nearby. "Your idea on Gene not pushing the button in Vegas, well Taeyoung has just played a Royal Flush. And Nagriza's in trouble."

He told her what had happened and the words she had used. The others listened on.

"But I've recorded it and kicked in a tracker. Check it out Leoni and see if you can find out where it came from."

Having read the statement, Nagriza threw the phone and paper to the floor. The gunman stood behind her.

"That is good. You see. It is easy. You do just what we say and all is OK." And he put his arms around her, his hands inside the torn jacket, feeling her breasts. She tried to swing round but he was too strong. The man laughed and moved from behind to kiss her. She spat in his face. The back of his hand cracked against her face.

"Bitch!" he barked at her. And on that the two men left, turning off the light so the room was almost totally dark.

Alone and feeling vulnerable, Nagriza sat for some time, listening, trying to hear anything that would indicate where the two men now were. After a while she stood, tried to stretch to see how her back would respond. The result? Pain! It subsided after a while and she moved over towards the windows and the blinds. They were not plastic and flimsy as she expected them to be. They were more like industrial blinds – metallic and rigid, working up metal rods. She tried to prise two apart which she eventually succeeded in doing. She hoped it would give her a view outside. But she was wrong. This was a well thought out safe house with blinds her side of the window and closed shutters on the outside. And, although she could not tell by looking at it, her bet was the glass would be reinforced. The brief thought she had had of using the chair to batter her way through the window disappeared in a moment of despair.

Back in Wapping, it took less than an hour for the call to Georgi's mobile phone to be traced to a domestic location in Dushanbe. Georgi immediately set about organising a rescue raid. Not that that would be easy under normal circumstances. Getting such an action together was now made far more complex and frustrating. He and his department were already under heavy scrutiny from Brussels for having to put into motion diplomatic attempts to retrieve two operatives from cells in South Korea where they were held after the raid on the R&D establishment in Pyeongtaek. It would all take time and time was something Georgi was running out of.

Chapter 36

Gene Bond flew out of Central Asia on March 17th. After two days of tedious but uneventful travelling, he was established in his new temporary home, the hotel room Angel Martin booked for him. He arrived late in the day and did no more than relax, try and shake off jet lag, organise to meet Angel Martin and Tim Crenshaw for breakfast next day, March 19th, and talk to Georgi. The news from London was devastating. For the first time, Bond heard about Nagriza's telephone call to Georgi who had debated long and hard as to whether or not to tell his friend what had happened. In the event he decided there was no choice. Bond had to know.

Georgi reported that he thought they knew where Nagriza was being held and a raid to try and secure her release was imminent but, because of all the troubles afflicting that part of the world, organising such a rescue was extremely difficult and there was no guarantee of success.

"God help us – I hope you can get her out of there. But if you can't, what do I do?" a distraught Bond asked Georgi.

"You don't hit the button," came the reply. "In fact, you need some way of making sure Crenshaw's whole technical system malfunctions. If you don't hit it, we need to be sure it won't work if someone else can by-pass it."

"You're joking," said Bond, knowing full well there was nothing funny in any of this. "I'll be writing Nagriza's death sentence!"

"Gene. Don't for a minute think I've not despaired about this. I've torn my brain to shreds thinking about it. But there's no choice, my friend. It's one life against God knows how many, two million? I don't know. If Taeyoung's attack is for real, the direct and collateral losses will be beyond calculation."

There was a silence between them before Georgi added. "The hard truth is my friend, Nagriza is expendable. It has to be that way."

"Fuck!" Bond spat out the expletive. "You've just got to get her out of there Georgi."

"As if I don't know that!" Georgi retorted, despairingly. "We're doing our best. It also raises other problems. It was my plan that either Nagriza or I would come to Vegas to help you there. Now I can't. I must stay here. There's too much to do."

"I understand," Bond agreed reluctantly. "What a bloody mess."

"Indeed," said his Georgian friend.

It made for a restless night for Bond. Sleep was impossible to come by. A mix of travel fatigue, paranoia about Nagriza and worry about his convention script all conspired to keep sleep away. As a consequence, he felt like a lump of lead as he headed for his breakfast meeting.

There was no mistaking Angel Martin. She was, Bond immediately thought, a big woman, a very big and very black woman. She exuded flamboyancy, eccentricity and energy. She was wearing a full length white robe – her signature fashion style although at this stage he did not know that. Ungraciously he thought it would look like a tent on many women of her size. But it did not on Angel Martin. She somehow radiated femininity, even sexiness, which seemed to clash with the religious collar she wore. Atop was a gold and blue African head wrap.

Alongside her stood a tall, thin, suited man with light, wiry, curly hair surrounding a bald dome. He looked pale and drawn with dark bags under eyes which flickered nervously about, even as Bond was to find, when he was speaking to you.

"Bond! Bond! My English aqua-hero!" Angel moved towards him. Her voice boomed. She smiled the biggest and warmest smile Bond thought he had ever seen and her eyes sparkled like jewels. As she approached, her arms extended in what became a bear hug and a bodily encounter the likes of which he had never experienced before. She seemed to engulf and almost suffocate him, dragging his head down so it became hard to breathe, smothered as he was by her enormous breasts.

"I am so pleased to see you," she hollered, releasing him from her all-embracing grip. The word 'so' was loud and extended. Bond thought it echoed round the hotel breakfast room.

With Bond getting his breath back from this overwhelming onslaught, Angel turned to the man alongside her and said: "Gene, this is Tim."

"Crenshaw," the man added, extending his hand in greeting. Contrary to the man's general demeanour, the handshake was firm and with authority. Opposite to the image he was portraying, Bond thought it was perhaps evidence that once this man used to be far stronger, far more confident than he now seemed to be.

"Welcome to Vegas, sir. And welcome to our convention. We're very pleased you are able to add so much value to our event."

"It's good to meet you both after knowing you only from a distance," Bond replied. "How's the event looking? How many delegates have you got? Is everything ready?"

And they were able to tell him that their target of 200 delegates had been exceeded, nearly doubled. It was now certain the UN was fielding a speaker. His presentation would challenge the skirmishing nations of the Ferghana Valley to re-establish the resource sharing scheme that once prevailed in the area. He would quote UN Director Deirdre Tynan's call for the *"development of a strategy focusing on reform of agricultural and energy sectors"* but one that be extended to embrace all resources especially water. The UN was now taking advantage of Angel's event by calling a Ferghana Valley Emergency Summit to be held the following day, thereby adding more prestige, status and global media interest to Angel Martin's event.

In response, Bond told them of his findings from his recent time in Central Asia. He made the comparison between the history of the Aral Sea and the current plight of Lake Mead. "We should learn the lessons of history" would be his closing statement.

"Oh my!" Angel Martin was on her feet and applauding the Englishman. "Inspiring!"

"I'll try and keep it upbeat," Bond promised her. "But around the world the news isn't good and we should ensure the message from the convention is the need for top echelon political acceptance of the magnitude and pressing nature of the challenge. We should demand an immediate, coordinated response. It sounds good but I bet not a lot will happen as a result."

"We must endeavour to ensure this event kicks butts and gets action," the evangelical church leader told him. "You're right, we're running out of time on this Bond. Responsible people have just got to see and understand that."

After a pause, she added, "Perhaps you could deliver the formal challenge from our convention, something along the lines of what you've just said. Maybe you'd consider saying – ," she paused to think, "on behalf of everyone associated with this, the first convention of the New Church of Acionna, we call for world leaders to action a comprehensive and coordinated response to the challenges affecting our most precious natural resource – water."

She clapped her hands – obviously pleased with her own efforts. Both Crenshaw and Bond felt obliged to join in.

"That's powerful stuff, Angel," said Bond. "I'll build it into my script."

They told him more about who was saying what on the 22nd and Crenshaw reminded him at the end of his speech, he was to hit a button to start a video sequence from three parts of the world.

"Can you tell me what that's about?" probed Bond. "Last time I asked, you were very cagey about it."

"Cagey! Cagey! Not the word for it," proclaimed Angel Martin, interrupting. "He's so secretive." Again the emphasis and extension of the word 'so'.

Crenshaw shuffled nervously and looked down at his feet. When he spoke, it was in a nervous mumble. "It's our big message to the world, a wakeup call about water. But there's an important technical issue here. We need you to hit that button right on four o'clock."

And although Bond pressed for more information, he did not get it. But they did agree to talk about how the video would work when they met at the convention rehearsal the next day.

"What are you planning for the rest of today?" asked Angel.

"I thought I'd take a drive out to Lake Mead," Bond told her. "I'd like to see it for myself."

"Good idea, Bond," she replied. "Sorry we can't be with you but with just today and tomorrow before the convention, we're under pressure. It's become a lot bigger than we ever expected."

Back in his hotel room, Bond called Georgi but there was no news from Dushanbe. "Believe me, Gene," Georgi tried to reassure him. "We're working on it."

The afternoon visit to Lake Mead reinforced Bond's view that he was right to draw the similarity with the Aral Sea. The startlingly obvious 'White Cliffs Of Dover' – or 'bath tub ring' as the locals called it – stood out as a white border to the lake and provided a dominant new feature to the beautiful area. He drove around, stopping now and then where he could walk down to the water's edge. He talked to anyone willing to pass the time of day with him, and most he spoke to were happy to engage with him. One local told him the lake had dropped to 1,080 feet above sea level this year from being 1,225 feet in 1983. At 1,000 feet, drinking water intakes would go dry to Las Vegas.

But, he thought, the Colorado River also showed resemblances to the plight of the Syr Darya River of Central Asia. From the various people he met during the afternoon, and reading information he picked up as he moved around, he found the Colorado River is the main water source for 25 million people. It runs through five states for nearly 1,500 miles and is fed one way or another by virtually every river in Arizona. It always used to flow into the Gulf of California at its delta in Mexico. But since 1983, it has only reached the delta five times.

He found that years of economic boom in the US Southwest has increased demand for water, coinciding with a drought that has gripped the region for almost 15 years. Seven states take water from the Colorado, plus some allocation to Mexico. The amount of extraction now often exceeds the amount of water the river carries. The economic consequences are already being felt with marinas losing business and, hundreds of miles away, farmers growing increasingly concerned about irrigation to some four million acres of farmland. Some farmers have already downsized their businesses.

"We're just hoping for snow and rain up in Colorado, so it'll come our way," a marina operator told him.

It was a worrying story with extraordinary parallels to the Aral Sea and it provided vital local colour for his presentation on the 22nd.

There was no way he could be in this area without seeing the Hoover Dam, something he had so often talked about in recent times but had never seen. With not enough time to do a proper visit, he drove into the hills to look down onto the dam, seeing it at some distance and through the curved span of the new road bridge with the Colorado River winding its way through the rocky canyon and into the distance. It was a massive and impressive structure standing in smooth and white grandiose comparison to the grey, black and reddish rugged terrain of the mountains in which it is located.

"It's quite magnificent," Bond thought and wondered if anything Taeyoung flew at it would make even a dent let alone a breach.

Chapter 37

Nagriza was cold. It was always dark with the blinds and shutters closed denying light to the room during the day and the switch to the solitary light bulb being on the other side of the constantly locked door. She only saw the two men when they came to feed her or to escort her to the toilet. These actions were taken with the utmost caution with one always pointing a silenced gun at her and both being extremely careful as to how they positioned themselves. They both carried assault guns as well as hand guns and were clearly well trained professionals who, by the way they responded to her, acknowledged she was also.

Time passed tediously slowly. It was difficult to track when it was day and when it was night. It was only on her toilet trips that she was able to tell which it was. She was aware it was stormy outside. She could hear rain and hail lashing at the shutters and there was the occasional crash of thunder. Her time was spent continuously straining for any sounds and trying to catch any words from the two men. It was only because of this concentrated focus on sounds, that she heard, amidst the dull rumble of the latest storm, the faintest of noises that most other people would have missed. She certainly hoped the two men somewhere in the house had not picked it up. If she was right in interpreting what it was, the sound – a short, sharp crack – was of a thin, bolt shaped listening probe being fired into the wall outside. If she was right, more would be fired into other walls around the house. It would enable people outside the house to get an understanding of who was where within the building. If she was right – and she prayed she was – it was the precursor signs of attempts to get her out of this mess.

Letting some time pass from when she heard the noise, Nagriza eventually started humming patriotic Uzbekistan songs. She hoped the two men would think it was a way by which she was keeping her morale up. But if she was right about what she had heard, this was how she could try and ensure those listening into the house knew exactly where she was.

On the morning of March 21st, Gene Bond, oblivious to developments in Dushanbe but frequently worrying about Nagriza, met Tim Crenshaw by the glass door and atrium entrance to the pink tinged modern structure of the Las Vegas Convention Centre. It was the start of another busy day and the place already bustled and teemed with people.

"How was your visit to Lake Mead?" asked Crenshaw.

"Informative," Bond told him. He did not like this man and had no inclination to pass the time of day with him.

Crenshaw seemed to get the message and they walked in silence into the huge complex of meeting and convention rooms, eventually arriving at the one allocated to the 1st Annual Convention Of The New Church Of Acionna as it proudly proclaimed on the banner above the door. Several people were busy sorting final arrangements for the following day. Bond followed Crenshaw into the auditorium where the civil servant searched out the event's senior technician. Together, all three headed onto the stage and to the very modern lectern.

"If you're running PowerPoint slides, we would prefer to load them onto our computer so they become part of a seamless show," said the technician in a very English voice.

"I have no visual aids at all," Bond responded. "You English?"

"Yes," replied the technician, "in this industry we get everywhere! And he went on to explain the equipment on the lectern and how the show would work.

"This is our traffic light system," he said, showing Bond a series of three lights set into the lectern. "Normally we would flash amber at you when you're five minutes to your allocated time. You get a red with one minute to go. The third is another red light. If you were to go well over your allocated time, both reds start to flash. It's a warning we're about to cut you off sound and spotlight. It's a tough call if it gets that far but it has happened."

"In your case the timing is critical. I'm told you need to hit this," he pointed to a large blue button, "right at four o'clock. It fires the video sequences. Because the timing of this is so critical we propose, Mr Bond, to flash the amber at 35 minutes into your speech, the red one at 39 minutes and flash both reds at 40 when you hit the blue one. Is that OK?"

Gene Bond had been listening intently. It seemed straightforward enough, if not a little nerve wracking. It was a sizeable convention room and he was aware delegates were coming from all over the world. A large media presence was expected. Presenting under normal circumstances was tough enough. The added dimension of the critical timing added an extra spice.

"What happens when I hit the blue button?" he asked as if still concerned about the presentation technology. What he was really after was information to feed back to Georgi.

They still had no idea how Taeyoung was going to achieve what he planned to do.

"That triggers two things, Mr Bond. I can show you part of it." He spoke quietly into his headset microphone, waited less than a minute, then hit the blue button. Instantly the large screen behind them started to divide into three elements.

"We're linking to three locations, Mr Bond, and each screen will cover one. In addition, when you hit that button, a signal will be triggered that will set things in motion at the three locations."

"What sort of things?" queried Bond.

The technician shrugged his shoulders. "Sorry, Mr Bond. We've no idea. You'll have to ask Mr Crenshaw here. The whole thing's shrouded in mystery."

They turned to Crenshaw for an explanation. "We're still keeping it secret," he told them. "We don't want the media to jump the gun."

They discussed the event before eventually leaving the stage. Bond asked to be excused to use the nearby toilets. As soon as he was away from the others, he phoned Georgi.

"Any news, Georgi?"

"No, nothing new Gene, what about your end?"

"I don't know much more. I'm at the Convention Centre. I now know I have to hit a blue button spot on four o'clock. The timing seems critical. Apparently in doing that, I send a signal to the three locations they're doing something at."

"Where the drones are."

"Yep."

"Can you find how the signal's actually sent? Where's it transmitted from?"

"I don't know. I'll try."

And on that he returned to Crenshaw and the technician.

"That was all very helpful," Bond told them. He turned to the technician. "You still got much to do?"

"As always," the technician sighed. "It's part of the job. We always have to work late into the night before a show like this. So many elements to get right then rehearse, rehearse and rehearse. That's why I know it'll run like clockwork tomorrow."

Back at his hotel, Bond put in yet another call to Georgi fully aware that it was now late evening in London. Georgi at last had some news from the Tajikistan capital.

"We know the rescue squad is on site. They've got listening devices attached to the house. They know where Nagriza is being held and they know she's still alive."

"Thank God." Bond interrupted.

"The less good news is the squad wants to black out the house by cutting off its main power. They've got access to that but they can't do anything until late into the night. They also want to go in just before dawn. They reckon that's the best bet to catch people with their guard down."

"What time?" asked Bond.

"It'll be four in the morning they tell me."

Bond did a quick calculation. "Shit, that'll be three o'clock in the afternoon here. Can't they go in earlier?"

"No," Georgi told him. "We've worked it out too. It's a problem. But they've two things that dictate time. The first is access to the street power and for reasons I don't know, they can't do that until after two o'clock. Then they want to hit what they call lowest awareness time. That's around four in the morning."

"That's not good, Georgi. In fact it's about as bad as it could be. I'll just be starting to talk then and won't know if Nagriza's going to be safe or not."

"Oh Gene," Georgi sighed. "What the hell do I say? There's no way either of us want to lose Nagriza but, operationally, we've got to clear her from our minds. We have got to stop Taeyoung and Crenshaw firing those drones. Millions of lives depend on it. What happens to Nagriza is irrelevant."

Bond felt a nervous wreck for the rest of the day. He tried desperately to finish his speech but his mind would not concentrate on it. Despite his best endeavours, he could not help but think of Nagriza. Georgi was right, but you could not just wipe her out of existence – out of mind.

Eventually, as darkness started to fall on Las Vegas and The Strip began to come to life, Bond made his way back to the Convention Centre and to the event room. Searching out the senior technician, he asked to again see the technology associated with the videos.

"I need to feel safe in my own mind that it'll work," he told him. Obligingly, Ian, as it turned out the man was named, showed him how the lectern button activated a radio transmitter, a small and innocent piece of electronic kit located just behind the large convention screen, close to where the event technicians would be stationed during the event.

"Just say the button fails," Bond challenged. "What then?"

Ian smiled with a look of confidence that suggested he always had every eventuality covered. "We'd hit the transmitter manually," he explained. Mentally Bond had to agree. Ian had every eventuality covered.

Chapter 38

Georgi Patarava sat at a specially prepared operations desk in his Wapping HQ with various screens before him and five clocks showing the local time in London, Beijing, Madrid, Las Vegas and Dushanbe. One screen provided him with live images from a head cam from the rescue attempt in Tajikistan and another, a live feed from Angel Martin's convention. Three other screens were hooked into outputs from the Vegas event including the video images from the drone attacks. He had already been at his desk for eleven hours. Members of his team and anyone else working on Taeyoung's Acionna Project remained in Wapping and would do so until the expected forthcoming action ended. Georgi's desk was the centre of operations and people came and went and now and then assembled for full team briefings to ensure everyone was up to speed with all developments.

In China, Spain and America, military teams were now deployed to find Taeyoung's drones and to establish appropriate defences. It had been challenging and frustrating to convince the appropriate authorities of a real security problem. As a matter of statutory procedure, this was conducted via Brussels which meant serious delays as one person after another became involved and slow and cumbersome bureaucracy creaked into action. Georgi's patience and temper passed the threshold of control and people in the Wapping HQ became accustomed to his loud, expletive-embellished outbursts. This was particularly the case when he and his team were accused by others of not allowing enough time for local countermeasures to be put into place.

The tension grew as he watched the operation unfold in Dushanbe, other members of his weary team gathering round him. In the Ferghana Valley, it would soon be three o'clock in the morning. It was nearing ten in the evening in London.

In Seoul it was eight o'clock in the morning. Unbeknown to Georgi, Sum Taeyoung was sitting alone in his home enjoying a slow and lazy breakfast. For him a very special day was dawning. And what a day it promised to be, a momentous and historic day, a day of unbelievable infamy. A day when he alone would wreak havoc across the planet and change the way people think and behave – from this day on.

To fully savour the occasion, he was treating himself. His breakfast was accompanied by chilled Henri Abele, a variety of champagne he appreciated because of its spicy undertones. Away from the hustle and bustle of his office, here he felt cocooned in a bubble of tranquillity. There was now no more he could do other than to watch his plot unfold, see his months and months of planning take centre position on the world's stage. Like Georgi Patarava, Taeyoung also had screens to watch, one picking up the feed from the convention at Las Vegas, and one each for the drone locations. Now he watched as a man he had tried unsuccessfully to kill several times approached the lectern at the convention in Las Vegas.

Some hours earlier, Gene Bond had arrived at the location of Angel Martin's event. Banners and flags decorated the reception desk where he checked in. A line of girls waited to greet everyone. They wore gowns and head pieces in the Angel Martin style but these were of deep red and bright gold respectively. It was a dramatically colourful and welcoming sight.

"You wait here please sir," said one of the girls behind the desk as soon as he gave her his name. "Angel Martin specifically instructed us to keep you here while we find her. She wants to welcome you personally."

Two or three minutes later, Angel breezed into sight like a yacht in full sail, her white gown billowing as she moved towards him. He braced himself for the bear hug that inevitably followed.

"Bond! Bond! We've made it. We've done it! And I'm so pleased to see you." Again that accentuation of the word 'so'.

And taking him by the hand, she led him into the convention room where a large number of people were already gathered in the catering area. Rounded up like sheep by Angel Martin, the speakers were introducing themselves to each other and talking about their particular contributions to the event. Though small in number, it was a seriously prestigious group and Bond felt delighted and privileged to be amongst them. Even so, part of his mind was locked onto what was happening a long way away. He had told Georgi he would keep his mobile phone on at all times, leaving it to vibrate if he called. It was his intention, he told his Georgian friend, to place it on the lectern so that even if he was speaking to the convention, he would be able to see if Georgi called. Beyond anything else, he needed to know Nagriza's fate.

That was about to be decided. Storms still raged across the Ferghana Valley, thunder rumbling and grumbling around the mountains, lightening flashing in the valleys. Occasionally there were eruptions of violent downpours of rain, roads being turned into instant streams, trees bending in the wind. Deep into the night of March 22nd, in Central Asia, International Water Day ended as if the Gods were ensuring enough water was deposited onto the planet to last to Doomsday. For anyone still outdoors, it was downright uncomfortable. In Dushanbe, squalls of tropical deluges lashed across the city's suburb and puddles of rainwater deepened and linked one to another to form growing pools and mini rivers. Where there were street lights, the water jumped excitedly in silver reflections, agitated by both the wind and the torrent of falling water. In the blowing gale, increasing amounts of bits of timber were mixing with general rubbish and flying in all directions. It was chaotic.

In the pitch black of the stormy night, three elongated canoes sped as fast as they could along the Gissar Canal, four commandos in each, all wearing black combat gear and now and then silhouetted as flickering lightening momentarily illuminated them. As far as they were concerned, the weather could not have been more helpful. The worse the noise from the storm the better it was. In unison, they cut their small outboard engines and cruised silently to an area of scrubland where they disembarked and fanned out to creep through the darkness, crawl in undergrowth, and slide along walls.

Within 20 minutes of landing, the house where Nagriza was held was surrounded, the sound probes fired and secured, noises from within closely monitored, and power cables located by which to send the whole district into blackness. The raiding party quickly identified through the sound probes where within the house, the two gunmen were – in one of two rooms at the rear of the building. Nagriza was in a front room to the right of the building.

Everything was in place for the attack to commence. It was just a matter of waiting for the agreed time of attack.

Eventually, as the second hand of the watch of the group's commander clicked to quarter past four, he gave the single command "Go!" At that instant, all lights in the area died. From three locations around the house, state of the art, laser controlled, computer assisted SAAB-Bofors grenade launchers hit their targets, house windows being blown asunder to open passage for the immediately following stun grenades, more popularly known as 'flash-bangs'. There was instant bedlam and chaos in the targeted three downstairs rooms but not, it was hoped, in the one in which Nagriza was locked.

As events started to unfold in Dushanbe, around the time the commando force moored its three canoes, it was three o'clock in the afternoon where Bond sat listening to a series of highly authoritative presentations including a plea from the United Nations for everyone to hold their nerve in the Ferghana Valley and for the conflict there not to develop into a new and major 'water war'. At three fifteen, the vivacious Angel Martin stood at the lectern to thank the last speaker and to introduce the English environmental entrepreneur, Gene Bond. By now his nerves were stretched like violin strings. He walked onto the stage with as much control and authority as he could muster. Unquestionably the 1st Convention of the Church of Acionna was a formidable occasion. He was very aware of the large and high profile audience awaiting his deliberations. His mouth was dry, his stomach churning and his legs a little weak. His only consolation was, knowing from experience, it was always like this and once he got going, all would be well. The major difference was his constant worry about Nagriza. It was now three twenty in the afternoon. He had forty minutes to speak and then hit the fire button for the videos – or not – to potentially dictate whether Nagriza lived or died.

Slowly and deliberately he placed his script down on the lectern and drew his mobile phone from his pocket to lay it alongside. As he did so, it vibrated. He looked down at it, shocked and horrified at the coincidence of the timing. A message from Georgi simply read – "Rescue launched."

He stared at the phone for what seemed eternity. In reality it was seconds, hardly noticeable to the audience. They watched as the Englishman slowly and deliberately established himself at the lectern, looked up at them and began to speak.

"Water scarcity," he told them, "could lead to conflict between communities and nations as the world is still not fully aware of the water crisis many countries and many millions of people face."

He paused. "These are not my words. They are from a report published two days ago by the United Nations Intergovernmental Panel on Climate Change. And I will quote from what IPCC Chair, Rajendra Pachauri, told the conference on water security where that report was launched. She said: "Unfortunately the world has not really woken up to the reality of what we are going to face in terms of the crisis of water."

"If anyone wants confirmation of the validity of these statements they only have to look at Central Asia where today we are on the threshold of a full blooded, 21st century water war. I tell you, we are on a knife edge of that happening."

Bond paused to take another sip of water but, more vitally, to look again at his phone. There was no more news from Georgi. He tried to put the rescue of Nagriza to one side of his mind. It was close to impossible to do so.

The first Nagriza knew of the armed assault on the building was an ear shattering explosion, followed by another and another. All her senses had been primed ever since what she rightly had identified as the 'crack' of a sound probe hitting the house. That the attack did not include the room in which she was held suggested her singing had done the trick. Those outside knew where she was.

Her instinctive response was to know that wherever the two gunmen were, if they were still alive, they would be trying to head in her direction. She was their only asset. Her imprisonment was their only task. Her freedom would mean they had failed and they would die. But they probably realised by now they had nothing to win in any direction. Nagriza's death would, to them, at least be some justification for their own. There would also be the remotest prospect they could use her as a shield or a bargaining chip but both seemed unlikely.

Her room only contained the single chair and the bed. With deafening noise all around the house, she broke the chair up into useful pieces and thrust its back framework under the door handle in forlorn hope it would stop or at least slow the progress of her captors in getting to her. She pushed the bed up against it as well. It was not much of a barrier but it was all she could do.

In the back of the house, the two gunmen rapidly recovered from the initial shock of the attack. In seconds, both donned breathing masks and night sights. One started to return fire to those outside. Immediately, his action attracted a barrage of incoming heavy calibre rounds, brickwork around what was left of the window from where he had fired, shattering and disintegrating in a chaos of flying mortar, metal and glass fragments. The room was quickly filling with dust and smoke as yet more flash-bangs arrived to add to the general carnage. He ducked down, his back to the direction of the window as chunks of wall cascaded onto him.

His colleague was opening the door leading to the short hallway off which were doors to the other three downstairs rooms and the front door. The noise was incredible. Flash-bangs seemed to be exploding in every direction, including the hallway. The front doorway had taken a hit from a grenade and the door itself hung at a crazed angle from one solitary hinge in its dislodged doorframe. Smoke billowed from a smoke grenade that nearly entered the house but instead, smashed into the remains of the front door structure.

Both gunmen were armed with Russian AK-12, lightweight, 60 round magazine assault rifles and carried several magazine packs plus grenades around their waist. The man in the hall crawled forward, anticipating the arrival of troops in follow up to the flash-bangs by firing blindly in short bursts through the smoke, not necessarily expecting to hit anyone but at least perhaps creating a deterrent to their entrance. It also provided a modicum of cover as he slowly progressed to the door of the room in which Nagriza was held.

Some ten minutes had passed since the rescue assault was launched; the commander of the assault team expected by now to have men in the house. Optimistically he hoped the whole operation might only take 10 minutes. He was being proved wrong. In the house, whilst trying to offer as much resistance as possible, one gunman resolutely maintained his defensive position to the rear of the building. Three quarters of the way down the hall, the other felt he should by now have got hold of the girl. She was potentially their only chance of living.

Back in Las Vegas, Bond was trying desperately to keep his mind off what was happening in Dushanbe. His phone remained silent. He was throwing volumes of statistical evidence at the audience mixed with case studies from around the globe as to how people endured a lack of clean water.

"Across our planet, diarrhea caused by inadequate drinking water, sanitation, and bad hand hygiene, kills an estimated 842,000 people every year – or approximately 2,300 people per day."

"Seven hundred and fifty million people around the world lack access to safe water. That's about one in nine of all the people living on Planet Earth."

"The World Water Council believes that by 2020, we shall need 17% more water than is available if we are to feed the world population. If we go on as we are, millions more than do so already will go to bed hungry and thirsty each night."

He paused, took a sip of water and looked at his phone. "Buzz you bastard," he said to himself. "What the fuck's happening?"

Roughly at that moment, a little over 7,000 miles from Las Vegas, the door to Nagriza's room was unlocked and kicked. The makeshift barrier withstood the first assault. The man in the hallway kicked it again but still it refused to open. Now he knew Nagriza had blocked it somehow. Turning his gunfire away from the front door and aiming it at the one immediately in front of him, he watched as it started to shred and disintegrate under the assault. Risking standing up, he stepped back then threw himself bodily at the remains of the door, crashing through it, sending the only bit of the chair that had survived the attack, flying across the room. He part landed on the bed then fell to the floor where Nagriza, using part of the chair she had previously broken off like a lance, clouted the man on the side of the head. It was a moment of triumph. But it was short lived.

The blow to her former captive was far from decisive. Keeled over by the blow, he rolled on the floor to retrieve the gun he had dropped, Nagriza arriving on top of him as his hand reached the weapon. Still holding the chair leg, she used it to try and strike a winning blow on the man's head but he twisted away just in time to avoid it, striking back at Nagriza as he did so. The side of his hand caught her with a swinging hit to her neck, throwing her off him. With one hand still holding the chair leg, she clutched where she had been struck with her free hand, struggling to breathe, taking in big gulps of air. It was enough of a lapse in her attack for the man to roll round to face her and to get to his knees. He was conscious their fight had taken them into the middle of the hallway, fully exposed to any incoming fire. He lurched forward and grabbed Nagriza, turning her so she was now between him and the front door. As he did so, two more flash-bangs arrived followed immediately by two smoke grenades. The noise was ear splitting, visibility now virtually zero. Clutching the squirming, choking Nagriza, the man heaved them both back into the room from where she had come, one part of the house to still remain with not much smoke. As he did so, two commandos arrived at the front door.

At the rear of the house, the battle had been raging for some minutes. Where the window had been was now unrecognisable, sizeable chunks of brickwork having been blasted away by incoming fire. The commandos had added tear gas to the mix of what they were firing into the house. Their target was finding his position increasingly untenable and opportunities to return fire few and far between.

Reluctantly he came to the conclusion that together he and his colleague could fend off the outside force better together than if they were separated. He made his way towards the door to the hallway, crawling as he did so through a chaos of broken furniture, concrete, metal and empty grenade cases. As he reached the door, so the commandos reached the outside wall and, from the closest range they had so far enjoyed, sprayed the room with gun fire. The gunman inside was hit three times, once in the back and twice in the legs. He was still able to open the door to the hallway only to be confronted through swirling thick smoke by the sight of two more commandos. Before he could fire at them, they fired at him. He died instantly.

Commandos soon filled the hallway either side of the doorway leading to the room in which the remaining gunman was now on his feet and holding Nagriza in front of him as a shield, her arms held together behind her and bound with snap on plastic cuffs. She was as tall as him and he was having to look around her to see what was happening. She had stopped resisting him and her main worry was breathing. With no mask to shield her, the gas was affecting her badly and she was gulping for air. She knew it was futile to try and break away and anyway, each time she tried to twist and turn from his grip, the man holding her twisted her arms up so it felt as if they would snap from the shoulder sockets. The pain was excruciating. Both she and the gunman were white with mortar dust. Her hair was disheveled and full of debris. Her jacket remained torn from where she had earlier been assaulted and her now partly revealed breasts heaved as she tried to take in air.

Slowly commandos approached the door from either side. In a well-rehearsed procedure, tear gas and smoke grenades were lobbed into the room, two commandos opened with random covering fire and a third dived into the room to arrive spread eagled on the floor, gun firing.

296

Instantly he saw to his right standing in the room's farthest corner, a tall woman, covered in dust and debris, her jacket in shreds and near naked from the waist up. Her chest was heaving as she fought to breath as smoke and tear gas filled the room. A handgun was being held to her head by a masked man standing close behind her holding an assault rifle in his other hand.

"Stop firing," the commando on the floor shouted. His colleagues shuffled forward so they too were in the room and could see what was happening. Across the house what had been a battlefield for fifteen or more minutes now fell silent. They had reached something of a stand-off.

With his mobile phone remaining silent and its clock showing the dreaded deadline of four o'clock relentlessly approaching, Gene Bond moved into the final parts of his convention speech.

"I came here direct from a week spent in the Ferghana Valley in Central Asia, tracking the Syr Darya River. The fate of people living in the various nations within the valley relies upon sensible decisions from the international community and local, national politicians. They are on the brink of war – the first modern day water war. Some have died already. On the evidence of political inabilities and incompetence of the past, I can only say God help them. What drove me to that area was the tragic and despicable story of man's destruction of one of the great natural assets of the world – the Aral Sea."

Bond paused, looked at his watch. It was now three minutes to four. Still the phone remained silent.

"What was once the fourth largest inland sea is today reduced to a toxic sump. Thanks to the work of man, this once picturesque and vibrant wonder is now massively reduced in size and contains a vile cocktail of obnoxious substances. Instead of providing economic benefit to the 40,000 or so people who made a living from it, today it is the source of materials that hospitalises and kills people. It is an environmental, economic and social disaster."

A look at the watch - two minutes to go.

In London, though the picture was limited, sometimes painfully difficult to see and frequently not showing them what they really wanted to see, Georgi and the team watched mesmerised by what was unfolding in the house in Dushanbe. They too were very mindful of the time. Via the head cam on one of the commandos who had now entered the downstairs front room, they could see Nagriza, dishevelled and obviously in serious distress, but alive. The gunman was trying to move off the wall, pushing Nagriza before him.

"Holy shit," muttered Georgi, seeing what was happening.

Slowly the gunman moved forward. The commandos moved back. Their leader sought advice from his superiors. Was the girl expendable? Where did the priorities lie? And while they waited for a response, so they backed off, allowing the gunman to get to the doorway then into the hall. There he stopped, shouting for his comrade. There was no response. He knew what had happened. The odds were it was always going to end that way.

Slowly, so slowly, events moved from the house to the small front garden. The gunman called out. He spoke in Russian. The leader of the commando group understood. He assured the man a vehicle would drive to the front gate and he could use it. It was only 20 yards from the front door of the house to the gate. It seemed to be taking eternity to get there.

In London, Georgi looked again at the clocks before him. In Las Vegas there was now just a minute to go to four o'clock. He looked back at the screen.

Clutching Nagriza before him, the gunman progressed towards the road. A 4x4 arrived and the driver got out, opened the passenger door then ran off, bent double to avoid any hostile fire. There was none.

In the street outside the house, a commando crept forward to establish a position by the corner of the front garden, hidden from sight by bushes. This man was a specialist and the equipment he carried reflected his skills. As fast as he could he prepared for his moment in the drama. Looking down the sights of his rifle, the sniper brought the crosshairs to bear on the fraction he could see of the gunman. Almost instantly he was out of sight, hidden behind the girl. Then the shot was there again, a fleeting moment when the gunman's head was in the crosshairs. The sniper squeezed the trigger and felt the rifle recoil. He watched in horror as the girl dropped, taking the man with her. In that instant he had no idea who he had hit.

In London, Georgi saw Nagriza and the gunman go down. He had no idea who had been hit by the sniper's bullet.

"Who was hit?" he asked those around him. There were shrugged shoulders and blank looks. Nobody knew.

After a moment's hesitation, Georgi sent a text to Bond.

"She's free!" it said. He prayed it was right.

In Las Vegas, Bond was concluding his speech.

"What happened to the Aral Sea and rivers like the Syr Darya should be profound lessons to us all. They are a clear demonstration that actions driven purely by short term economic targets often only lead to economic failures, environmental and social devastation. But it is blatantly obvious here in Las Vegas, that lessons have not been learnt. Unless a drastic rethink in the value of water is immediately undertaken here, the Colorado River is likely to follow the example of the Syr Darya with devastating consequences to Lake Mead. And if Lake Mead follows in the footsteps of the Aral Sea, Las Vegas and many other communities in this desert area will surely fail."

He looked up towards the audience and picked his papers off the lectern. People were starting to applaud. He looked towards the blue button on the lectern. Should he push it? Should he not? Should he let Nagriza live? Should she die? At that moment, his mobile phone buzzed. He saw Georgi's message. It was unbelievable. Fantastic. He reached forward, grabbed the blue button in the tightest grip he could achieve and pulled with all his might. He heard and felt cables snap. The audience looked on incredulously. Bond leapt from the stage, leaving the convention in chaos.

Chapter 39

From his viewpoint in the Convention Centre, Tim Crenshaw watched Bond's departure from the stage in disbelief. In London, Georgi Pavarati saw it on his video screen and hoped what Bond was doing would work. In Seoul, Sum Taeyoung nearly choked on his champagne when he saw what was happening. That man Bond – again!

Crenshaw had been viewing the presentations while leaning against the wall at the rear of the auditorium. It was a day of mixed emotions for him. At its start, he felt a sense of enormous relief. The day of the convention had finally arrived and everything seemed to be in good order. But any feelings of elation or satisfaction were overwhelmed by worries dominating his mind about what would happen at the end of the programme when Taeyoung's plot was activated. How much blame would come his way? Could he weather such a storm? If he lost his job, what then? What of his marriage? It was a bleak and black outlook – near terror as to where life went from this day on. He now had not been home for several days nor spoken to Susan. Hardly a thought about her or the family or the future of his marriage had crossed his mind during the run up to the event. Now all the preparatory work was done, a dark future and a thousand unanswered questions rolled around in his head. The last few nights were spent at a hotel near the Convention Centre but there had not been much sleep, what with pressures at work and the final organisation of the convention. In the last two or three weeks, working days had averaged nearly 20 hours. He was physically wrecked and mentally shattered. Almost zombie like, he circulated around convention delegates, speakers and VIPs and kept an eye on the proceedings to ensure they were running to order and time. They were, thanks to the team in charge of the day. His work was done. After months of relentless hard work, the convention was nearing its finale. The big reveal of the videos and the link to locations around the world was minutes away. The event was, he subconsciously thought, round the last bend and on the home straight. He watched Bond speaking from the lectern but the words bounced off him. He had heard it all through rehearsal. There was nothing for him to do, except think. And thinking was not good for Tim Crenshaw. Like water circulating in a bowl before disappearing down the plughole, the same thoughts went round and round his head before disappearing into a black hole of despair.

His eyes did not deceive him but it was a while before his befuddled brain caught up. Blue button in hand and wires dangling from it, their ends torn and shredded after their brutal disconnection, Bond leapt from the convention stage, the applause of delegates still ringing out in appreciation of his contentious and challenging presentation. Seconds later – although it seemed like an age – Crenshaw moved and left the auditorium.

In blackness at the rear of the stage were the event technicians and appreciable amounts of equipment. Bond knew exactly where to locate Taeyoung's radio transmitter. He had seen it at yesterday's rehearsal. Consisting of a black plastic box with two aerials on top in a V formation, it stood in isolation from everything else and only a few strides from the back of the stage. Bond was there in seconds. There were no niceties about this. No time for anything subtle. He leapt at it, both feet first, crashing onto the box with all his weight. It burst into fragments, bits flying in all directions. The startled technical crew looked on in amazement.

Crenshaw, having left the rear of the convention room, ran as fast as he could down adjacent corridors to a door leading into the same room but behind where the technicians sat. He thrust the door open in time to see the aftermath of the Englishman wrecking the transmitter.

"Stupid bastard," he cried, launching himself at Bond who buckled and was sent backwards into scaffolding on which projectors sat. The whole rig rocked violently and precariously under the assault and looked for a moment as if it would topple over. But while the audience on the other side of the screen saw images fly off and distort, the scaffolding did not quite collapse. At the lectern, Angel Martin, trying to recover the end of her otherwise triumphant event sent into disarray by Bond's unexpected and unrehearsed rapid departure and attack on the electrics, was interrupted as, with most of the audience, she heard Crenshaw's outcry and the crash that followed.

Bond was trying to protect himself and to roll away from the onslaught. The body of his attacker held him pinned down on broken boxes and bits of presentation equipment and the remains of the transmitter. Some of it was cutting into his back and the pain was excruciating. Crenshaw was grunting and almost frothing at the mouth in an uncontrolled rage, his arms flaying as he tried to strike blows on Bond. Two technicians who initially watched disbelievingly as events unfolded right in front of them, now decided the fight needed to be stopped if for no other reason than to protect their equipment. Rushing forward, each grabbed one of Crenshaw's arms and heaved him off Bond who was busy trying to extricate himself from the crushed convention gear.

"You fucking lunatic," Crenshaw was shouting at Bond, trying to shake off those who held him and kicking out with his feet. "You've destroyed me."

Like a demented wild animal, in one mighty heave, Crenshaw freed one arm and with that was able to strike out at the technicians. For a split second he escaped their hold but he was free enough to be able to turn and run from the room. The technicians, not knowing who was the bad guy or the good guy in this unexpected battle, were trying to help commiserate with Bond but at the same time detain him until some representation of authority arrived. Still recovering from the onslaught, feeling decidedly battered and with real pain from some parts of his back, Bond suddenly became aware his phone was vibrating in his pocket. The text message was from Georgi.

"For fuck's sake, don't lose Crenshaw."

"Bloody hell," Bond muttered to himself. He had seen Crenshaw flee the room and before the two men who had saved him could make any real attempts to stop him, he was after his assailant. Outside the convention room he caught the briefest of glimpses of Crenshaw heading through a door, some 100 yards away. Bond followed and found it was an external door leading to loading bays where large trucks waited to take away shows dismantled at the end of the day. Crenshaw was still running, now towards an area where some ten or so cars were parked.

As he ran towards it, Bond saw signs that this area was reserved for Centre and event officials. Presumably Crenshaw's car was amongst them. Sure enough, he saw the civil servant unlock a Ford saloon which, engine screaming and wheels spinning furiously and laying black rubber lines on the road, drove past him, just missing him.

Bond looked on, hopelessly. He pulled his phone out and called Georgi.

"I've lost him," he admitted.

"Shit," came the reply. "How?"

"He's leapt into his car and driven off. I haven't got a car here."

"We've got a tracker on his car," Georgi told him. "The Secret Service attached it for us the other day." And he instructed Bond how to use his phone to lock onto Crenshaw's tracked car. As he fiddled with the buttons on his phone, he heard another car start off in the car park. A small car was pulling out. He could see a young woman at the wheel. Thinking back some time afterwards, Bond was amazed at what he then did.

"I'd seen it on the movies," he explained some days later to Georgi. "And I wasn't thinking. I just did it."

Taking his wallet from his pocket and holding it high in front of him as if it represented some form of authority, Bond moved into the path of the exiting car. It stopped a foot away from him. He could clearly see a young dark-haired woman behind the wheel. She could not have been much older than twenty. She looked petrified.

Bond strode towards the driver's open window.

"I'm commandeering this vehicle on behalf of Her Majesty's Secret Service. You drive. I'll tell you where to go." He grabbed the car keys from the ignition before she could do anything, ran round to the passenger side and got in.

"Who the hell are you?" the girl screamed at him.

"Just do as I say," he shouted back.

"Why the fuck should I?" she responded.

"I haven't got time to muck about. We do this the easy way or the hard way. I throw you out or you help me. Which is it to be?"

"Are you really a British spy?" the voice was a bit more controlled.

"Sort of," said Bond. "I'll explain it all but you've got seconds before I throw you out and steal your car or you decide to help me. Which is it to be?"

"I don't seem to have an option," the girl admitted.

"No you don't," agreed Bond passing her keys back. "Now drive the bloody car."

With a shrugging of her shoulders, they drove off. Looking at his phone, he gave her directions. Keeping an eye on the tracker, he phoned Georgi.

"I'm onto him."

"How the fuck did you do that?" asked an amazed Georgi.

"I've commandeered a car and a glamorous driver," Bond told him, the flattery towards his reluctant driver was well intended and she looked at him with the briefest suggestion of a smile.

Georgi was astounded. "You're fucking joking!"

"Now let me concentrate on the job." And Bond cut the link.

It did not take long to fathom where Crenshaw was heading. Out of the city and through Whitney, his progress along Highway 93 and ultimately through Boulder City could lead to only one place – the Hoover Dam. Bond reckoned they were less than ten minutes behind him. Crenshaw was taking risks, travelling fast. The last thing Bond needed was any delay by being stopped by the law so he told the girl, who he now knew to be Angie, to drive just on the limit.

For a good half an hour, he watched the dot that was Crenshaw follow the 93 towards the dam, then veer off. When they too reached the junction, they found the turning took them onto the Hoover Dam Access Road, the old highway road that eventually crosses the Colorado River on top of the dam. It had been a dry spring day but windy. That wind was blowing dust everywhere off the moonlike, baron, dust-red rocky lunar-like landscape with its giant electrical pylons carrying power away from the hydroelectric plant at the Hoover. Within a couple of miles or so from the dam, Crenshaw's car slowed and turned left, then made progress along a side road that seemed from the map to go nowhere. Bond was puzzled. What was he doing? Where was he going?

They eventually reached the same turnoff, an area surrounded by numerous gigantic pylons and massive switching stations. All this electrical engineering amidst the moonlike terrain created an alien scene. Bond told Angie to slow right down. He had no idea what to expect. The road was a tarmac track. Sometime ago, someone had blasted their way into the mountainside, scooped up the debris and gouged their way in with an earthmover, then laid a strip of tarmac on top. Both sides of the track were filled with pylons, switching gear and sub stations behind tall, metal meshed security fencing which glinted in the sunshine. Behind it all, the craggy rockiness of the mountain climbed steeply upwards. Bond and Angie were now two hundred yards from the Access Road, slowly driving round a left hand bend. Then ahead was Crenshaw's car and Crenshaw himself, remonstrating with a group of youngsters. They were all gathered round what Bond immediately recognised from all the photos Georgi had shown him. It was a Taeyoung drone!

"Keep him away from it," Bond shouted, leaping from the car and heading towards Crenshaw who spun round to become aware of the Englishman's arrival.

"For Christ's sake, fuck off," Crenshaw shouted back. "You don't know what you're doing. None of you know what damage you're doing." It sounded as if he was crying. He lurched towards the drone only to be held back by those who were standing close to him.

"Keep him off the drone," Bond shouted, now only a few strides away. "I'm a policeman," he lied. It had the desired impact. In that instance, he became the goody and Crenshaw the baddy in the minds of the youngsters. They held him off the drone. Bond had no plan in mind but just wanted to restrain the civil servant. As he reached Crenshaw, a deafening noise heralded the arrival of a police helicopter. It came from nowhere seemingly , appearing a mere 50 yards away from over the summit of one of the hills surrounding the dusty road but keeping high enough to avoid the dozens of electricity cables and the pylons. Before Bond could grab him, Crenshaw wrenched himself away from the somewhat half- hearted, indecisive hold of the youngsters. The arrival of the helicopter seemed to have taken him one stage further beyond the demented state he was already in. Like a madman, he lunged at the arriving Bond, sending him flying to the ground. But instead of following up the attack, Crenshaw leapt into his own car and in a cloud of dust and screaming, spinning wheels, drove straight at Bond, the youngsters and the drone. Everyone scattered. Crenshaw missed them all but crashed into the side of the drone which toppled over and partly disintegrated. Slamming the car into reverse, Crenshaw tried again to ram anyone he could but again missed. To the sound of tortured gears, his car now dived forward, narrowly missing Angie's car and sped off in the direction of the Access Road.

"Follow him!" Bond shouted at Angie, diving into her car and at the same time hearing the sound of police car sirens not too far away. "And fuck the speed limit."

Angie obliged and chased after Crenshaw whose car turned left at the junction with the main road almost without slowing, its back end sliding round at a crazy angle, nearly side-swiping a car and caravan heading in the opposite direction. Miraculously Crenshaw saved the car from spinning and got it pointing in the right direction. He was driving fast, getting close to the car's maximum speed limit and leaving Angie trailing far behind. Another police helicopter came flying towards them, just above the height of all the power cables and from the direction of the dam. Crenshaw's car swerved violently from side to side again on the edge of control but still continuing on its crazed passage towards the dam.

Bond watched from a distance. As Crenshaw reached the point where the road curves round in a grand right hand sweep and onto the top of the dam, tourist visitors either side of the road dived to be as far away from the road as they could as the car with its maniac driver, roared into the bend at a speed far, far too fast. The police helicopter was now above the car as, at undiminished speed, it left the road and crashed mightily into the wall between the pavement and the drop the other side. There is an entrance here to a short footbridge leading to one of the circular pillars that tower up from the Colorado River below. The front of Crenshaw's car caught the concrete corner of the footbridge and crushed as the back end flew upwards. Angie and Bond arrived in time to watch it lift and easily clear the two foot high wall and disappear from sight.

Others were running to the point where the car had dived over the edge as Bond leapt from Angie's car as it skidded to a halt. He ran to the wall and joined the growing crowds of people looking over. As he did so, there was an explosion from below. A large cloud of thick, black smoke headed upwards from the blazing remains of the car, now far below at the bottom of the dam and nearly submerged into the water. Overhead the smoke swirled, agitated by the blades of the police helicopter that hovered overhead.

As he looked down, a hand grabbed his. Bond looked at Angie.

"Jesus," she said in horror. "Who was in that?"

"A tormented man," Bond replied. "He's left one Angel. I hope where's he's gone, he might find some more."

Chapter 40

"It was a head shot and she took it full on," Georgi told the group of grim faced people around him. "Death must have been instantaneous."

The atmosphere in the Wapping communications centre was morgue-like.

"I didn't lie to you Gene. I just told you what I had to tell you. At that stage, we didn't know what had happened. It was seconds before four o'clock your time. We had seen blurred images of Nagriza and the gunman fall after the commando sniper fired. It was a 50/50 guess who he'd hit. We now know he hit Nagriza."

It was two days after the astonishing scenes at the Hoover Dam. Almost instantly as Bond, Angie and a growing crowd of people looked down at the blazing car as it slithered slowly into the water, several police cars arrived where black smoke rose epitaph-like for Tim Crenshaw. Gene Bond, still clutching the hand of the young and bewildered Angie, demanded to speak to the senior police office on the scene.

"I work for the British Secret Service," he lied. He dialled up Georgi and told him to speak to the officer. "Get him to get me out of here before the media arrives," he told Georgi after explaining what had happened to Crenshaw. And the police had obliged, whisking Bond and Angie away and back to Vegas. There he was interviewed by senior officers and plain clothed people he took to be from the CIA. He was beyond caring. He was desperate to know what had happened to Nagriza but, strangely, he failed to get links to Wapping. After an emotional farewell to Angie, he was taken to his hotel then on to the airport where arrangements had been made for him to take the first flight back to the UK.

Eighteen hours after Crenshaw's death on the Hoover Dam, Bond joined the remains of the team at Wapping where Georgi conducted a post-project debriefing.

"Nagriza's death is the tragedy of all this," he told them. "I'm not sure I can say any more about that without cracking up. She was sacrificed to save enormous numbers of people – possibly millions."

"We prevented Taeyoung's plot. No drones flew. Gene smashed Taeyoung's transmitter and Crenshaw failed to hit the manual override on the American drone that would have fired off the others in Spain and China. So no dams were hit. Nobody died in subsequent flooding. Sum Taeyoung did not achieve the chaos and cataclysmic disaster he wanted to achieve but the message he said he was keen to deliver to the world, has been headline news across the planet. The media were all over Crenshaw's spectacular death on the Hoover Dam and the crashed drone was found by some of them. That let the cat out of the bag and we issued news releases from Brussels about how an international plot had been thwarted. Angel Martin added to that so the media picked up the message big time that water is a resource under global pressure. A lot of people quoted you, Gene, about the knife edge danger of the Ferghana Valley becoming a 21st Century water war that spreads."

"Sum Taeyoung has got away with it – again. There's no evidence anywhere to connect him to anything. Bernhard Gedeck has been forced to leave Esca International after what was disclosed as being "inappropriate use of corporate funds." The major accusations were about reckless attempts to expand the company. Again Taeyoung was not implicated. Gedeck did not dare finger Taeyoung without dragging himself further into severe difficulties."

"The French students were cleared of any illegal activity and seen to be what they were – young, naive and somewhat spellbound by Taeyoung. However, they did capitalise on the situation by distributing their message as far and as wide as they could."

"What that message was, is best stated by using the words Angel Martin is always quoting. 'Truly, truly, I say unto you, unless one is born of water and the Spirit, he cannot enter the kingdom of God.' There clearly is no resource more important to us than water. Maybe through all of this, more people now understand that."

"I don't know whether Crenshaw has entered the kingdom of God. He was obviously a man overwhelmed by his problems and ruthlessly exploited by Taeyoung. From those problems he will now have been released. Clearly the importance of water is demonstrated by those now losing their lives fighting over it in the Ferghana Valley. We now do have a modern day water war. Let's pray that battle doesn't spread. And let's pray for Nagriza and for Oska. It's been a bugger of a few days – a tragedy for us. Gene, let's get pissed. I'll take you to the Russian Bar."

The Acionna Projects

Fact & Fiction

Fact
- All environmental/water shortage statistics
- UN International Water Day – March 22nd
- Cult of Santez Anne
- Gallo-Roman water goddess Acionna
- German Red Army Faction
- Banlieue(everything)
- "Hwanung", the mythological first king of the Koreans
- The State of Islam and the Mosul Dam in Syria
- The first recorded water war involved the armies of Lagash and Umma
- The Stele of the Vultures
- The Caithness Flowlands- the largest blanket bog on the planet
- The Dubh Lochan Trail
- Johnny Cash fan and "A Boy Named Sue."
- The biggest sheep auctions in Scotland at Forsinard
- Tibetan Plateau (everything)
- TEEB, the Economics of Ecosystems and Biodiversity.
- Scottish cottage (different location)
- Aral Sea in Uzbekistan (everything)
- SNB – the Uzbekistan National Secret Service
- Douglas Laing's Big Peat
- Island of Uido-ri (not the detail)

- Buckingham Palace Garden Party (everything)
- Honorary Corps of Gentlemen at Arms
- St. Denis suburb of Paris
- Café bar at Rue du Faubourg Poissonniere and Rue Bleue junction
- Laboratoires d'Aubervilliers
- douk-douk pocket knife
- Front de Libération Nationale (FLN)
- Hôpital Saint-Louis
- European Satellite Centre; the Intelligence Division; Joint Situation Centre.
- Historic foot tunnel built by Marc Isambard Brunel
- Prospect of Whitby inn
- Flying Bird Tea Shop in the Insadong district of Soule
- Casino losses in Las Vegas
- Nevada State Administration in Carson City
- National Hydrological Plan of Spain
- Albufeira Convention
- Orthodox Church of America and the Great Blessing of Water
- National Church of Bey launched in Atlanta by pop singer Beyoncé Knowles
- John 3:5 – "And Jesus answered, 'Truly, truly, I say unto you, unless one is born of water and the Spirit, he cannot enter the kingdom of God.'
- The Hoover Dam (everything)
- Hoover Dam Bypass
- Lake Mead (everything)
- Southern Nevada Water Authority
- Las Vegas Office of Emergency Management
- Dam Busters (everything)
- China's military UAV WJ-600 drone
- Eleanor Revelle, League of Woman Voters in Washington and her quotes.
- Digging for wells in Beijing (media reports)

- Plight of Wanquan River (media reports)
- Danjiangkou dam (everything)
- CL-20
- Guadiana River and dams (everything)
- Water wars quote in Spain (media report)
- Russian Bar (but moved from Liverpool to London)
- Portcullis House (everything)
- Badajoz (some liberties on dam locations)
- Arroyo de Albarregas; Merida and the Cornalvo Dam
- Las Vegas Convention Centre
- Mount Wudangshan
- RAF Predator B-003
- The commercial movement of water
- City of Las Vegas Drought Contingency And Emergency Plan
- AAA – American Association for the Advancing of Science
- Caucasus brandy (and associated quote)
- Statistics on illegal movement of migrants
- Ferghana Valley (tensions exist but no military conflict)
- Ferghana Valley – all locations
- Munak – everything
- Syr Darya River
- Deirdre Tynan, the UN Crisis Group's Central Asia Project Director, and his quote
- Dushanbe – everything except house in which Nagriza is held
- Khujand – everything
- Swiss State Secretariat for Economic Affairs and the European Bank of Reconstruction and Development
-
-

Fiction
- All characters except those listed above
- Paris Guerriers Urbains

- Esca International
- EscaEau
- Wandora (everything)
- European Secret Service (everything)
- Sustainable Development Brokers International (everything)
- Wapping HQ of European Union Intelligence Service
- Drifters Nightclub (based on former Opposite Lock Club in Birmingham)
- New Church of Acionna
- Las Vegas Journal (everything)
- Specialist company in Pyeongtaek